CERTAIN
REQUIREMENTS

CERTAIN REQUIREMENTS

by

Elinor Zimmerman

2018

CERTAIN REQUIREMENTS
© 2018 By Elinor Zimmerman. All Rights Reserved.

ISBN 13: 978-1-63555-195-2

This Trade Paperback Original Is Published By
Bold Strokes Books, Inc.
P.O. Box 249
Valley Falls, NY 12185

First Edition: May 2018

Credits
Editor: Cindy Cresap
Production Design: Susan Ramundo
Cover Design By Melody Pond

Acknowledgments

I am an incredibly fortunate person with wonderful people in my life. I could go on for quite a while with gratitude, but I'll try to keep it simple. Thank you, Angel, for being my "writing dominatrix" and making sure I saw this through, for being an early reader, and for years of writing friendship. Thanks to Caitlin Hernandez, for being hilarious, encouraging, an insightful early reader, and an excellent writer. Thanks to my mom and my sister for always believing in me. Thanks to all my trapeze and lyra teachers, especially at Wise Fool New Mexico and Paper Doll Militia.

Thanks to Bold Strokes for welcoming me in the writing family and getting this novel into the world. Thanks to my editor, Cindy Cresap, for making it better. Thanks to Kathleen Knowles for coming across the Bay to give me advice and talk about books.

Most of all, thanks to Kasey, my first reader, who was a good sport about listening to me type at six a.m. every day when I wrote the first draft and who took our baby on adventures so I could edit it. I love you, like you, and appreciate you.

Dedication

For K

CHAPTER ONE

I'd never been so happy in all my life. Every morning since I'd given notice at my job, I'd woken up smiling. I recited the affirmations my New Age friend and performance partner, Sasha, had insisted I try months earlier, but unlike in the past, I believed the hokey words I told myself. The whole drive to the office, I calculated how many hours I had left before I was free from my job. When I got bored at work, I imagined what I would be doing in two weeks, when I was done with nine-to-fives forever. Nine more days and I'd be a full-time aerial dancer and not a receptionist spending all her free time rushing between trapeze classes and the occasional performance gig. Finally, after three and a half years of saving and struggling to be an aerialist without a day job, I could live my dream.

It had been a long slog of classes, rehearsal space rentals, and many years of training, but it was over. At last, I'd devote myself full-time to aerial dance. I'd never make it into Cirque du Soleil, but I could have a career teaching my skills and dangling upside down off a trapeze at corporate parties. I'd lined up a few teaching gigs at studios around the Bay Area and arranged two afternoons a week working the front desk at my favorite aerial school, Kirkus Radix, in exchange for open studio time for practicing my routines. I'd created an extremely tight and creative budget. Dining out, alcohol, recreational shopping, and using plastic baggies only once were to be things of the past. With my savings and the half dozen classes I was teaching, I had about eight months to start making better money from aerials, or else find another nine-to-five. But I had an absurd amount of optimism about the number of performing gigs I'd book and how much they'd pay.

Nothing fazed me. I wasn't bothered by the snooty clients, the tedium, or the flickering fluorescent lights of the office. I beamed all day at everyone. I sang along with the radio on the way home. I skipped up the steps of my battered West Oakland apartment building. Humming, I grabbed our mail. Even the junk made me happy.

Halfway up the stairs, I stopped in my tracks. A routine-looking letter from our management company revealed that our rent was going up in sixty days, and it was jumping fifteen percent.

"Fuck," I hissed.

"What, honey?" asked Mrs. Lester from down the hall, fiddling with her purse as she passed me.

"Did you get one of these?" I held up the offending letter.

"Oh, that," she said with a sniff. "We saw that."

"Are you going to stay in the building?"

Mrs. Lester shook her head. "We might move in with my daughter. They have a cottage in the back. This building is going to get filled with San Francisco people." She said "San Francisco" like a slur.

Fucking hipster techies, I thought as she lumbered down the stairs. I dragged myself through the door to my apartment and started calling for John.

"Cooking," he answered cheerily.

His boyfriend, Ollie, added, "He's making blondies."

I burst in with the letter held above my head. John was wearing his bright blue apron, his shoulder-length dreads held back by a rubber band. Ollie was still wearing his tie from work but had rolled up his shirtsleeves, glass of wine in hand. They looked so perfect and happy, Ollie with his bright gap-toothed smile and his hazel eyes set against his brown skin; John tall and handsome, his dark poreless skin and his seemingly endless muscles. They looked, I thought, like they should be in an ad. I ruined the domestic scene by blubbering, "Did you know about this? They're hiking our rent up by hundreds of dollars!"

Ollie and John froze.

"What are we going to do?" I screeched. "I just quit my job."

One of my favorite things about Ollie and John was that they were untroubled by my lack of preamble or social graces. Maybe they were just nice people, or maybe being my roommate for almost six years had made John immune, and being John's boyfriend for three of those years had done the same for Ollie. But that evening, they exchanged a long look, the kind that was a silent conversation.

"Actually, Phoenix, we have something to tell you," John said gently.

"Ollie's going to move in, yeah, I know," I said impatiently. "You guys have been talking about it for a year. So maybe that will solve the problem, but really, if they're raising it this much, they could do it again. Do you think we need to look for another place? Everything's getting so expensive."

They shared another look, and John set aside the batter he was mixing. "Maybe we should all sit down," Ollie suggested.

"Huh?" I stared at them, not understanding.

"Come on," John said. He took me by the arm.

Once we were all settled on the couch, John held my hand. In his gentlest voice, the one he used with his rowdy preschool students, John said, "Ollie and I are moving in together, Phe. But the thing is—"

"I got a librarian job," Ollie interrupted. "It's really great, at a public library, with a focus on the young adult section just like I wanted."

"That's awesome!" I cheered. I jumped up and hugged him. "Congratulations!"

One more look between them, and finally John said, "It's in Boston."

"What?" I whispered.

John squeezed my hand. "I love Oakland. I'm always going to love Oakland. Ollie's going to keep an eye out for librarian jobs here. Hopefully, we'll be back soon. But right now, I think moving is best for us. I've got a couple of interviews lined up, one at a school that looks like a really good fit. We just decided for sure yesterday, and we were going to tell you tonight, you know, with food. I'm sorry we had to tell you like this."

My eyes welled with tears. "But there's snow in Boston!"

"I know." He put his free hand on my arm.

"Your family, your community, it's all here. How can you leave that?"

"I want to try something new, Phoenix. I'm excited. I'm nervous, but I'm excited."

"But what about me?" I said softly, and selfishly.

"We're sorry," Ollie said sadly. "We'll miss you like crazy."

That did it. I burst into tears. "I'm going to miss you both so much. I'm proud of you, Ollie, and I'm happy for you guys, but I'm going to *miss* you."

"I'm going to miss you too," John said. He blinked away tears of his own. "You're going to be okay. We aren't leaving until the end of September. We can cover our share of the rent while you find another roommate."

I shook my head. They couldn't really afford it, especially with the rent increase, but of course they would offer. "What am I going to do without you?"

They wrapped me up in a hug, but none of us had an answer to my question. My aerial dreams, my plans, vanished.

CHAPTER TWO

I'm going to be homeless," I whined to my dear, patient friend Meghan the following Saturday.

"Actually?" She sighed.

"No, I'm being hyperbolic. But I am fucked. I just gave notice at work and now my rent's going up fifteen percent. Fifteen percent! Can they do that?"

"Not if you have rent control, but in Oakland new construction is exempt. Your building isn't new construction, is it?" Meghan tapped her chipped coffee cup with her nails and raised her eyebrows.

"The building's old, but it used to be a house. They converted it to apartments like in the eighties."

"New construction, then."

I choked back tears when I added, "And John's moving out."

"Wasn't that always the plan? He and Ollie have been talking about moving in together for, what, a year? You knew that was coming."

"I knew they were moving in together, but I thought Ollie was moving in with *us*. My share of the rent was supposed to go down. I had it all figured out. But they aren't just moving out, they're moving to Boston." I laid my head on Meghan's kitchen table.

"Oh, Phoenix, I'm sorry," she said.

"What am I going to do?"

She patted my back. "Have they hired someone else yet at your job?"

"No." I braced myself for the advice I knew was coming.

Without my roommate and with the increased rent, I'd need a steady paycheck months earlier than I'd planned. Because of the competitive job market, I'd need to start looking almost as soon as I stopped working.

"If you can't afford to do this right now, then why don't you work a little longer? Save a little more?" Meghan was my most sensible friend.

I turned to face her, my cheek still pressed against the table. "Because I already lined up all these teaching jobs and a work exchange at Kirkus Radix. It took me months to get everything arranged. People have signed up for my classes, and if I cancel, it could hurt my teaching reputation. If I stay at my job, I can't do any of the things I arranged. A normal job wouldn't work around my teaching schedule because I'm teaching at all these different times."

"Waitressing? It can be really flexible."

I groaned. "Teaching an aerials class and then waiting tables for a whole shift? That sounds awful. And who would even hire me? I haven't waited tables since college, and I was terrible at it."

"You do what you have to. You can make it work, Phe," she said firmly but not unkindly.

"Okay, but first I get to complain about it. I can't believe this, Meghan. I've spent the last year training five days a week and performing every weekend I can and teaching Saturday and Sunday. I can't keep up this pace. And I'm twenty-seven! If I don't start soon, I don't think I'll ever do this."

Meghan knitted her eyebrows together. She was, as always, dressed more like a high school student than the respected and fierce lawyer she was. With her bright pink pants, ballet flats, and her second-hand cardigan over her T-shirt, I had trouble believing that she'd actually been working on cases until I came over. She was a do-gooder, an immigration rights lawyer, rather than the better-paid kind who wore dry-clean-only clothes all the time—not just when they had to go to court. But still, with her plastic glasses, makeup free face, girlish freckles, and her long red hair in a perpetually messy ponytail, she was often mistaken for an intern, despite being thirty-two.

"You'll need another roommate," she said. "Maybe you can find a couple willing to pay a little more?"

"Who?" I asked. "The only couple I don't hate besides John and Ollie is you and Bill."

She patted my hand. No way she and Bill would leave their sunny, rent-controlled Berkeley apartment for my crumbling place with an inept building manager who never fixed anything correctly the first time. "Craigslist?"

"So I can get murdered?"

"You're being ridiculous."

"The last time I had a Craigslist roommate, he used to throw his dirty socks in the backyard and leave them there until we threatened to kick him out. I had a whole yard filled with rotting socks! And then he got a girlfriend who'd once dated my girlfriend at the time and they hated each other."

"When was this?"

"College. Sophomore year. I'd just started seeing Carolena."

"That was a long time ago and now you can be more discerning. Besides, you don't have a girlfriend, so you don't have to worry about that."

I glared at her and grumbled, "Very helpful. " I lifted my head finally, brushing my hair out of my face. "What was that financial domination site you used to be on?"

In addition to lobbying for the rights of undocumented immigrants while dressing like a teenager, Meghan was the most dedicatedly kinky person I knew. Long before we met, back when she was in college, she worked as a phone sex operator, a verbal dominatrix. This was hilarious to me, since Meghan generally sounded even less commanding than she looked. But she was a domme to her core. She told me when we first met that she'd never had a vanilla relationship and never wanted to. I was still in college at the time, bruising from my breakup with Carolena, and a little naïve. I was kinky too, but I wasn't basing my relationship decisions on it. I'd asked Meghan what she would do if she met the perfect person and they weren't kinky at all. "If they weren't kinky," she'd said calmly, "they would not be perfect for me."

When we met, she was in law school at Stanford, dating mostly via internet, using profiles that made her tastes clear from the start. Meghan was bisexual, and she was more concerned with an interest in submission than somebody's gender. She messaged me on OKCupid because I hinted at BDSM experience and because I spoke some Spanish. She said she was learning the language and wanted a conversation partner, so we went on a date. As it turned out, I didn't know how to talk about legal issues *en español*, she was only marginally interested in the kitchen-oriented New Mexican Spanish I grew up with, and we had no sexual chemistry. We did, however, get along well enough to become friends.

Meghan told me that though she preferred kink for play than for pay ("it isn't about what I want when they're paying me, and I like it to be about what I want"), she dabbled in pro-domme (professional dominatrix) work. At the time, she did financial domination, something that was very lucrative. Through a website that hosted a variety of fetish-focused independent phone sex operators, Meghan had set up a profile offering her services as a domme, one who'd also use up your wallet as a financial dominatrix. After establishing what a client wanted, she'd answer his calls with a curt, "I don't have time for you," and put him on hold for fifteen minutes, charge him two dollars a minute for it, and then taunt him and demand gifts of cash via PayPal. Some of her clients barely interacted with her at all and did nothing more than pay her bills. Others doled out big bucks to have her berate them on the phone or via email. Thanks to this, she finished law school with less in student loans than I owed for my BA.

As soon as Meghan got a job as a lawyer, she quit her paid domme work. Around the same time, she met Bill, a nice, responsible guy who worked at a bike shop. Bill was also happily submissive, with kinks that lined up pretty neatly with Meghan's. They'd been together ever since, and she'd never looked back at her old job.

I'd always wondered if I could make money like Meghan had, but I'd never told her this before. Her response when I did was laughter that lasted several minutes.

"You are way too submissive to be a findomme."

"I could fake it!" I objected. "I can act."

She shook her head. "You'd be better off subbing for money. But the clients would mostly be guys."

I wrinkled my nose. "A sugar mama?"

"Good luck finding one," she said and rose to pour us more coffee, then paused with the coffee pot in her hand. Meghan stared at me.

"What?" I asked.

"It's the funniest thing. A couple of weeks ago, Bill and I went to a play party, and we met somebody who's looking for a live-in sub. She has, uh, certain requirements."

"Like what?" I asked cautiously.

"Female, queer, submissive, femme." I nodded as I fit the categories. "I don't know all of it, but she mentioned she wants a woman to cook and clean for her."

"That's a little strange."

"She was hot, if that helps. Sort of a dapper butch. About my age, maybe a little older. She works in tech, some hotshot thing. I bet her place is amazing."

"I could cook and clean. But I've never met a tech person I could stand."

"She seems like a good person. But you probably don't want to be a live-in sub." Meghan refilled our cups. "It's sort of sex work. That's not your thing."

"I don't know," I said thoughtfully. I'd always been curious, but unlike Meghan, my experience with bondage, domination, discipline, submission, sadism, and masochism had been entirely within the bounds of romantic relationships. I did not go to play parties or munches, did not have a Fetlife profile or any serious training beyond a few rope bondage classes and a knife play workshop I attended with my post-college girlfriend, Ronnie, years earlier. But in my fantasies, I dove into submission, deeper and more completely than I ever considered in real life. I read erotica about countless tops dominating an eager-to-please submissive, and about relinquishing control in ways I'd never discussed with my girlfriends. Sometimes I thought trying my fantasies would be liberating, but I worried that I was too scared for liberation.

Desperation was a pretty powerful motivator, though, and I wondered if submission could keep me afloat financially while I pursued my dreams. "So subbing for a room, huh?" I asked. "That's unusual. Why does she want that?"

"Ask her yourself." Meghan dug her phone out of her pocket. "I'm texting you her email."

I checked my phone. An email address and the word "Kristen" flashed at me.

"Give it a try or don't." Meghan shrugged. "It might not be a good fit. But at least you'll have explored it. And anyway, you aren't allowed to say that you're going to be homeless anymore."

I blinked. I thought of the affirmation I'd been saying for months. "Everything I need comes my way," I'd intoned that morning while staring at myself in the mirror. I looked at my phone. *Everything I need comes my way.*

CHAPTER THREE

I emailed Kristen while I walked to the BART station. My palms were so sweaty that I thought I might drop my phone. Luckily, I'd spent the previous year dating online pretty exclusively, so I had my virtual charm down pat.

Hi, I typed, in an email with the subject line, *This is awkward.*

My name is Phoenix (and yes, my parents did give me that name, which makes sense if you know my parents). In addition to really liking parentheses, I'm an aerial dancer, a kinky queer femme, and a friend of Meghan's. Meghan said she met you the other night and that you and I might hit it off. She also said you had a room you were looking to fill with somebody who met 'certain requirements.' I'm incredibly curious about what those might be.

Because some folks do better with a visual, here's my YouTube channel, so you can see me dangling off silks, ropes, a lyra hoop, and some trapezes. Notice that my costumes are basically underwear. If that piques your interest, drop me a line, yeah?

I then spent the entire ride back to West Oakland obsessing about how to sign off. Peace? Sincerely? Best? Some cute little emoji? Should I turn off my automatic email signature on my personal email account: "Phoenix Gomez, aerial dancer," with a link to my aerial Facebook page? Did I want this random stranger to have access to my full name and my profile? But if I included a link to my performance videos, she'd be able find me easily enough. Should I skip the link to my videos? But as I'd realized pretty quickly through all that online dating, those videos were more alluring than I ever was in real life. While I was cute in person, in those videos I was magnetic. Every girl I'd directed to that channel had gone out with me at least once, if only out of curiosity. I was strong, flexible, sexy, creative, and powerful in those videos. Whatever the situation was, those videos would almost guarantee me a follow-up from Kristen.

In the end, I left my automatic signature on and finished my email with, *Thanks for considering my unsolicited interest in possibly maybe being your sub. I hope receiving this sort of bid from a complete stranger wasn't completely off-putting.*

Obediently (maybe),

Phoenix.

Then I freaked the fuck out. This freak-out had to be contained however because as soon as I got home, I changed and headed off to an advanced trapeze class. Forty minutes after I'd sent that terrifyingly flirtatious email, I was upside down, hanging by one knee, while the instructor called out positions and 90s music blasted in the background. Before I knew, all my worries faded away.

I loved low-flying, mostly static aerials. This meant no trapeze swinging back and forth through the air, and usually being able to reach the bottom of the apparatus from the ground. It also meant no safety net so I was careful not to risk a fall. I couldn't let my attention wander when I twisted myself around the ropes of the trapeze or balancing on the trapeze bar.

I also performed on silks, long pieces of fabric rigged from the ceiling, and on ropes. Though these let me go higher up, there wasn't a net with these either. Even after years, I still occasionally got jitters if I looked down from the top of these before a trick. The key, I'd learned, was not looking.

My favorite apparatus was lyra hoop. Like a big Hula-Hoop hung vertically from the ceiling by one or two ropes, it was no safer than anything else I performed on, but I always felt more secure on it. Maybe it was because it was so solid, even as it spun, or maybe it was because I'd put in the most hours on it. If I was ever still stressed after an aerials class or training session, I tried to sneak in a little time on the hoop. Twirling up in the air always cleared my head.

Sending that email had made me wonder if I'd need a little hoop time after trapeze class, but by the time I was done with my class, I felt like I'd been wrung out. I was dripping with sweat, pleasantly exhausted, and had gotten out of my head and into my sore body. Aerials always made me put aside my worries and pay attention to my body, to the present moment, to the line between pushing myself and hurting myself so I didn't go too far. Who needed to meditate when you could go upside down?

Kristen and my little email were a distant memory by the time I got home and jumped in the shower. As I pulled on sweats, I realized my phone was dead and plugged it in without a glance. I joined John in the kitchen just as he finished cooking, because my timing was perfect, and settled in for a night of Netflix and John's latest experiment from *660 Curries*.

When I stumbled to bed, stuffed and sleepy at nearly midnight, I was shocked to see not one but two emails from Kristen. The first was simple if a little formal. She thanked me for reaching out and pointed me to her FetLife account. Then she suggested that if I thought we had "common ground," I could email her again and we might meet for coffee. She did not mention the room or give me any more information about herself or even her last name. This was not promising.

The next email was sent an hour after that one and was much more encouraging. It read, *Whoa. I started watching your videos after I emailed you and I have not stopped. You're amazing. Let's meet. Even if we don't have chemistry, I'd love to see one of your shows.*

Sincerely,

Kristen Andersen (but you should call me Kris)

I smiled to myself. I debated emailing her back, but decided it could wait until the morning. She was hooked. I clicked on the link

I'd sent her and watched myself unspool from red fabric, dropping dramatically close to the ground. In another, my hair brushed the floor as I hung by my heels from a trapeze. The camera zoomed in on the left side of my face as I winked suggestively. In some videos, I was all lean muscles and olive skin, my curves barely concealed by sparkly bras and hot pants Sasha had made. I was short with a relatively big butt and thick, strong legs, which made finding clothes a pain. Plus, people who didn't know assumed I was weak because I was a small woman. But in these videos, I was nothing but sexy and powerful.

One of the videos zoomed in on me tightly, the background barely visible. My wavy hair tumbled over my shoulders wildly. It wasn't the best video because it didn't catch every trick that well, but it made me look like a silent film star, glamorous and enigmatic.

Half of the videos on my channel were just me, and the rest were me with partners performing duo acts. Almost always, that partner was Sasha. Her short blond hair and fair skin made it easy to tell us apart. Sasha and I moved in synchronized rhythm. We hung off each other's limbs and folded our bodies around each other in artistic shapes. Of course Kris was hooked. Those videos were hot. The only question was if I could live up to my own image.

❖

The next morning, I realized that that wasn't really the only question. I also needed to find out about Kris, her place, and whether I really wanted to sub for her. I skipped my usual Sunday yoga class in favor of some vigorous googling. I learned Kris was the CEO of tech start-up that I'd heard of but never thought much about. Tech stuff bored me tremendously, so all I really understood was the company developed apps, had started in 2008, and that it seemed to make a stupid amount of money.

The word "wunderkind" was thrown around a lot when anyone wrote about Kristen. As a teenager in the early days of the internet, she'd taught herself how to code in her native Seattle. She earned a computer science degree from the University of Washington while moonlighting building websites. After college, she moved to California and got a job at the then relatively young Google. There wasn't a gap in her résumé from then on, with years of freelancing on top of working at major tech companies before she launched her start-up. At thirty-six, she was successful in a way that sort of made me nauseous.

Also? She was cute. In all her pictures, she wore an elegant V-neck sweater or blazer over a tie and button-down shirt, like that was her uniform. She had bright green eyes behind stylish, masculine glasses; glossy, short brown hair that clearly got cut in some expensive barbershop; and pretty lips on a handsome face. Her mouth seemed to rest like she was about to laugh in every picture, but always at a joke that only she knew.

Next, I poked around Kris's FetLife page, which meant joining FetLife. I gave myself a username that was pretty close to my real name and hoped it wouldn't be a problem. Though I'd been experimenting with BDSM since college and curious before that, I'd been strictly a private player. I read some books and owned decent restraints, but I'd kept myself separate from anything that could be classified as a "scene." I couldn't quite take a lot of the BDSM stuff seriously, mostly because I could not get into the terminology. Looking over profiles and picking out a "role" for my own made me feel like I needed a kinkster dictionary.

Kris's profile was accessible enough at least. Her screen name was pretty generic, nothing that made me embarrassed like, say, "Mistress Kristen." She identified as dominant, which was no surprise. Her picture was her outside on a sunny day, wearing sunglasses and a tank top. Her picture revealed that she had nice arms and also that she totally had the same tank top as Ollie. She had another picture, too, one of her in a very sharp three-piece suit.

Her profile said, "I work long hours, so I'm not as active in the scene or on the site as I want. I'm also not as available as many potential partners might want. I like partners who have their own lives and their own interests. I especially love topping alpha femmes who run the show professionally and have their shit together, and bringing them to a place where they can let go and then past that. I'm not good at being a girlfriend, but I give great aftercare. I'm primarily interested in regular play partners. I'm interested in sharing my home eventually, though not in a strict 24/7 D/s relationship, or a traditional vanilla one. I'm still friends with just about everyone I've ever played with, and I want to like the people I tie up. I'm interested in women. I'm a cisgender butch lesbian, in case you weren't sure."

Her profile also gave me a list of her turn-ons. Giving: face-slapping, biting, bruises, hair pulling, flogging, spanking, bondage, rough sex. Receiving: service, oral sex. Everything to do with: butch-femme, control, aftercare, and femmes. Watching others wear lingerie and red lipstick. Putting bratty bottoms in their place.

Yeah, let's meet, I emailed her as soon as I read that. *When do you want to buy me coffee?*

Weekdays are crazy for me, so it will have to be the weekend, she replied right away. *Next Sunday, 10 a.m., Philz in the Mission.* There wasn't a question mark in sight.

It seemed to me that the place she was putting this bratty bottom was her spare bedroom, rent-free.

CHAPTER FOUR

Would I have gone out with Kris if I hadn't been hoping to sub for a room? I thought about it as I took BART to the 24th Street Mission stop in San Francisco. Historically, I dated people who'd eventually be something big, but who were sort of a mess when I met them. My first girlfriend, Amanda, had gone on to get a PhD in English lit (with an eye toward feminist intersectionality) by thirty and adapt her thesis for an academic press. When we met, though, we were seniors in high school in Albuquerque. She was still using her given name and the male pronouns she'd been raised with. She was tortured about her gender identity, unfocused in her ambitions, and showing only hints of the brilliance she actually had.

My next girlfriend, Carolena, was a fantastically political, furious student activist who never did her homework, and a wannabe rapper under the name La Verde. After college, she went to New York and became a full-time, well-respected activist.

My kinkiest ex, Ronnie, spent most of our two years together working as a dog walker, getting faded in her ample free time, and stopping around the Bay Area to rescue stray dogs. After we broke up, she got into veterinary school and eventually joined a practice with a spotless reputation.

My last ex, Beth, had been a sulky barista who constantly gave me just enough attention to keep me hooked. She took me out for a weekend trip to Napa and dumped me on the drive back to Oakland. Then she started therapy about her commitment issues, got a promotion to manager, met a genuinely nice woman, and was engaged before I'd updated my OKCupid profile.

I thought it was notable that I loved these women before they really bloomed. Though I helped some, and in Amanda's case, my sympathetic professor parents helped as much as I did, it wasn't that I improved them. I just loved people unfinished and untidy, but most people don't stay that way. On less generous days, I thought maybe I just couldn't stand to be with someone who had it together when I didn't. I couldn't imagine myself with someone accomplished and sure of themselves when I was worrying about how long I could go without replacing my three-a-pack underwear from Target. Or when I was still toiling away and unsure if my dreams would ever come to anything.

I couldn't imagine how Kristen and I would have met in real life. We didn't exactly move in the same circles. I also couldn't imagine feeling brave enough to approach her, or any situation in which she'd approach me.

But since we both knew Meghan and we maybe had complementary interests, there we were. Kristen stood outside Philz Coffee, wearing jeans, a T-shirt, a hoodie, and sneakers. She was on her phone, frowning, when I approached her. I was already sweating, running slightly late, and worried about my outfit. What did you wear to something that was a date, job interview, possible new roommate meet, and kinky get-together all in one? I'd settled for black flats, fishnets, and a curve-hugging sleeveless red dress, topped off with giant hoop earrings. Seeing Kris, I worried I was overdressed.

As soon as I waved, she gave me a big smile that revealed slightly crooked teeth. I'd never seen those in the pictures, I realized. She put away her phone. "Phoenix?" she asked.

"Hi," I squeaked and gave her an awkward hug. She was not as tall or imposing as I'd imagined, but she was still half a foot taller than five-foot-one-inch me.

After she bought me coffee, we tried and failed to find an empty table. "Maybe we could walk over to Dolores Park?" she suggested.

I nodded. I was so hopeful it would work out with Kris that I was a gulping, sweaty ball of anxiety. This was not my most attractive look.

It was a beautiful August day, actually hot for a change, and Kris shrugged off her hoodie. She kept the conversation going for our short walk to Dolores, giving me a little background on herself. I was too nervous to do much more than nod along. When it became obvious that I wasn't going to pull my own conversational weight, she told me she'd seen some of my aerial videos and was impressed.

"Which did you watch?" I asked.

"You and another woman were going up and down fabric in sync to Jenny Lewis." She smiled.

"I liked that performance." I nodded, thinking of our careful climbs and drops on the silks. "The other woman is my friend Sasha."

"I saw another where she took your clothes off and put them on herself. You were on a trapeze."

I blushed. We'd done that low-flying trapeze act for a burlesque show years earlier. Sasha started the performance wearing only lingerie, but by the end I was the one stripped down to little more than pasties and a thong. She lay on the ground and pulled my shirt off while I dangled in a one-knee hang. I had held a crucifix pose as Sasha, kneeling in front of me, took my pants off. One night the zipper had gotten stuck and I stayed in the position so long that the rope had rubbed a patch of skin off my arm. I still had a scar.

"And one of you by yourself," Kris said as we entered the park. "You were on a hoop in the air, spinning around and flirting with the crowd."

"That's my favorite."

"You were great."

"Thanks." I gulped my coffee too fast and burned my tongue. We silently found an empty spot and sat on the grass.

"So what do you want, exactly?" I blurted as soon as we were sitting. With my shot nerves, I couldn't help myself, despite the stunned look on her face.

She exhaled slowly. "Let's start with getting to know each other a little."

"Right, right, of course. I'm sorry. I'm just nervous. Meghan told me you might be looking for a live-in sub, and my roommate's moving out, and I gave notice at my job, and basically, I'm freaking out. So I'm being weird."

"It's a weird situation," she said diplomatically. "I've never had a live-in sub before. I don't normally meet with complete strangers who might live in my house."

"I don't normally even meet up with strangers who I'm just looking to sleep with," I mumbled. "I mean, I date. But I'm not, I don't know, in the scene or whatever. I don't go to sex parties or find people just to do kinky things with. So this is…"

"Are you wondering what you're doing here?"

"Kind of."

"You're having coffee with somebody. If it doesn't work out, it's not a big deal, is it?"

I nodded. When I told Sasha that I was losing my roommate, she offered to let me stay with her and find me a place in her co-op. Unfortunately, Sasha lived in a repurposed walk-in closet. It was incredibly cheap, but living with a dozen people and attending weekly co-op meetings with all of them did not appeal to me. Still, I had options.

"I noticed your profile wasn't filled out," Kris said. "I thought maybe you were pretty new to this, and I was hesitant about that."

"Why?"

"I don't generally play with someone who's this new."

"I'm not new to it. I'm just not…public. I've done lots of stuff. In private."

"Oh yeah? What kind of stuff?"

I blushed again but made myself sit taller. "Wouldn't you like to know?"

"I would, actually. That's why we're having coffee."

I took another scorching gulp. *Way to flirt, Phoenix.* "I've been tied up."

"With what?"

"Restraints, fabric ones. Ropes. Not, like, chains or anything."

"And you liked it?"

I grinned. "Very much."

Kris reached over to capture a curl that had fallen in front of my shoulder. She tucked it behind my ear. "You saw my whole list. I'd like to know yours."

"I've never exactly made a list. I guess I've tried things, and I liked them or I didn't."

"What have you tried? What have you liked?" she asked cheerfully. "What didn't you like?"

My upper lip began to sweat, a sign I was exceptionally nervous. I chugged the last of my coffee and excused myself to throw away the empty cup. I was hoping she'd forget about it by the time I got back, but when I sat back down, she just looked at me expectantly. I shook my head. "I'm new to talking about it with someone I barely know."

"You don't know me well enough to talk to me about your kinks, but you know me well enough to consider moving in with me and having kinky sex with me?" Kris arched an eyebrow.

"Touché. But where do I start?"

She sipped her coffee slowly, then asked, "Have you ever made a yes/no/maybe list?"

I shook my head.

"Why don't you try one, and if you want to meet again, we can compare what we like. They're kind of cheesy sometimes, but they're useful. I'll send you a link."

"Okay." I shrugged. "Not to be too forward, but why are you interested in this? I mean, I'm a broke wannabe aerialist. But you're successful and you must meet tons of women who share your, um, interests. You're involved in BDSM stuff, and you could pay a professional if you wanted. So, why this?"

She flashed me the smile from her photographs. "I've been thinking about this fantasy for a while, and I'd discussed it with a couple of partners in the past, but it never worked out. I do okay with play partners, but it can be hard to meet people because I work so much. My last sub moved to San Diego a few months ago, and I've been looking for a new one, asking people in the scene if they know anyone for me. I told Meghan I was looking for a sub. She asked more about it, and I told her my dream is to have a hot, live-in, femme sub who'd clean and cook. She made a joke about me getting a sex housewife in exchange for rent, and I said it didn't sound half bad and to send anybody who fit the bill my way. Before I knew it, I was watching those videos you sent, and now here you are."

"Ask and you shall receive."

"It's worked out for me. Or at least, we're having coffee. I'm interested in exploring this. What about you?"

"I'm interested. I mean, I want to see your house." I nudged her playfully with my shoulder.

"If our interests line up, let's play, and then we can talk about the house. Any interest in the party at Mission Control next weekend?"

I raised my eyebrows. "I've never gone to anything like that before. I'd be much more comfortable if we played in private first."

"Really?" She looked shocked.

"Look, kink in public is new to me. But kink in private? I know how to do that."

She looked worried. "It's been a long, long time since I played with a new person in private. I always play with new partners for the first time in public."

I chewed a hangnail. "Is that something you can compromise on?"

"I think so. But I'm not used to it."

"I'm not used to any of it."

"But you're interested?" She took my hand and I jumped at the unexpected jolt it gave me.

"Very." I leaned closer to her. "Though I think we should test if we have chemistry."

"And how would we do that?" she asked huskily.

I kissed her slowly, lightly. Her lips were soft and yielding. It lasted just for a minute, but I felt a spark, a rush of desire.

"So," she said after we had pulled apart. "When do you want to come over?"

"Now?"

She pulled out her phone and frowned again. "Actually, I have to get back to work. Tomorrow?"

"Sure."

"Bring the yes/no/maybe list. I'll text you." She gave me a peck on the cheek. She was already calling someone and walking away.

CHAPTER FIVE

We met in the same place the next afternoon. It was my first Sunday as an unemployed person, and I couldn't quite believe it. John and Ollie were leaving in six weeks. If it didn't work out with Kris, I'd need to find another solution pretty fast. If it were possible, I was even more nervous than I'd been the day before. When I told John I was going to see Kris's place, he frowned and told me to please be careful, which didn't exactly help matters.

After we grabbed coffee, Kris and I walked to her house a few blocks away. I'd been expecting an ultra modern loft with a million-dollar view. Instead of sleek and stark, her house was a skinny Victorian with bay windows and intricate details. It sat so close to the neighboring houses that they almost looked connected. A treacherously steep driveway led down to a garage door exactly the size of one car. A single row of planter boxes filled with flowers separated the descending driveway from the ascending staircase to the front door. It was classic San Francisco, the kind of house I'd dreamed of living in since I moved to the area for college at San Francisco State University nine years earlier.

"It's beautiful," I breathed.

She beamed. "Thanks. When I bought it, it was a mess. I had it restored."

She led us up the stairs to an even lovelier interior. Gleaming hardwood floors and a wooden staircase to the top floor greeted us. There were French doors in the back of the house showing glimpses of a yard. There was also a small room with a closed door off the kitchen. The living room, dining room, and kitchen were all open to each other, and the place looked like it could have been the last five minutes of a remodel show on HGTV. It wasn't huge, but it was big for San Francisco, and comfortable.

The living room had a window seat in the beautiful bay window, a cream-colored love seat and a blue velvet chair, along with a plush cream rug, a rustic coffee table, and a flat-screen TV mounted above the fireplace. The dining area was filled with a square table I recognized from John's West Elm catalogues, four high-backed chairs with blue velvet cushions, and a funky chandelier. The kitchen was full of high-end appliances, marble countertops, and featured shining pots and pans hanging from a pot rack over a butcher-block island. French doors in the back of the kitchen opened out to a teeny patio. I peeked outside, where there were two chairs and a bistro table. Another row of planter boxes lined the edge of the patio, and behind those was a simple wooden fence. Above the patio was the underside of a deck, and the wilting flowers in the planter boxes were the only things getting any sunlight out back, but any yard at all was a big deal in the city. I wandered back into the kitchen. It was all impossibly clean and perfect.

"Wow. It's like something out of a magazine." As I said it, I realized that it was also impersonal. Other than a few framed pictures on the walls of Kris and what had to be her parents and siblings, this house could have belonged to anyone. It looked staged to sell. The little I knew about Kris wasn't reflected anywhere. On our walk yesterday, she told me she never cooked, but she had a gourmet kitchen. She'd devoted her life to working in tech, but there wasn't a gadget or even a computer in sight. She'd told me she'd lived alone since she'd bought the house, but her dining room table was set for four.

"I bought in 2011," she said. "My contractor and designer did so much work."

"Did you pick this out?" I pointed to a gorgeous stainless steel saucepan.

She shook her head. "I told the designer what I liked and what I didn't, and I wrote her a check," she said apologetically. Then she continued the tour with the half bath under the stairs and the stacked washer/dryer squeezed into a former linen closet. I wondered about the room with the closed door, but Kris put her hand on the small of my back and led me up the stairs.

The first bedroom had a bay window with another window seat. Like the downstairs, it was perfect but somewhat anonymous, like a quirky boutique hotel room. The queen bed looked inviting and topped with what looked like a dozen red pillows in different prints, a white comforter, and a soft black throw. The hardwood was partially covered by another plush rug, this one black. Other than that, there a white side table, white desk, and a small white chest of drawers, some abstract art, an accent wall painted red, and a medium-sized closet. "This would be your room, if we go forward with this," Kris said. "Furnished if you want, or we could get rid of this stuff."

"This is all way nicer than what I own," I said. If I sold my furniture I wouldn't even have to rent a U-Haul.

Opposite the bay window was a red-handled door that opened to the bathroom. Like the half bath under the stairs, it was tiled in cool greens and whites, with thick white towels, lots of mirrors, and a spa-like feel. Unlike the downstairs, it was big with a white claw-foot tub and a separate glass shower large enough for two. Another door in the bathroom led into Kris's room.

It seemed like Kris's room was the only place in the house that was actually used. It was larger than the other bedroom, but cluttered and overstuffed. Other than a dark blue accent wall, it seemed to have left the decorator's tastes behind. A weight bench and a set of free weights blocked one of the doors to the closet doors. The windows above the headboard were covered by blackout blinds. A concert poster from 2003 was tacked over the unmade king-size bed. Next to the bed, a table with a tower of books partially blocked the door to the upstairs deck.

The dark wood furniture was covered by scattered papers, a tablet, an iPod, a laptop, and a smartphone with a cracked screen, even though Kris had her phone in her pocket. The desk had a desktop computer, a pile of books, and even more papers. A TV was mounted on the wall, with an Xbox on the dresser below. A shelf ran around the top of the room, stuffed with books, games, and DVDs. The floor was clear, with a plush rug in navy blue, but the half-open walk-in closet overflowed with clothes on the ground, kicked off shoes, and clear plastic storage boxes.

"A little different than the rest of the place," I teased her.

"This is one of the only rooms I actually use. And one of the only ones my cleaning lady doesn't touch."

"I thought part of the idea of me moving in is that I'd be your cleaning lady." I clucked my tongue. "Am I making somebody redundant?"

She laughed. "She's retiring, so I have a vacancy. C'mon, I'll show you the best part."

Kris took my hand and led me through the narrow door. Outside was a deck. There was an oversized mahogany chair with huge white cushions and a matching ottoman, a sleek chaise lounge, and a metal side table. Lights were strung up overhead, and I saw the tiny garden when I peered over the railing. The view was just neighboring houses mostly, but it was quiet, sunny, and peaceful. It was the kind of thing I'd dreamed of in a home, a private sanctuary.

"Now this is amazing."

She stretched out on the chaise. "I work out here whenever I work from home. I love it here."

"Is this for sharing?" Even before I asked, I already knew the answer.

Kris looked sheepish. "Sorry, but I want to keep this all to myself."

"I can't blame you. If it were mine, I probably wouldn't share either. Even with a hot sub."

"I think it's important we have boundaries, you know? It's already an unusual situation, and I don't want to make it messier than it has to be. So if you want to do this, your room will be yours, and mine will be mine, and there'll still be separation. Speaking of which, let's go back downstairs." I followed her to the living room, worrying the whole way.

Once I was settled on the incredibly comfortable love seat, I blurted, "Can we talk more about what that would entail, if we decide to do this?" I bit my lip.

She plopped down in the blue chair. "I want a woman who will clean my house, do the laundry, run errands, and keep a couple of home-cooked meals in my fridge. I want to come home from work and fuck her, then go to my bedroom and close the door."

"So, what, I'd need to be waiting around for you to come home every night?" I fluffed a pillow and arranged it behind me.

Kris shook her head. "We'll pick a time and keep that hour set aside for sex, for kink and domination. And a few extra hours on the weekend for longer scenes or play parties."

"And if the hour passes without sex?"

"I might text you instructions to follow. But if I miss it, then I miss it." She spoke without hesitation or shame, looking me right in the eyes. I couldn't meet her gaze.

"So it's every day?"

"We can pick a day off, two if we really need to, but I want at least five days a week."

That sounded like dream come true to me. I'd never dated someone with a libido as high as my own. I chewed on my lip. "What about the cooking and cleaning? What standards are we talking about?" I picked at my sparkly red nail polish. I wanted to know more about the sex and the kink, but I felt incredibly shy.

"Neat and tidy. It doesn't need to be shining all the time, but the dishes need to be done, I don't want dust all over, and I don't want the laundry to sit around for two weeks. I'll give you a list. As for food, I'm not picky, I just can't cook. There's a chef at work, but sometimes I'd like to eat something at home other than takeout."

I nodded. "Is this a twenty-four seven thing? Do I have to call you 'Master' with a capital M and always refer to myself in the lower case?"

She shook her head. "No. I want you to call me Kris, whatever we're doing. Here's what I like…" She paused and leaned toward me a little. "I like a woman who has her own life and is her own person, who won't indulge me all the time, and then, for this window of time, submits to me completely. I like taking a woman down and afterward having her go back to her independent life."

It sounded too perfect, too much like my own fantasies. "Are you an asshole or something? Are you going to say you 'don't do drama' or some other bullshit?"

"Do I seem like an asshole?"

I raised my eyebrows. "You're a hot butch top with money in San Francisco and you're offering me free housing in exchange for kinky sex and moderate housework. It's sort of too perfect. I want to know what the catch is."

She frowned. "I work eighty hours a week, minimum. Usually it's more like ninety hours, sometimes more than that. I haven't taken a vacation in six years. I even work when I visit my parents. The day my house was finished being remodeled, I went to work for fourteen hours. I've been working full-time since I was in high school, and working the hours I do for almost fifteen years. My life is work. Kink's my only hobby. On a good week I go for a run once or twice, lift weights in the mornings, and play video games for a few hours on Sunday, maybe binge-watch *Doctor Who* one evening." She sounded a little embarrassed at that admission. "That and kinky sex are all I do with my free time. I never have time or energy to go to a girlfriend's friend's birthday party."

I smiled. "Which Doctor is your favorite?"

"I really liked Matt Smith," she said conspiratorially. "But I'm incredibly excited for Jodie Whittaker."

"For me, it's David Tennant forever."

We laughed nervously.

She looked at her hands. Her phone vibrated in her pocket and she winced a little. "I've tried to be a girlfriend, and inevitably, I disappoint because I never have time for normal things. My last girlfriend started out perfectly happy with what I had to offer, but by the end, she wanted someone who'd be home for dinner, who she could marry and who'd spend Sunday morning getting brunch with her."

"Fuck brunch." That made her laugh, a big, loud guffaw.

"It's not unreasonable. But I'm not going to change how much I work or how I live my life. So I can't be what most women want from a girlfriend. But I still have things to offer."

"Is that what happened with your last sub? She wanted more?"

Kris shook her head. "We were involved for two years, but we weren't exclusive. She had other partners. I didn't have time for other regular partners, but once in a while I played with someone else if the stars lined up. She and I saw each other about once a week. I wanted to play more often, but my schedule was tough and she couldn't drop everything when I happened to be available. After a while, I told her about my live-in sub fantasy. We talked about it, but she wasn't interested. She moved to be with her partner in San Diego. We're on good terms though."

I eyed her suspiciously. "You seem too good to be true."

She lifted her hands in a helpless gesture. "Look, I won't ever be your girlfriend. I'm not available for a lot of things. I work too much and that makes me boring. Those sound like small limitations now, but eventually, they become a problem."

I rolled my eyes. "The last thing I'm looking for is a girlfriend. I have plenty going on in my life as it is."

"So is this an option?" she asked.

I looked around the perfect living room. "This is an option."

"Good. I think so too."

"Your house is amazing, by the way."

"Thanks."

"But, ugh, where am I going to park?"

"Do you really need a car? It's only a fifteen-minute walk from BART, and there are buses, and the Muni."

"On Mondays and Wednesdays I teach two classes an hour apart at different studios. It'd be cutting it too close getting there on public transit."

"You could use my car," she said. "I can walk to work. I could schedule around when you need it."

My eyes widened. "Really? Isn't that a little much?"

"It's just sitting in the garage most of the time anyway. If you figure out the insurance, it's no problem to me."

I stared at her. I noticed that she'd kicked off her shoes and they were half-hidden under the couch. Her bare toes dug into the rug.

"If you don't want it, say no," she commanded me, the first hint of what she sounded like in dominant mode.

I considered it as I uncrossed my legs. My old Hyundai was paid for, and I could probably get a couple thousand for it. Without the cost of rent and a boost from selling my car and meager furniture, my budget could relax. I'd need to stay frugal, but I could get a massage every now and then, see a show, buy a sandwich. And even if the arrangement only lasted a little while, my budget would still be eased during the early months of striking out as a performer.

"Thank you," I said. "I'd really appreciate using your car."

"So do you want to get together next weekend and decide if we're doing this?"

"What's left to decide? I'm on board."

She frowned at me. "The sex? The kink?"

"Right." I gulped. "Well, I find you attractive, so I'm on board for that too."

"There's also the STI talk," she said.

"Um, I haven't had sex since the last time I got tested, so I'm good. You?"

"Same here."

"So, we're settled?"

"Phoenix, we need to negotiate about what we like," she said seriously.

"Oh, yes, right. Sorry."

"So, what do you like?"

I blinked at her.

"Your list?" she said.

I dug my list out of my purse and handed it to her. I'd printed it off the night before and labored over it all morning. The list was four pages long, an alphabetical list of kinks, each with space to mark whether or not you've had experience with said kink, rate your willingness about it on a scale of zero to five, and room to write notes. I'd written a lot of notes.

Despite years dabbling in kink, I had never looked over a list like that before. When I'd told Amanda of my recurring fantasies of being spanked and ordered around, she'd recoiled and said she could never do something like that. Our one attempt at anything kinky had ended with me handcuffing her, something neither of us enjoyed, and that marked the beginning of the end for us. Carolena and I had stumbled into BDSM ignorantly, buying restraints from Good Vibrations with nothing more than a sales clerk's explanation of basic safety, trying on roles and games with enthusiasm but no clue what we were doing, or what to do if either of us got uncomfortable in the middle of it. It wasn't until I met Meghan that I actually read a BDSM book or blog.

I'd only gone to kinky spaces with Ronnie, and then just to learn specific skills that we hadn't mastered via YouTube videos. Ronnie was barely more experienced with kink than I was, and other than one wild play party before we met, was not part of a BDSM scene either. By the time any fantasies or preferences had come up in my life, I'd already been invested in the relationship, and sexual and kinky likes and dislikes had been discussed gradually, a little at a time over months. When I tried to broach the subject with Beth, she'd told me the only thing she wanted to know about kink was the "psychology that made people like stuff like that." For our whole relationship and the year since we'd split, I'd never even mentioned my interest in BDSM while on a date.

So the list made me think about what I wanted in a way I hadn't before. Some were an easy yes in terms of experience and a five in terms of willingness, like being bitten, light bondage, hair pulling, face slapping, following orders, giving and receiving oral sex, wearing high heels and lingerie (with a note that she was very welcome to buy me these), a wide variety of spanking and hitting with and without implements, punishment scenes, all sorts of genital sex, and strap-ons (with some notes about the many, many ways I enjoyed strap-ons).

Some were an easy no and a zero in terms of willingness, like permanent marks, piercing, suspension bondage, cages, gags, filming or photographing what we did, vomit, feces, and urine (with a note that I guess I could pee on her if she really wanted, but nobody was going to pee on me). But a lot of them left me stumped. How did I feel about body paint, leather or rubber or latex clothes, corsets, uniforms, or shoe and boot worship? Mostly, I felt that these things weren't particularly sexual to me, and I thought I'd feel silly, but it wasn't a hard no, so I wrote that again and again.

Others left me confused, like Saran wrapping, manicures, and wearing symbolic jewelry. I wrote, "I'm confused by this," next to them, and marked them a one. I noted that I had to look up "Violet Wand" and "metal thumbcuffs" and marked zero willingness to try these. I wrote "meh" next to some and marked them a two, like "standing in the corner," tickling, blindfolds, hot wax, ice cubes, and erotic dancing.

I marked four for things I'd never tried but wondered about, like intricate bondage, group sex, fisting, and "play kidnapping," and then immediately worried that Kris would think I was too weird. Some I marked moderate interest in, like stocks, with the note, "This seems complicated, and I would not want to set this up." I made an elaborate note next to "anal sex," reading, "I'm not usually into anal, so don't ask. If it's the one day a year I'm in the mood for it, I'll tell you," and then worried it was too bossy. I crossed out things about blood four different times before scrawling, "No drawing blood, but period sex is okay."

I worried a lot while filling it out. What if she loved outdoor sex and I marked it "no"? I said the backyard would be fine, but not somewhere we could get caught. What about exhibitionism or voyeurism? I marked them a two and said I didn't feel any particular way about them. What if she had strong preferences about types of restraints? I said they were all fine. Slutty clothing? I wrote, "Most of my clothes are slutty clothes," and then worried I sounded too flippant. Food play, teasing, kneeling, wrestling? "I think it depends and maybe warrants a deeper conversation," I wrote, and then thought I was too vague. Domestic service? "Duh," I noted. "That's what we're doing, right?" but I was afraid she'd hate my answer.

The thought of her reading through my weird, vulnerable answers while I just sat there made me squirm. Luckily, she pulled her own list from her pocket and handed it to me. "I thought you'd like to see my answers too," she said. I breathed a sigh of relief.

Kris's answers were not covered in notes. She'd tried a lot of things, and had plenty of zeroes and ones on her list, along with lots of fours and fives. She didn't have as much in the middle as I did. I relaxed seeing she wasn't interested in anyone peeing on anyone else, or choking, breath play, age play, or either of us pretending to be any kind of animal. I was disappointed, though, that she'd marked "zero" next to "weapons (knives, guns, etc.)."

"Oh, period sex, I'd never thought about that on this list," she said without looking up from my list. "Change my answer to that. Period sex is good."

"What about knives?"

"What about them?"

"I, um, like knives."

"If one of us isn't comfortable with something, we shouldn't do it together, even if the other likes it. Are knives essential for you?"

"No," I said too quickly. "I just, I don't know, it was different with my exes. We just tried things." I thought of an elaborate doctor scene I'd done with Ronnie, despite how un-aroused it left me. "No medical play," I added. "I didn't write that down, but I want to add it."

"Okay." Kris went back to reading.

At the bottom of the list was a space for allergies, medical conditions, aftercare requests, and other comments and ideas. I'd marked "none" for allergies and medical conditions, requested only water and somewhere soft to sit for aftercare, but written a lot for "other." So much that it spilled over to the back of the page.

"Don't call me a bitch. Don't tell me I'm ugly. Nothing racist or homophobic," I'd written, thinking of a particularly miserable encounter when Carolena had attempted to incorporate painful words that had been slung her way in high school. As much as eroticizing it took the sting out for her, they hit too close to home for me. It shut me down and turned me off. Just thinking about it, even years later, made me feel queasy.

"Don't hit me with a squid or anything," I'd written, with the explanation, "(I read about it in an article on edgeplay). Humiliation is a maybe. Being stripped could be hot but being made to cry would not."

I'd followed that with, "I don't like tons of pain. I don't want to be screaming in agony. But I like being hit safely! Don't punch me in the stomach or the kidneys or things like that. Don't damage me. The kind of performance I do hurts. I get rope burns and calluses and abrasions, and I'm proud of being able to withstand it so I can do something beautiful. It also grounds me and puts me in my body. There's an edge of pain that's good and satisfying, and it's different from pain that's telling me to stop, and I like finding that edge. I don't like going over it. I want to feel, not just hurt. That's how I feel about pain in a scene too. I like it, to a very specific degree."

Kris's answers were simpler here too. About aftercare, she'd written, "I like string cheese and apples, water, to hear all the things you liked, verbal reassurance, and occasionally cuddling." For "other," she wrote, "I don't like subbing, but I like bottoming sometimes."

"What's the difference between subbing and bottoming?" I wondered if I should already know.

"I like being fucked and touched and getting head, but as a dominant," she said. "I like to be in charge when that happens. Well, I like to be in charge always, but especially if that's happening."

"Oh, okay." I looked back down at her list.

"Yours is very thorough." She sounded impressed. "It's very helpful. Like here." She pointed to my comments on the back. "Now I know that when you say that's enough pain, it doesn't go further. This gives me great guidelines."

"Thanks. I felt like I wrote too much."

"No, it's perfect."

"You didn't say as much." I pointed at her list.

"I didn't have as much to say."

"I don't believe that. You have this whole domestic service fantasy, but you barely wrote anything about it here."

Now it was her turn to look embarrassed. "I don't talk about it much."

"No fair! I never talk about my fantasies and I didn't get to use that as an excuse."

"Okay," she said slowly. "Most of all what I like is to give orders and have them followed, and to reward or punish according to whether or not they were. Whatever a reward is for you, we'll talk about it beforehand, and I'll give it to you. And you'll tell me how to punish you too. I like taking control and giving someone exactly what she wants, without her having to ask in the scene, without her needing to say anything. And sometimes, I just want to take a beautiful girl, hold her down, and control her. But I don't want to control her completely. I tried twenty-four seven before, if I can't be a decent girlfriend, I really can't be a good twenty-four seven dominant. It's too much energy for me, and it doesn't fulfill the need I have."

"Which is?"

"I've had this fantasy since I was in middle school, of a beautiful woman in a red coat, long hair, heels. She has an entire life outside of me, but for a little while, I take her into a room and do anything I want to her, and she lets me. She gives in to me, and when I'm done, she puts her coat back on and walks out the door, back to her other life that has nothing to do with me, that I don't have a part in. She's so close, but she's never exactly mine. I can have her, but I can't keep her. What makes it hot is that she is powerful the rest of the time, that she can say no to me—sometimes she does, sometimes she shuts me down and I can't do anything about it—and she has all this power, and chooses to let go with me. She lets me take control, but she doesn't need me to. I want that feeling that I have to give her exactly what she wants, even as I take what I want. I have to give her the things she wants but won't ask for. Because even though I'm in control, I have to earn that control from her. Do you understand?"

"Yes, but where do the domestic service fit in?"

"I want to be reminded of that dynamic every time I look around my home. I want to pick up a T-shirt in the morning and think it was put there by a hot, naked woman as an act of service. I want a woman who will let me make her do these things, even when I'm not there, but who won't give up control of her whole life to me either."

I fidgeted, feeling my clit starting to throb at the description. "I like the sound of that," I said.

"Which part?" She leaned toward me.

"All of it."

"How would I punish you?" She laid a hand on my bare knee. "And how would I reward you?"

"You'd reward me by making me come."

"Happily. Any which way in particular?"

"I like almost everything. Mouth, hands, penetration, all of it works for me. Sometimes, being tied up, or being hit for a while, anything that brings that edge of pain, makes it more intense. That could be part of the reward."

She grinned. "What about punishment? What do you want then?"

"Just use me." I shocked myself with how shameless I sounded. "Make me wait, don't let me get off, deprive me. Use me to make yourself come."

My cheeks felt hot.

"Excellent."

"What about you?" I asked. "How do I please you?"

"By doing what you're told whenever we play," she said a little sharply. "Do you have a safe word? Or do you just use 'no'?"

"Red, yellow, green," I said. "Sometimes I like it when I say 'no' and it's ignored."

"As a reward or a punishment?"

"A punishment. But also, sometimes I'll come, and I'll say I'm done, but if someone keeps going, I'll keep going, you know?"

"And you like that?"

"Yes," I exhaled. "A lot."

"Come here," she said. I got up and sat next to her on the arm of the chair. She pulled me onto her lap. "You want to try this?"

"Yes." I turned toward her face. Up close, I could see a dusting of freckles on her nose, and how unexpectedly long her eyelashes were. Her lips looked soft.

"Usually, I'm home by eight o'clock." She ran her left hand up my thigh. "At eight thirty Monday through Thursday, I'm going to tell you it's eight thirty, and for an hour we'll play and have aftercare, and then we'll stop. I'll give you any orders during that hour, and the rest of the day, your time will be your own. How does that sound?"

I could feel myself getting wet. "Yes."

"I want one longer evening and one afternoon on the weekend. Pick which day you want off."

"Saturday," I said. "I'll be teaching on Saturdays, and that's usually the night when I get gigs."

"So Friday night and Sunday afternoon, you're mine?" she said, her voice low.

I nodded. I didn't teach at all Friday, and Sunday I finished teaching before noon.

"Friday at eight, for two hours, and Sunday from one to four. How is that for you?"

"I think it's good. But what if I get a Friday night gig?"

"You'll tell me and we'll reschedule. But you have to tell me right away, and you have to say please."

"Yes." I moaned as she slipped her hand between my thighs, resting it tantalizingly close to my hardening clit.

"If I can't get away from work, I'll text you. I'll tell you what I want you to do, and you'll do it, even if I'm not there to reward you or punish you right then."

I nodded. I edged forward, trying to press my pussy against her hand. She moved her hand away.

"If you want something from me, you'll ask and you'll say please."

"I'll try," I said.

"You'll do it or you'll be punished," she snapped.

I asked, "What if I safe word?"

"Then we'll stop. We won't do anything you don't want," Kris said, much more gently.

"Even if it's eight thirty?"

"Even then."

I scrunched up my face. "This is new to me in a lot of ways. What if something comes up, or I need something, and I don't know it already?"

"We'll figure it out." She shrugged.

"What if I say no too much?"

"If we try this and it doesn't work, for either of us, we'll reevaluate together. Let's try it and check in."

"I'm at a disadvantage," I pointed out. "If it doesn't work for you, you're out a sub. But if it isn't working for me, I have to move out and I can't even afford my old place."

"There is a huge imbalance. Do you think it's too unequal to work?" she asked calmly.

"Or…" I said quietly, looking at my lap. "Or maybe that's part of the appeal. You do have this power over me."

"But it doesn't exactly make it easy for you to have your own independent life and to feel free saying no, not if you're worried that you'll be out on your ass if you don't keep me happy. Part of what's hot for me is that you aren't helpless. You're incredibly talented and obviously hardworking and ambitious, and I don't want this to make you feel like you aren't."

"So what's the solution here?"

Kris thought a minute. "How about this? I'll make sure you have housing for the next three months. If living together isn't working, you can move out and I'll help you pay your rent until the three months are up. If it is working after three months, we'll decide if we want to sign on for longer."

"That's incredibly generous. Maybe too generous"

"I like being generous. I like being able to support somebody's dream. And this makes the footing a lot more equal, doesn't it?"

"Only if you don't change your mind."

"We can talk to Meghan about writing up a housing agreement or something. To protect both of us."

Smart, generous, hot. Who was this person?

"Sound good?"

"Would you please kiss me?"

Kris took my face in both her hands, pulled me in, and gave me a soft, sweet kiss. I kissed her back a little harder, and she nipped at my lower lip. As our kisses became more heated, I climbed onto her lap, straddling her thighs.

She wrapped a hand in my hair and yanked my head back. "You didn't ask," she chided me.

"Please?" I moaned, ready to grind myself on her.

"No." Her eyes sparkled. "Because now you get to see the last room."

She led me to that closed door I'd wondered about. She opened it and revealed another bedroom. The walls were painted lavender, and it had soft, dark gray carpet wall-to-wall. In the center of the room was a full-sized bed done in pale cotton sheets and a purple knit blanket. The room had several lilac lanterns in different sizes casting the room in soft, tinted light. The ceiling was dotted with eye hooks ready for rope, and restraints hung out from under the mattress at the head and foot of the bed. There was no headboard, but two small bedside tables, both black and with drawers. I opened the matching black wardrobe to reveal a collection of dildos and harnesses, high-quality vibrators in a range of styles, lube in large bottles (the good stuff, I noticed), a basket of condoms, gloves, and dental dams, and several blindfolds. Kris opened the closet for me, revealing a well-lit display of floggers, paddles, riding crops, ropes, clamps, and other toys.

"Every other room, I told other people to use their best judgment on, but I decided every detail here," she said proudly.

The slatted dark blinds were open slightly. I could see the garden and the back fence.

She pointed to a small black mini fridge next to the wardrobe. "It will be your responsibility to keep that stocked with everything we want for aftercare."

"Huh?"

"I don't want to go to the kitchen after I play," she said. "Or are you giving me that look because you aren't sure you're interested?"

"I'm so interested that I'm moving in. That is, if you'll have me."

Kris smiled at me. "Get on your knees."

I dropped to the soft ground and let my ballet flats fall from my feet.

"Take off your dress."

I lifted my cotton dress above my head and tossed it to floor, wearing only my black panties and my skimpy black push-up bra that made my generous C-cup breasts spill out. I looked up at her standing in front of me, her loose jeans clinging a little over her strong thighs, her biceps defined and peeking out from her T-shirt.

She ran a finger over my cheek. My hands were calloused from aerials, but Kris's hands were soft.

"You're going to suck my cock." She went to the wardrobe to select one.

I wanted to. I wanted to do anything she told me to, to submit, open up, release. But I also wanted to be like her fantasy woman and make her work for it.

"Actually, it's not eight thirty."

She whipped around, a black harness and an enormous blue cock in hand. "And?"

I stood and put my hands on her narrow waist. "It's not time to play yet," I said coyly. I bent down and retrieved my dress, making an exaggerated show of my ass.

"Damn," she muttered, half-frustrated and half-admiring.

I pulled my dress on, "I'd love to play. I just play by the rules."

Kris looked me up and down. "When can we start?"

I considered for a moment. Maybe it would be better to play while living apart for a while before rushing in. Maybe I didn't need to add the upheaval of moving in with a stranger to my life at the moment. Maybe I could take it slow and still have everything I wanted.

But I didn't want to take it slow. I'd been careful and responsible for years. I'd been nothing but safe. For once, I wanted to dive in, to be reckless.

"We can start when I move in." I sounded much more in control than I felt.

Kris trailed her fingertips along my side, then dug them into my hip. She looked straight into my eyes. "Start packing."

CHAPTER SIX

I cannot believe you're doing this," John told me with a sigh while he helped me tape boxes. "We're going to be here another month. Why don't you stay at least that long?"

"Because rent is due in a week here, whereas no rent is ever due at Kristen's." I considered a pile of books, then dropped them in the box gracelessly.

"Uh, I think you mean rent is *always* due at Kristen's. Because you are paying every single day."

"It's not a price I mind paying," I answered in a singsong.

"How would you know? You haven't slept with her yet. You haven't even seen her since Sunday."

I paused. This was technically true. However, Kris and I had been flirting via text every evening for the past three days. In fact, the night before, I'd called her to discuss my move. It had quickly turned into something else. At eight thirty, I pointed out the time, and Kris responded by telling me to touch myself. She spent the next half hour describing to me what exactly she planned on doing to me, as I followed her instructions and tried not to be too loud. So, no, we hadn't had sex. But I did come on command.

The thought of it made me blush.

"I'm fine."

"Why the rush though? Like you said, you still have a week until rent is due. And we're paying next month's rent anyway, so we're not rushing you out. You could stay for five more weeks without paying more—and without having to sleep with anyone."

"Maybe I want to sleep with her."

"Then sleep with her and stay at your own apartment. See if you like it. Take some time, try things out. You don't have to jump in like this." John huffed as he started taping another box.

"I want to jump in." I stretched and put an arm around him. "I just want to." I couldn't explain the magnetic pull I already felt toward Kris.

John sat on my bed. "This isn't like you, Phe."

I sat down next to him. "I know. I've been being sensible and planning ahead and being responsible all my life. I never hop on a plane or go out partying on a weeknight or move in with somebody too soon. I don't even sleep with somebody too soon. For once in my life, I'm doing something without overthinking it. I want to do something, so I'm just doing it."

"Is there some other way you can be impulsive that doesn't involve you trading sex for housing starting in three days? Can't you get a tattoo or something?"

I pointed to a spot on my back where, under my shirt and bra, a snake curved over my skin. "If you'll remember, this took me six months of planning and I'd wanted it since I was a teenager."

"That's my point! You were so careful with something that at worst might look bad, but you're impulsive about who you're living with? About where you sleep at night?" Concern strained his voice.

I put my head on his shoulder. "Want to know the rest of my reasoning? If it's awful, I can come back home to you guys. If I try it now, there's a safety net."

He slung an arm around me. "Isn't there a safety net in her paying for you to have a place if you move out?"

"Yeah, but I meant emotionally. I can't try this new thing— this living situation, my new artist life—with you gone. I need you around for me to try new things."

John squeezed me. "We're going to talk all the time, I promise. Even with me on the other side of the country, I'm still here for you."

"It's different. You know it's going to be different."

He nodded. "I know. Part of the reason I don't want you to move out is because I don't want you in some other place for the time we have left."

A tear escaped my eye. "We'll hang out all the time."

"Of course." We both knew it was a lie, but we pretended it wasn't. Quietly, John helped me pack.

The next day, I loaded up my car with all the nonessentials I was keeping and drove it across the bridge. Kris was at work, like most people were on a Friday. I picked up a key from her at her office, then shoved boxes into my room and headed home to a mostly empty room in Oakland. After teaching Saturday and Sunday morning, I stuffed my car with the last of my things, said a tearful good-bye to John and Ollie, and made the drive again. Even though it was Sunday, Kris was around for less than an hour. She lugged my heavier boxes up the stairs, then went back to work for the rest of the move. After dropping my unpacked car back in Oakland and taking a noisy train into San Francisco, I was in my plush new room, all my possessions in boxes around me. I was also completely alone in the house and not ready for the silence. It was never really silent in my old apartment. The walls were thin, the pipes a chorus of sounds, and the street noise never far away. Plus, half the time I could hang out with John and/or Ollie, just by sticking my head out of my room. But this place? It was really, terribly, horribly quiet.

I felt very lonely. I texted John, even as I knew he and Ollie were having their "no phones" Sunday dinner. I texted Meghan, knowing that she and Bill were likely at trivia night at their favorite bar. I texted Sasha, who invited me to a musical movie night sing-along she was having with her housemates, something that did not appeal to me at all. I thought about my old coworkers and debated reaching out, even though I wasn't actually close to any of them. I thought about other aerialists I knew, but again, there was no one I was close enough with to randomly text at 8:47 on a Sunday night. I wanted to ask Kris when she'd be home, but that was not the spirit of our agreement.

What did lonely people do on Sunday nights in empty houses? I changed into pajamas and plodded downstairs to enjoy the fancy living room and its television. I made popcorn and poured myself a soda. After five minutes of channel surfing, though, I realized why the house didn't look lived in. It was eerie to be so alone in such a perfect-looking place, to have so much beautiful space to yourself in a crowded city. It felt like the beginning of a horror movie. I took my snacks back to my room, opened my computer, and put on season two of *Buffy*.

I ate popcorn in my fluffy new bed and rewatched my favorite episodes, but the lonely feeling did not abate. I kept listening for the door, hoping Kris was home, but I never heard her. I zoned out with my show and fell asleep. When my alarm woke me at seven, my laptop was dead and I had popcorn in my hair.

I got up to a house that still seemed empty. Kris's door was closed, but there was no evidence of her. Downstairs I found a note that said, "Welcome! Sorry I couldn't be there yesterday. I'm off to work. The car's in the garage. See you tonight." I made coffee and had some cereal, and wandered out to the patio. It was only a little chilly, and I wrapped myself in one of the many blankets from the living room. All the loneliness from the night before disappeared when I sat outside in my new yard. Maybe everything would be fine.

I went about my day as best I could, with no more word from Kris. Everyone returned my texts. I felt loved by my friends, a feeling I appreciated as I rushed between three different studios. I was completely in the zone as I taught, and my students were excited and attentive. After I was done with work, I threw together a stir-fry and unpacked a little.

At eight o'clock, I sat down in the living room. My palms were sweaty and I couldn't get comfortable. I kept looking at my phone aimlessly. Five minutes later, Kris walked in the front door.

"Hi," I chirped.

"Hi."

"Where have you been?" I sounded needier than I meant to be.

"Working." She shrugged. "What have you been up to?"

"Moving, aerials, you know." Damn, this was awkward. "So, are we going to…?"

Kris laughed. "Maybe we should start a little slower." She sat next to me. "Are you all moved in?"

"All my stuff is here, but I'm not unpacked. I'm selling my car this week, and then I'll be totally out of Oakland."

"So, are you liking it?"

I chewed on my lip. "Honestly? It's awesome, but last night when I was here by myself, I got completely freaked out. It's weird here alone."

She nodded. "I basically live in my room. I didn't live alone until I was twenty-six, and then I lived in a tiny studio. I didn't think about what I'd do with all this space by myself."

"So why did you buy a three-bedroom house? Why live alone?"

She leaned back on the couch. "It was always my dream, you know, owning a home. I got to the point of my life where I could buy a house, and I looked for a long time. My agent told me about this place before it was even listed and I made an offer the minute I saw it. The location was perfect, and I knew it could be amazing. I felt like an adult buying this place. But then I moved in and it was uncomfortable. I didn't know what to do with it. I didn't want to move out, but I didn't feel like I could have anybody else live here either. Adults live alone, or they live with a partner, their kids. I was too old to be living with roommates, and I didn't need the money anyway. The thing is, I'd liked living alone in a studio, so I never thought I wouldn't like living alone in a house."

"A giant house," I pointed out.

"Giant for San Francisco. Not for anywhere else."

"Giant for one person, anywhere," I said.

"True."

"Can I ask you something? Did you buy this thinking, you know, that you were going to meet somebody, get married, have kids, that kind of thing?"

Kris scratched her head. "No. It was in terrible shape and I was thinking about fixing it up, not who I'd want to live in it with me."

My forehead wrinkled in spite of my efforts to stay casual. "Are you, like, opposed to that?"

"I just haven't really thought about it in a long time. When I think about my future, I think about my professional life."

"Don't you worry, though, about being alone?"

"I'm not alone. I work with great people. I have friends, and I almost always have play partners. I have parents and a brother and a sister and two nephews and a niece, even though I don't see them much. I have people."

I folded my legs up into a pretzel. "I ask because I always worry about that, about being alone."

"Because it's important to you to get married and have kids?"

I shook my head. "No, it's not. I'm not against the idea, but that's not my dream. It's more like a compulsion. When I'm single, I worry about meeting someone, and when I have a girlfriend, I worry about moving our relationship along. But when I try to imagine the most perfect future possible, it's all about living as a performer, being creative, things like that. Not about being a mom or a wife."

"Why do you think that you worry so much about something if it's not really your dream?"

"Your career doesn't love you back, no matter how good it is. Talent doesn't keep you warm at night."

Kris leaned toward me. "I know I don't know you that well yet, Phoenix, but I need to tell you something. Your career might not love you, but there's no guarantee about anyone's love. Doing things that matter to you, that you feel good about, can give you confidence and pride and self-worth. Your work can make you happy. People tell women it can't, but they're lying. I'm happy with my life, even when I'm lonely, because I love what I do. You can have that too."

I looked at my lap. In every relationship I'd ever had, I'd prioritized keeping my girlfriend around over, well, everything else. And it had never worked. It had, however, drained my savings when I helped keep Ronnie afloat during a few months when she spent more time lighting up than working, which probably kept me in a nine-to-five half a year longer than I otherwise would have been. It certainly wore down my sexual confidence when certain exes rejected my kinks, but I stayed anyway. And I missed more beginning aerials classes than I could remember thanks to processing sessions with Carolena.

"So if you're so happy," I said, "why exactly am I here again?"

She gave me an unhappy look. "Because of something we both wanted, remember?"

"What's that?" I played dumb.

"You're being a brat," she said.

"You like brats."

"Not exactly. Now might not be the right time for it, but what I like about brats is stripping them, hitting them, fucking them, and making them do what I say."

Heat rose up my face. "Who said now isn't the right time for it?"

Kris looked at her watch. "We have plenty of time. But you seemed nervous."

I batted my lashes. "Maybe I needed some convincing."

She smiled. "Let's start slow."

"How exactly?"

"Take off your clothes."

I stood and pulled off my T-shirt without a word. I wiggled out of my yoga pants. My heart racing, I unclasped my bra and dropped it to the floor.

"All the way," she said.

I slid my panties down my legs and stepped out of them. I stood in front of her, completely exposed, as she watched me.

"Are you ready?"

I nodded.

"Give me a color."

"Green," I said.

She reached up and pinched both my nipples, hard. I startled, and Kris looked at me cautiously.

"Green," I said again.

"Good, pretty girl. Now go upstairs. It's time for your first chore."

I walked up the stairs with Kris following close behind me. We got to her room and she handed me the hamper. "Every week, you need to wash the clothes. You'll also need to clean each room except mine, wash all dishes every night except on Saturdays, and cook three dinners a week, along with buying groceries and any other household items we need. On Sundays, I'll examine your work. If you haven't done your job, I'll obviously punish you."

"Of course," I said.

Kris smiled and pulled me close. She kissed me, soft and sweet. Then she twisted one of my nipples again. "Take that laundry downstairs and get to work."

I trudged the hamper down the stairs and loaded the washer. When I glanced behind me, Kris was there, blatantly staring at my bare ass.

"Good. Now, down the hall." I did as I was told. In the lavender room, I waited as she rummaged through drawers and then settled into a chair.

"Turn around," she said. I walked in a slow circle until my back faced her. She dug her fingernails into my hips and pulled me to her. Kris fastened one fabric cuff on my right wrist and held the other with her hand.

Her face was inches from my lower back, her breath warm on my spine. "I'm going to tie you up and play with you. I'll try a lot of things on you. When I ask you, you'll tell me what you liked and what you didn't. Your only job is to take it and then to answer honestly. Don't pretend for me. Do you understand?"

"Yes," I said.

"Good girl." She grabbed the thick fabric hanging from my right wrist and led me to the eye hook. I saw that she had already rigged for this. When did she do this? I wondered what she had planned as she looped the restraint through the rope she'd hung. Once it was secured, she ordered both my arms above my head and tightened the other cuff around my left wrist.

"Too tight?"

"No, it's good." My voice had become smaller, higher than usual.

"Wiggle your arms. Fingers too." I obeyed. "Good, your arms aren't locked. Is the height all right?"

"A bit lower."

She adjusted the strap on the restraint. "Don't lock your knees. If you can't keep standing, tell me and I'll untie you. Don't push yourself." Kris showed me a large floor cushion, mine for the kneeling if I needed it. "Do you understand?"

"Yes."

"Good." With that, she smacked me, open-palmed, on the ass. I squealed in obvious surprise, and she grinned.

"Wait until you see what's in store for you." She laughed.

What was in store for me? First, some gentle thwaps from a flogger, warming up my back, my butt, the backs of my thighs. It felt like a caress, like a massage from the leather. I relaxed.

"Scale of one to ten," she said, "with ten being the most humanly possible, how much do you like this?"

"A seven," I said.

"I think we can do better than seven," she said. The next thing I heard was the sharp whoosh of a riding crop. I felt its concentrated sting on the fleshiest part of my backside. My breath caught in my throat. As slow and tender as Kris had been with the flogger, she was merciless with the crop. She hit my legs and ass a dozen times in rapid-fire succession. The speed of the hits made it impossible for my nerve endings to keep up. I wrapped my hands around the fabric that bound me and squeezed.

"Give it a number," she said.

"Three," I said through gritted teeth.

Just as the sting became too much, she stopped. "Your skin's so red now." She soothed my inflamed skin with her fingertips. She traced the marks she'd made on my skin, so sensitive to her careful touch. Once in a while, she pressed deep and gave me a start, only to rub it away with the lightest massage a moment later.

"Number?"

"Eight."

Then she got out the paddle.

We went on like this, alternating soothing and pain, inching up the edge of what I could take and then backing away. I lost all sense of time in this play. Kris experimented with the heaviness of her hand, with the instruments, with the angle, with the points of impact. She raked her short nails over my body, stroked me back to equilibrium, and then began it all again. Despite the strength of my shoulders and arms, I eventually couldn't stand with my arms tied above my head. Kris untied me and bound my arms behind me as I knelt. She used this opportunity to dabble with clamps on my nipples, screwing them tighter and releasing them, then flicking and teasing the swollen results.

Even that was too much over time, but I was so deep in my submission I could only slump. Nothing else existed as she made contact with my skin. The sensation, the silence of the room, her dominance over me, all became absolute and complete. I felt—not broken down exactly, but cracked open, raw and spilled out.

"Are you okay?" she asked when I sank into the cushion.

I mumbled something incoherent.

Kris released me, freeing my nipples from the clamps, then my wrists. Gingerly, she helped me to the bed.

"Water?" she asked.

I nodded. I took a huge gulp from the bottle she handed me. Slowly, I came back to myself. "Whoa," I said. "Intense."

"How are you?"

"I'm good. I'm…I've never gone so deep into it before."

"Did I go too hard on you?"

"No. This was good. This is what I wanted." It was true even though I had not known, before this, that it was what I wanted.

"I tried to take it slow," she said.

"It was perfect." I took another long drink of water. I glanced at the clock. Our time was more than up.

"We didn't have sex."

Kris laughed. "Do you want to?"

"Not right this minute." I realized that I was so slick that I was practically dripping on the bed. It would be my job to clean it, I mused.

"Want to try for tomorrow?"

"Not just try. I want you to fuck me. I want…" Suddenly, I felt my complete nakedness. "I want you to. Please."

Kris cupped my face in her hands. "I'd love to." She kissed me, as sweetly as before. She stroked my hair, helped me get dressed, and promised me a list of chores to do. I put the laundry in the dryer, and she told me she'd be thinking of me, undressed and cleaning her house, all day.

But as soon as she said it, she rushed off to her room. Once again, I was essentially alone in a big, empty house.

CHAPTER SEVEN

Sasha held the ladder as I rigged our trapezes in the Kirkus Radix studio the next day. It had just opened for early morning free time, and we were alone except for the girl at the desk out front. I was meeting with a buyer for my car that afternoon, and John and I had organized a yard sale the following weekend for the rest of my things. I hadn't booked a single aerial gig yet, but I was optimistic about my new life. Everything was lining up.

Sasha, of course, couldn't make sense of it. As we rigged, she questioned my move to San Francisco, which she thought had to be more expensive than my previous digs. I demurred vaguely until she suggested we take a terrible gig doing an elaborate children's birthday party. We'd done a show for the same family months earlier for their spoiled six-year-old. Not only was it a headache to find space suitable for our equipment and for thirty kindergartners, we had to create a whole new act for the occasion, and the children didn't even like it. One of them threw cake at us. The prospect of repeating the situation with the family's four-year-old sounded unbearable. She called up at me, "We need to do this if you're going to make San Francisco rent."

I made a face as I double-checked the carabiners. "Actually, I don't pay rent," I muttered, thinking she wouldn't hear me.

"WHAT?" Sasha exclaimed. Sasha had superhuman ears.

I climbed down the ladder. "Nothing! What are you thinking for our warm-up?"

"What are you talking about, not paying rent?" Sasha tapped her foot. She shot up an eyebrow.

"Kris and I have an arrangement." I tried to sound casual. "I buy all the groceries and household stuff, and I cook and clean and do all the laundry."

"How is that possible?" She put her hands on her hips. "And what about utilities?"

"She pays them." I cringed. Why on earth did I have to open my mouth about this?

"Your roommate pays the rent and the utilities and you... what? Do some dishes, make dinner, and buy food?"

I nodded as we put the ladder away. "Technically, it's a mortgage and not rent, but, yes."

"Your *one* roommate?"

"It's her house. She's giving me a deal."

"*Obviously*. How do I get in on something like that?"

We started our warm-up stretches. "There's a little more to it than that," I said.

"Of course. Do you have to babysit her dog? House-sit while she travels? Host cult meetings? What is happening here?"

I pressed my lips together tightly.

Sasha stared at me with her intense blue eyes as she balanced in a perfect warrior three. I blushed, thinking of my intense evening, and Sasha nearly fell over. Her blond bob hung over her face as she righted herself and shoved me. I toppled over onto the crash mat we'd set up under the trapeze. "Oh, Jesus. You're sleeping with her. Oh my God, you're ridiculous. Come on, Phe. You've known her for like six seconds. Don't move in with a brand new girlfriend just because your roommate's leaving. What are you going to do when you two break up?"

"She's not my girlfriend," I said.

Sasha shook her head. "So you two aren't fucking?"

"I do have sex with her." This was, of course, somewhat true. We'd certainly played, but we hadn't had sex. Still, for the sake of simplicity, and because the intent was certainly there, I figured "sex" was the easiest way to explain it.

Judging by Sasha's glare, though, I'd guessed wrong. "What is wrong with you?"

"There's nothing wrong with it. It's sex work, basically. I just happen to get paid in housing."

Sasha rolled her neck. Her glare didn't let up. "Don't shit where you eat, Phoenix."

"Does that really apply here?" I circled my arms.

"Either she's your girlfriend or she wants to be, and that's going to end badly. Drama and heartbreak and awfulness, I promise. Or maybe you really are a very well paid prostitute, in which case you're living with the person you're working for, which always sucks. Remember when I was a live-in nanny? Remember how badly that went?"

"That's because you hate children."

"No, I hate children because I was a live-in nanny." She folded herself forward and rolled back up. "What if you want to date somebody else, Phe? What if you want to have friends over, or have a party, or spend the day in your sweatpants? Is it your home or is it your workplace?"

"It's my home." I felt uncertain as I said it.

"So what about my other questions?"

"Sweatpants are fine. And I can have people over. Kris works seven days a week. She leaves before I'm up and she works late. Other than our, uh, time, I hardly see her. I'd ask her about a party, but that's just courteous. I would have asked John before I threw a party at our place."

"And dating?"

"It hasn't come up." I pressed my palms high on the wall and leaned in for what we called the "getting arrested" stretch. "Like I said, she works a ton, so she doesn't have time to date. And I'm focused on my aerial career right now. I don't need complications."

Sasha snorted. "What an obnoxious thing to say."

"Come on, do you date?" I dropped under a trapeze bar for shoulder shrugs and she followed suit.

"I sleep with people who don't bore me. You know I don't like relationships. They restrict the natural flow of sexual energy."

"How is this different? It's not a relationship, but it meets my sexual needs. So what if it helps me out at the same time?" I flipped myself upside down to practice my knee hangs.

"It's different because I kick the guys out the second it stops feeling good, and if you get tired of this chick, you're stuck. Besides, you're a compulsive girlfriend. You nest anytime you start sleeping with somebody."

"That's not true!"

"Oh come on, who was that girl you were seeing last year? Beth? You said it was just fun and then you were so heartbroken when you guys broke up." Sasha stood on her trapeze and lifted her knees into her chest, holding her weight in her hands as she gripped the ropes.

I was confident I could indeed have a good time without falling in love, despite my history as a serial monogamist. Sasha's assessment during my last breakup had been that I was "prone to fall in love." She'd said it like it was a disease.

"This is different," I said. "The boundaries are clear. I know what to expect."

She shook her head. "So she's gross? Or horrible?"

"Not at all." I smiled to myself. "She's very cute. Six days out of the week, she dresses impeccably, all these nice ties and pocket squares. You know I love a well-dressed butch. And we don't spend a lot of time together, but I like her. She seems honest, and levelheaded, and generous. She's kind of geeky."

"Ugh. She's like your dream girl. Is she closeted? Way too old for you?"

"Out since college and she's in her mid-thirties. Totally acceptable."

Sasha looked at me, her nearly invisible blond eyebrows knitting together. "Is the sex bad? Is that why she's turning over a room for pussy?"

"It is so good," I said, though of course I wasn't sure. But the mere thought of what was planned for the night left me feeling distracted and dreamy. I fell behind Sasha's warm-ups and sat there, leaning against the rope to my left.

"Eeww! Phoenix! What's going to keep you from falling in love with her?"

"She's successful."

Sasha laughed.

"No, really," I said. "I fall in love with people who do not have their shit together. I need somebody who's a fixer-upper. Once they are fixed up, we stop working."

"Oh, honey, you're an idiot. You're going to fall for her."

"I'm really not. I can't love somebody who's not a mess. It's the way I'm broken."

"And what's to keep her from falling for you? If she hasn't already?"

I rolled my eyes. "She's not going to fall for me."

"Why not?"

"Because I'm a weirdo artist and she's an adult. I, like, have a nose ring and wear ripped fishnets half the time, and she's clean-cut. She's serious and I'm frivolous."

"So? Business folk can't like aerialists?"

"Like? Yes. Have a relationship with? No."

She shook her head. "Really, why wouldn't she fall for you?"

"She works all the time. She meets tons of important people. We're on different planets."

"You're in trouble," Sasha said, but I ignored her. Sasha prided herself on never getting serious with anyone, so her standards for no-strings-attached were a little high. She teased me as we ran through our latest choreography. I let her words fall away while I focused on feeling myself move through space. Aerials always made me feel calm.

Aerials also left me sweaty and a little wiped out. This was one of the things I'd always loved about it. On that particular day, the training wore me down. Moving and the scene from the night before had drained my stamina. I managed to complete my chores once I got home, but by seven forty-five, I was ready to fall asleep.

As a remedy, I hopped in my luxurious new shower. I hoped I'd get cleaned off (and woken up) before Kris came home. Just in case I wasn't, I didn't lock the door.

"Phoenix?"

"I'll just be a minute. Sorry, I'm in the shower."

I heard the door to the bathroom open. "Ready?"

"Five minutes," I said.

"It's eight thirty." I could barely hear her over the water.

I looked at her. The steam on the glass shower door blurred the edges, but I could still make out her slacks, her neat dark hair, the line of her tie. "I was just so tired, I was trying to wake myself up…"

"Is that a no?"

I shook my wet head. "It's not a no."

"Is that a green light then?"

"Yes, green."

Kris opened the shower door and reached in. I thought she was reaching for me, but instead she turned off the water. "We're in a drought," she said. "Can't waste water while I'm fucking you."

In the heat of the steam, I felt my nipples harden.

"Get out."

Naked and dripping, I stepped onto the bathmat.

"Today I'm going to give you a taste of reward and punishment both, so when I give you directions later, you'll know exactly what to expect if you follow them, or if you disobey." She ran her hands over my wet arms. "But first I'm going to look at you. Get your hair out of the way, then hands at your sides."

I wrapped my hair in a towel on top of my head and stuck my fists by my sides. She skimmed my body with her hands, staring at each inch of me. She brushed her hands over my breasts, my stomach, my hips, my closely trimmed pubic hair, then dropped to the ground to touch my legs. Once her fingers touched my feet, she told me to turn around and inched her way up the back side of my body. Even this light touch was igniting me, making my stomach flip with anticipation and my pussy clench with need.

She squeezed my shoulders as she stood behind me, her body pressed against mine. "Do you want your reward first, or your punishment?"

"My reward."

"That's too bad, because I'm in charge, and I've decided you'll need to be punished before you get that. On your knees."

On all fours facing the door to my bedroom, I heard her zipper slide down. I looked back to see she'd already strapped on a large purple cock, smaller than the blue one but not by much. "Did I tell you to turn around?" she snapped. "Keep your head forward and don't move unless I tell you to."

I looked back at the door. I was worried that I wouldn't be wet enough yet, that the cock was too big, that the fantasy appeal of being taken on her terms and used wouldn't translate to real life. She teased the opening of my pussy with her fingers, then explored my clit and labia with the same gentle, curious caress she'd used on the rest of my body. She nudged a finger inside me, and the ease of entrance surprised me. I was wetter than I expected.

Without a word, I heard her snap open a bottle of lube and squirt the liquid on her cock. "I'm being so nice," she said. "I could probably fuck your slick little pussy without this, but this will make it easier for you to take. You should thank me."

"Thank you," I gulped.

She eased the bulging tip inside me. I gasped. Slowly, she inched it in me until I felt the leather of the harness against my ass. Fully enveloped, she stayed still for a minute and took my breasts in her hands. She handled them roughly, pinching my nipples, as she started a slow rhythm with her hips. Her cock pulsed back and forth, still startlingly large for me. The thought of being taken by her like this, of belonging to this woman I barely knew, undid me. I melted around her and gripped the bathmat whenever her cock rocked deeper inside me.

"What color, Phoenix?"

"Green," I moaned. "Green, green, green."

With that, she picked up speed. Kris yanked herself so far back she was almost out of me, then she slammed back in up to the hilt in one hard, fast motion. I shrieked in surprise and a flash of pain that gave way to overwhelming fullness. I moaned as she dug her fingers into the flesh of my hips and began fucking me— relentless, fast, hard. The movement untangled my towel, and it dropped to the ground.

She kept on like this for I don't know how long. I lost all sense of the world outside of the sensations in my body, just like I had the day before. My moans and cries were the only sound other than the slap of our bodies meeting. I felt more than just pleasure, more than the ache inside me. I felt like I was completely in my body and at the same time like I was dreaming.

Unexpectedly, she sped up even more. After a minute of jarringly fast motion, Kris slumped onto my back. Her silk tie felt soft against my skin.

"Kris?" I asked.

"I came," she panted.

"From fucking me?"

She nodded against my neck.

"Am I done being punished then?"

"Uh-huh." I slowly eased her cock out of me and turned myself around to rest against the wall. Kris collapsed on the floor.

"So, my reward?"

"Give me a minute."

"But I need it." My pussy felt tragically empty all of a sudden, and my clit ached.

"Don't try to be the boss or you'll get punished again. Go downstairs and lie on the bed. Just lie there until I tell you otherwise." Despite her commanding words, she was still out of breath.

I was tempted to tease her, but I didn't want to delay my reward any longer than I had to. I stood up. "When will you be in?"

"When I'm in. Go downstairs."

I reached for a towel.

"No, as you are."

Naked, my hair still wet, I walked through my bedroom and then down the stairs. In the lavender room, I lay down on top of the covers. A clock on the wall ticked away the minutes she made me wait. Finally, she came in, sans button-down and tie, but wearing her pants still, and a white undershirt.

"Were you waiting nicely?" she asked.

I nodded.

"I like making you wait. But that's your punishment, and it's over now. Ready for your reward?"

"Yes, please."

Gingerly, she strapped my wrists and ankles into the fake-fur-lined fabric restraints at either end of the bed. Spread out like a star, I felt even more exposed than I had in the bathroom.

"So pretty." She checked the tightness of the restraints. "So good. How's it on your wrists and ankles?"

"Perfect."

"You're ready then?"

I nodded quickly.

"Say please if you want it."

"Yes, please, Kris. Please."

She lowered her face to my pussy and began slowly licking. "I'm going to try things, and you'll tell me which you like best. Just like yesterday."

"Like another experiment?"

"Yes," she said, her breath on my swollen clit. "Now, this is option A." She circled her tongue on me, teasing me everywhere but the place I most wanted her mouth. I tried to buck against her and shift my body into place, but the restraints held me fast.

"This is option B." She moved her circling tongue where I wanted it, swirling over the most sensitive part of me.

"Option B," I cried. She sped up the pace, bringing me to the edge. Just as she started to pull away and say the words "option C," I felt the clench deep within me. I wanted to grab her head and pull her back, but of course I couldn't. As if sensing what I needed,

Kris pressed her face back where I wanted it, resumed that perfect motion of her tongue, and brought me over the edge again and again and again, until I couldn't anymore. Finally, Kris lifted her face to look at me. I lay on the bed whimpering.

"Is that a good incentive to do your chores?" she asked from between my legs.

"Yesss," I breathed.

"Good." She stood and unstrapped me. "Do you need anything?"

"Just water."

She got us both waters from the mini-fridge. Tentatively, she put her hand on my head and lightly stroked my damp hair.

"How was that?"

"So good. I can barely move it was so good." I chugged my water.

"You don't need to flatter me," she said. "I like praise, but I don't need exaggeration."

"So fucking good, Kris," I said. "How was it for you?"

"A dream come true," she said. "But I had a lot more experiments in mind."

"You'll just have to save them for tomorrow."

"Provided you deserve them. Which reminds me, I want to give you your chore list."

I leaned my head on her shoulder. Kris pulled a list out of a drawer. "Things to do every week," it read. I was tempted to give her a skeptical look, but stopped myself. Following her orders was the fantasy, and at least they were clearly laid out. When I read the list, the tasks actually weren't much, and all were things we'd discussed. I looked over at her and nodded.

"Anything else you want? We have a couple of minutes left."

"Just one request, if that's okay."

"Sure."

"I'm naked and you haven't even taken off your shirt. You didn't yesterday either. I want to see you."

Kris gave me a small smile that revealed just the hint of her slightly crooked teeth. "Sometimes I like that, being dressed when my sub isn't."

"Please?" I batted my eyelashes.

She hopped out of bed and pulled off her undershirt. "I'm feeling generous."

"Thank you," I said.

She chucked her pants, which she'd never fully zipped up again after our session in the bathroom. I admired her lean body in just a harness and a binder. I looked up at her hopefully.

She pulled the binder off, then unbuckled the harness and dropped it on the bed. Kris stood there for a minute, letting me look at her gorgeous, full breasts, the neatly trimmed dark hair between her legs, at the body that was hidden from everyone but me.

"Thank you," I said.

"Consider this part of your reward. If you want to keep being rewarded, you need to do all the chores properly."

"I will."

"I'm warning you, I'll check."

"Well, if I do a bad job, you'll just have to punish me, right? And then I'll learn my lesson."

"Next time you get punished, you won't get rewarded afterward," she said and walked to the bathroom, giving me a long look at her firm, smooth ass as she did.

CHAPTER EIGHT

Over the next few weeks, everything was how I wanted it to be. I felt the ache of attraction with Kris, but not the pull of romance, probably because I almost never saw her outside of our play. It was practically like living alone. By the time I woke up at seven, Kris was usually gone, or at least showering. On Sundays, the only morning she didn't head to her office early, she went running first thing and was in her room with a video game or a show by the time I came back from teaching. In the first month I was there, I caught her eating cereal while I made my morning coffee only once. I spent the day busy with aerials, and came home to an empty house. The cleaning and cooking and laundry and errands, once I fit them into my schedule, were only a few hours more a week than I had always done. Every night, she came home around eight, and only a few minutes earlier on Fridays. Sometimes she grabbed leftovers I'd made, but often she'd eaten at work. For the most part, I made the kind of simple meals I had always made, but when she ate them, Kris always told me I'd done my chores well.

And the sex? Most nights she found me reading in the living room, waiting but pretending I wasn't waiting, and told me, "It's eight thirty," before ordering me to strip. Every night was unique but familiar at the same time. Some days she had me pick an implement from the closet and hit me in the slow, methodical way that let me release into my body, before she buried her face between my legs or touched me with her long, talented fingers. Other nights she spread her legs—sitting on the living room sofa, or on the purple bed—and ordered me between them, telling me how to touch her or ordering me to use my mouth. On nights following some slipup on my end, like forgetting to unload the dishwasher or failing to restock milk, she never let me come with her, leaving me dripping. Afterward, I'd go to my room and touch myself, and come within minutes. Some nights she strapped on and used my mouth and my pussy without letting me orgasm, and other nights she strapped on and rewarded me with release again and again. A few times, she didn't make it home in time and texted me directions: where to be, what to use, and how long I had to wait before I came. Usually on those nights she timed it to walk in the door just before I screamed out.

One Friday when I was wearing a skirt, she told me to give her my underwear, and we went for an evening walk, her whispering hot, filthy promises in my ear, the night air cool against my wetness. When we got home, she let me grind myself onto her bare leg until I came. Usually, Fridays and Sundays involved long sessions of elaborate bondage with those lovely eye hooks in the ceiling and intricate knots she tied; a selection of floggers, paddles, riding crops; and plenty of orgasms for both of us. One afternoon she played with my nipples until they ached, then sat in the room reading erotica to herself while pretending to ignore me, just to make me wait because I'd failed to clean the bathroom. Sometimes, I forgot half on purpose.

It was like living with a ghost. A kinky sex ghost. It was also the best fuck buddy arrangement in the world. During the few hours Kris was home and not playing with me, I still had the house to myself. She wasn't unfriendly; she just wasn't there. Sasha's concerns seemed laughable. How could I fall in love with someone I barely knew?

Our living arrangement was the exact opposite of what I'd had with John. John and I had been the sort of roommates who shared meals most evenings, who went to donation-based yoga classes together, who cuddled on the couch while staying up too late talking. The only problem we had was a compulsion to hang out together, and hurt feelings when one of us wanted space. We didn't just share an apartment. We shared our lives in many ways.

Of course, that started to change in the months leading up to quitting my job. I'd become single-minded about launching my artistic career. He'd been spending more and more time at Ollie's, and it was clear that them moving in together was only a matter of time. But even then, John and I were a team, albeit a team that was increasingly busy with separate activities.

In those first weeks at Kris's, I saw John two or three times a week and talked to him or texted him nearly every day. Since I was not getting much in the way of performance gigs, I spent Saturday evenings at his place—my old place. Right around when I moved out, Ollie moved in, leaving his spot in a housing collective full of obsessive bicyclists. But because a cross-country move was in the works, nothing was actually unpacked. Every time I came over, another stack of boxes greeted me.

A week before John and Ollie began their drive to Boston, John came over to my new home for the first time. We'd been pretty social as roommates, hosting big dinners (that he cooked), brunches for all our friends, movie nights, and the occasional party. Plus we were always having someone over for a cup of tea and some gossip. But in my new house, I'd never had a single guest. My friends all lived on the other side of the Bay, where I was teaching or training half the time anyway. I didn't really know anyone who could actually afford to live in San Francisco, so any invitation to see me came with a quick but smelly journey on public transit or a possibly traffic-ensnared nightmare with nowhere to park.

But more than that, I wasn't totally comfortable hosting in Kris's house. She never had anyone over. Of course, she was hardly there herself, but still, it seemed strange to invite guests to her house when she didn't. One thing Sasha had been right about was that I sometimes thought of myself as a servant in the place, rather than a full-fledged housemate, despite all Kris's assurances otherwise. And servants didn't go and bring around folks to the boss's house.

John kept bugging me to see the place, though, and finally I relented. One sunny morning in September, I welcomed him in as he whistled at my fancy new living situation.

"Gorgeous," he said over and over as I gave him the tour. He caressed the kitchen counters for so long that I took our coffee to the backyard without him.

"This place is *ridiculous,*" he said with a smile when he finally joined me. "What even is this?"

"It's how rich people live, I guess. And their sex maids." I sipped my coffee.

"How is it living with someone who has all that money?"

I gestured at our surroundings. "Mutually beneficial."

He shot me a look of disbelief. "There's no disconnect there? She has a nice house in one of the most expensive cities in the country, and six months ago you were worried you might need to move back in with your parents in Albuquerque if you wanted to be a performer without a day job."

"It wasn't because I was *that* broke. And it was my sister and her family in LA I thought I'd need to live with, not my parents, remember? She was complaining about childcare and we had this strange fantasy that I'd take care of my nephew and then perform and teach. LA is a better market for aerial dancers than San Francisco. Plus you know I've got my yoga teacher certification, and LA always needs yoga teachers, right?"

"Ugh, I must have blocked out the idea of you living with your sister," he groaned. "Thank God her husband said no. You and Connie would have killed each other."

"We're not that bad."

"I remember her visit when we first moved in together, in our old place. What did you two end up shouting about? How you organized your closet? Or was it about a flat iron? And that lady who lived downstairs came running up and saying she was going to call the police because you two were so loud? Honestly, I started looking for other roommates. I was so relieved when she went home and you went back to being a regular person."

My sister was six years older and a lot more conventional than I was, and yes, we did fight. Maybe more than was normal. "Okay, so maybe that LA fantasy wasn't a great idea."

"You think? And you did say you were going to move home to your parents' at one point. I remember I had this terrible image of you off in some tiny miserable room surrounded by desert, counting your change to pay for gas."

I laughed. "Why do you always forget that I grew up middle class? My parents work at the University of New Mexico. Honestly, their house is bigger than this place. Way less expensive, but bigger. I mean, it's not worth commuting to Santa Fe for aerials all the time, but the part of Albuquerque I'm from isn't the windswept poverty you're picturing."

John gathered his dreadlocks in a rubber band. "You know why I misremember your family? It's those stories you told about your dad being a Brown Beret and your folks getting arrested at protests. I think of them as, like, impoverished laborers, but they're humanities professors."

I grimaced. "Yeah, I overemphasized a pretty small part of my family history there for a while."

"You were trying to impress Carolena," he said.

"Her dad was a migrant worker, and all she talked about on our first date was Marx! What could I say?"

He shook his head and laughed. "She was so weird."

"You loved her."

"I did! I thought she was great. But Carolena was so serious all the time. And she could not rap for shit. Her hip-hop aspirations were painful."

"In fairness, she wanted to be a revolutionary rapper, and how many words rhyme with 'proletariat'?"

John cocked his head and considered. "Chariot," he said. "Harriet. Carry it. Bury it. Marry it. Really, a lot of verbs followed by 'it.'"

I laughed. "Okay, okay."

"But really, Kristen's good for you? It's not an adjustment?"

"I will remind you again that I didn't grow up poor, and while Kris has made an absurd amount of money, she's not exactly the one percent."

"I mean, is it an adjustment coming from who you used to date and where you used to live?"

"Well," I said slowly. "Sort of. But we're not dating. I mean, we don't talk that much. I think it was weirder with most of my ex-girlfriends, actually. Because they had their problems, whereas Kris is…"

When I didn't elaborate, he asked, "Kris is what?"

"An unknown. We have what we have, and outside of that, I barely see her." I bit my lip and changed the subject. "Remember Beth? Remember that time we were talking about student loans and she said, 'Wow, you're still paying off student loans'? Her parents had just written a check for her tuition, no big deal."

John laughed. "A barista with family money. And that time you said you were Chicana?"

I traced the rim of my mug with my finger, remembering. "We were talking about where we were from. I said New Mexico, and she did that thing people do, that 'But where originally?' thing. She said, 'Gomez, is that a Mexican name?' I said no, I'm Chicana. And do you know what she said?"

"'Chicana? Is that part of Mexico?'" we quoted together, cracking up.

"And then you gave her that speech! Oh my God, that speech." John straightened his back and imitated me. "'No, actually both sides of my family can trace their heritage back three to four hundred years in the Southwest, and for most of that time they were technically citizens of Spain, but for a little while that land was owned by Mexico. The United States took over the area shortly after that. My family is part Pueblo on one side, and the Pueblo Nations are Native American. Mostly, though, I'm part of a unique ethnic group that speaks a slightly different dialect of Spanish than other people. We didn't cross the border, the border crossed us.'"

"I was channeling Carolena," I said.

"You were channeling your dad. I have met the guy once, and he gave me that speech. And I knew what Chicano meant! It wasn't prompted by anything."

I laughed. "That's my dad. My mom will just give you a book about the subject passive-aggressively."

"And how exactly did you think Beth was going to fit into that family picture?"

"I don't know. She wasn't just that. She could also be really kind, and she was funny. She was open, I guess. Emotionally open in an incredible way, until she got scared and shut down completely. I mean, girlfriend-wise I'd had the most cerebral person in the world, and then somebody who made every personal thing super political. And then Ronnie, who was all about kink and running and dogs and getting stoned in nature. Ronnie was so physical, and so only about that. Beth was, I guess, the first person I dated who was a balance of qualities, even if they weren't the best qualities. Being with her felt like being with a whole person, a whole, imperfect human. I really loved her. And she loved me too, however limited she was."

John exhaled noisily. "You were a lot more patient with her bullshit than I was. She was old enough to look up what Chicana means if she doesn't know, instead of making it your job to teach her. She didn't need to make you feel bad about your kinks."

"She didn't know they were *my* kinks."

"She didn't need to dump you at the end of your vacation."

"Better than at the beginning?"

John rolled his eyes. "This is why you got trampled in most of your relationships. You're too nice."

"Well, even if I am, I'm living in this place rent-free, so I must be doing something right."

"That's right. I was asking about Kris and then you deflected. So, how's it different? If Amanda was the brains, Carolena was the politics, Ronnie the body, and Beth the asshole, what is Kris?"

"A mystery. Or, no, just compartmentalized. She's the sex and the kink and the money, period. At least to me."

"What do you think she's like outside of that?"

"I think her world is pretty limited. She knows a couple of things really well, and then everything else, not so much. It's like she doesn't even know how to cook or live in her house or have people over, you know? There are some parts of adulthood she excels at, and other parts she doesn't engage with at all."

"Isn't that boring?"

"I'm not looking to her for deep emotional connection." I patted his hand. "That's what I have you for."

"And when I leave?"

"Don't talk like that."

"Phe, our going-away party is on Saturday. We're getting in a car in a week and driving to another time zone. You and I aren't going to be hanging out for a long time."

My eyes welled up. "Uncool, friend. Don't make it something real."

He squeezed my hand. "I just want you to take care of yourself. Please don't get swallowed up by this thing you're doing with Kristen. I love you and I know you're amazing, and I don't want you to forget that."

"I won't," I said. "It isn't a big deal."

"Come on. Do you really think that this is healthy for you long-term?"

"It isn't going to be long-term. Besides, it's fun. I'm having fun. What's wrong with that?"

"You're living with someone who isn't there for you. You're making huge changes in your life right when your network of support is shrinking. It puts you in a vulnerable place."

"Ugh, stop. The world 'vulnerable' is making me gag." I followed this with exaggerated faux retching.

"No, I will not stop. I want you to take this seriously. I love you, but you have a blind spot when it comes to girls you're sleeping with. You're still defending Beth a year later, and she was not worth it. I worry about you."

"I'm not a codependent mess, John. I can handle myself."

"I know you can. But I also know that not everybody is careful with your heart and you don't always see it. This situation, it sounds intense. Even if it isn't love, feelings are going to come up. I don't want you to be alone when it happens. I think it's important for you to have people who really see you. You are a wonderful person, and I'm worried that you're living with someone who doesn't get you."

"I have Sasha. I have Meghan."

He sighed. "Okay, that's a start. But promise me you'll take care of yourself."

"I'll try." I rolled my eyes. "But I think you're worried about something that isn't actually a problem."

"Even if I am, try, okay?"

"Okay." I hugged him again.

"And you're coming to the party?"

"I won't miss it for the world."

"Bring Kristen," he said. "I want to see whose hands I'm leaving you in."

"Sure." I tried to sound casual. "Won't be a problem."

Of course, I knew it would be a problem. Part of our agreement was that outside our activities, Kris and I had separate lives. I doubted she'd join me at the party. Would I have to go to John's going-away party alone? The thought of coming home to a lonely house by myself after saying good-bye to John made me want to cry. What had I gotten myself into?

CHAPTER NINE

John and I first met in an art history class our sophomore year. I was heartbroken and lonely from my breakup with Amanda over the summer. When I'd headed to San Francisco State University at eighteen, Amanda had gone to the University of California at Berkeley just across the Bay. For my first year of college, she was not only my girlfriend and my best friend, but my only friend. Amanda was kind, and even though she was blooming in college and finding people who shared her interests, she devoted a lot of time to me our freshman year. I knew we were growing apart and we'd need to break up, but I also knew she wouldn't leave me when I was so unfocused and alone. When we were back home, I ended things. Amanda was relieved—she wanted time to explore her interests and for the new people she was meeting, plus our sexual relationship had pretty much ended after the failed bondage attempt that spring. Though we weren't unfriendly after the breakup, she wanted some distance. I went back to college that fall without a single friend.

That's when I met John. John was probably the easiest person to talk to in the world. He welcomed me into his life from the first time we spoke. He encouraged me to try new things. He invited me to my first aerials class. He weathered my breakup with Amanda, me falling for Carolena before I was ready for a new relationship, and the heartbreak that ensued. He helped me set up my online dating profile after that, and later put up with goofy Ronnie and insufferable Beth without pretending he thought either were good for me. Everyone should have a friend like John.

Best of all, from our senior year onward, John was happy to be my roommate. He was the main person in my life for most of my adulthood. Though I got wrapped up in girlfriends, John brought me back to myself and reminded me not to neglect the other people in my life. Through his example, I established some pretty good habits by my mid-twenties, habits that kept me from having the sort of post-breakup friendlessness that I'd experienced after Amanda.

I called my parents every week, and Connie almost as often. Seeing them at Christmas was usually my only vacation, other than occasionally camping with Meghan and Bill. When I wanted to talk about pursuing my dreams, go out dancing, or see a performance, I turned to Sasha. When I wanted to talk kink or get a levelheaded perspective, I called Meghan. For adventure, I went on day trips with John and Ollie. For everything else, I knocked on John's door.

John also came with a social network like you wouldn't believe. Literally any time I asked, he knew "just the person for that!" Did he know anyone who'd want to spray-paint and glitter some headpieces for a performance if I bought them coffee? Of course, he'd call the Queer Femme House he knew through his most beautiful coworker. They had household glitter and would love to. Did he know anyone who could revive the miserable herbs we were trying to grow on the windowsill? Obviously, he'd text the green-thumbed vegans he knew from volunteering at People's Grocery. Where could I get a haircut? His cousin did hair and lived just down the street. My car was making a weird noise? His best friend from high school was a mechanic less than a mile away. I needed to mend a costume and Sasha was out of town? Let's stop by his mom's. Should I be worried about this spider bite? His nicest ex was a nurse. You name it.

The flip side of this was that when we hosted parties, I invited maybe eight people, half of whom showed, and he invited thirty, who all came with a date and a couple of friends. He had to have three separate going-away parties: one just for family (almost all of whom lived in Oakland), one at the preschool where he worked that kids and parents could participate in, and one for his many, many friends. Like me, Ollie sometimes got swept along for the gregarious ride, so his going-away party would be combined with John's third one.

There wasn't enough room in the apartment for that party so one of John's college friends offered to host it at the giant Berkeley housing co-op she lived in. I'd only been there once before, and was impressed and slightly repulsed by the place. On the one hand, the housemates had four bedrooms plus a little converted shed in the back; a huge yard with a fire pit, raised bed garden, and a couple of chickens; and common areas that combined to be bigger than the whole of our West Oakland apartment. On the other hand, nine people lived there with three cats, and most of the furniture had been pulled in from the street. Everything was sort of shabby and dirty. There were people everywhere, cat hair on every surface, and a faint sweaty weed stench even when no one was smoking. How did anyone live like that?

But I had to say one thing about the house: it was perfect for huge parties. The lack of anything expensive or completely clean made the place seem immune to trashing. The giant yard and abundant common space allowed for tons of people. The free couches, harvested from Bay Area curbs, meant there was always a place to sit. And while the college student-style living grossed me out, it also provided with seemingly limitless alcohol. Plus, weed for anyone who wanted it.

The thing was, I hated huge parties like that. I hated them even more if I didn't have anyone to go with. Meghan and Bill were going to be out of town, and Sasha had other plans. I knew John and Ollie would be swamped with good-byes and wouldn't be much company. Desperate not to go alone and remembering my promise to John, I invited Kris. I waited, though, until I'd gotten firm "nos" from everyone else. I knew that asking her last minute would almost guarantee that she'd say no too, but I tried to steel myself by remembering that she wasn't my first choice companion for my good-bye with my best friend.

After we finished playing on Thursday, as we were getting dressed, I tossed the idea out like it was nothing. "Hey, it's no big deal, but my old roommate and his boyfriend are moving to Boston in a few days. They're having a going-away party, and I wondered if you wanted to go with me. It's no big deal if you can't." I approximated nonchalance as best I could.

Kris ran her hand through her hair. "When is it?"

"Saturday, starts around eight."

She frowned. "It's our night off. I made plans with a friend."

Kris had friends? I was completely surprised but tried to act cool. "It's not a problem. I know it's last-minute."

"I mean, is it important to you?"

"No, no, it's fine," I said quickly.

"Okay. Yeah, I can't make it. Sorry." She sat on the bed and buttoned her shirt. Kris paused just as I went for the door. "Actually, Phoenix, I think we should talk about something."

I forced myself not to sigh. I knew I shouldn't have even asked. "All right." I leaned on the door.

"This is a new arrangement for both of us, and it's easy to be unclear about the boundaries. It's important that we decide what those are, outside of what happens here, or what you do around the house. We need to be on the same page emotionally—and socially."

"Is the part where you say we can't be seen together in public? Because that's fine. I was just asking."

"I'm not saying that. But we need to have the same expectations."

"We'll keep it professional," I said coolly. "Now if you'll excuse me—"

"Phoenix, I'm not saying that. We can be friends, if that's what you want. But we haven't discussed doing things together outside of our dynamic, and I don't want to confuse things. What do you want? That's all I'm asking."

"What do you want?" I was being a brat, but I didn't care.

"I'd like to spend time with you, when it works out, and get to know you outside of this. I'd love to see you perform. I don't want to go on dates. I don't want to be your plus-one. I don't like parties, and I don't want to go to any unless they're play parties. I don't want to pretend we're a couple, and I don't want to be in social situations where we need to pretend we aren't sleeping together either."

"So were you just trying to get out of the invite when you said you had plans?"

"No, I'm going to have dinner with a friend," she said calmly.

"Like a date?" I played with my hair. What was wrong with me?

"Phoenix," she chided.

"What? Are we dating other people or not?"

"Of course we can date other people if we want. As long as we use barriers if we have sex with anyone else."

"I'm not talking about sex. I'm talking about dating." I pouted. I had no real interest in dating anyone, but I was offended that she might be seeing someone else when she barely had time for a conversation with me.

"I'm seeing a friend. It is not a date. But Phoenix, what do you want?"

I felt unexpectedly stung by her impatient tone. "I don't want to have to explain our situation either." I straightened my shoulders. "I don't want to date you."

"Good. Do you want to spend time with each other as friends?"

This was a weird question from someone who'd been shoving fingers inside me and pulling my hair fifteen minutes earlier. "Yeah," I answered with a noncommittal shrug. "Sure."

"Okay. Was that so difficult?"

I shook my head. But honestly? It was. It was one thing to say you had no illusions about a situation. It was another to have reality laid out starkly without flattery.

Back in my room, I wondered about my reaction. I didn't want Kris at the party, so why was I upset when she said she didn't want to go?

❖

The party was just as rough as I'd expected. I felt awkward and out of place. Some guy tried to hit on me. I spent most of my hour there standing around by myself and trying to catch John or Ollie whenever I could. They were both glad I came and apologetic that they kept getting pulled away. I understood, but it didn't make it any easier. John was upset that Kris hadn't come with me, and I was too sad about him leaving and miserable about the party to offer much reassurance about my situation. I cried the whole way home.

The next afternoon with Kris, I asked her to play harder than usual. The sensation of the toys pounding against me brought me out of my sad mind and into my skin. I didn't need another friend, I thought. It didn't matter if Kris understood me. All that mattered was that feeling, the ache of coming into my own body and feeling only the current moment. The pain of it, yes, but the pleasure too.

❖

Monday morning, bruised and missing John, I reminded myself that I also had other friends. I called Meghan after I was home for the day, while Kris was at work. Meghan and I hadn't seen each other very much though in the previous month. I realized when I called her that I was becoming wrapped up in my new life, neglecting my friends. Maybe I was at risk for being swallowed up? I was relieved when Meghan agreed to pay me a visit. Not only did I want to see her, I craved her perspective on my situation.

The following Saturday, Meghan came by. I was feeling shy about my upgraded living situation, but at least Meghan would understand how I could afford it. After she thoroughly admired the place and got the tour, we sat down for coffee and cookies at the dining room table. It was the first time I'd ever seen it used. Meghan caught me up on her work adventures, Bill's latest health food obsession, and the general events of her life. I showed her some of the road trip pictures John and Ollie had sent me, and to my surprise, started bawling immediately.

"I know," she said and rubbed my back. "He's your person."

I wiped my tears on my shirtsleeve. "It's so stupid. I knew this was coming, but I can't wrap my head around the fact that they're actually gone. Up until John said they were moving, I never even considered that he wouldn't be. I assumed that John would be here no matter what."

"That makes sense. He was so committed to Oakland."

"But now he's committed to Ollie. Who I love! But, Meghan, when did this happen?"

"When did people pair up?"

"Yes! When he was talking about moving, he kept saying how they'd decided together and how it was the right thing for them, and you know what I thought? 'When did you become part of a them?' When did all these priorities in life shift?"

"You know it happened gradually. You were there."

"Why isn't it happening with me?" I asked.

"Is that what you want?"

I shook my head and stifled another sob. "I want to be important enough to somebody that they wouldn't fucking decide to move away without me. I want to be the person somebody decides things with."

"You know the corollary of that is that you'd need to decide things with somebody else," she said gently. "You'd need to be willing to move or not move depending on somebody else too. Is that really where you're at right now? If you got offered your dream aerial job, would you really want to decide with somebody else whether or not to take it?"

"I guess not. I'm wallowing."

"Any idea how long the wallowing might last? Should I buckle in?"

"Just one more thing. John told me not to get swallowed up by my situation with Kris, and I was worried that he had a point, but also kind of pissed off, you know? Like, why do I need to watch out about not being swallowed up when he's the one moving because of someone else's job?"

She raised her eyebrows at me.

"I know, it's not the same. I'm wallowing. But Sasha said the same thing, about how I was going to get all wrapped up emotionally and how it was a bad idea for me to do this with Kris. I want to know why people keep putting this on me, like they don't think I can do this."

Meghan sighed. "Because they love you and they're worried, Phe. You're doing something that doesn't make sense to them and that you've never done before, at a time when you're already in a lot of transition. And with Sasha, there's a huge part of your sexuality that she knows nothing about too. They're trying to make sense of this with the information that they have, and it doesn't always add up."

"You're right," I grumbled. I picked at my nail polish, gold that day. "But do you think I'm going to get swallowed up, Meghan?"

"I don't know, Phoenix. This kind of thing gets intense. It challenges you and it doesn't always stop when you're not doing it. It can mess with your head, but that's not necessarily a bad thing. Sometimes our heads need to be messed with. I think the question is if you feel like it's challenging or changing you in a way you aren't comfortable with."

"That's the thing, though—I'm having the best time! I've never played like this before. I'm never felt so free, not just sexually or financially, but creatively too." As I said it, I knew it was true, even though I had been upset with Kris when we'd talked about the party. "But I'm also so wrapped up in everything I'm doing, I'm not spending time with my friends as much as I used to. I didn't feel like I got a proper good-bye with John, you know? And I haven't seen you in weeks."

"Things change, and friendships adjust." She shrugged. "That's part of being an adult. You won't always hang out with your friends every night."

"I guess."

"Is there an emotional component to things with Kristen?" she asked.

"What do you mean?"

"Is part of your arrangement emotional support? Do you take care of her beyond taking care of the house?"

I shook my head. "I don't know what she's feeling most of the time. We're blank to each other in that way."

"So you don't turn to her either then?"

"Why would I? We're there for each other during aftercare, but that's it." I said it a little sharply, thinking of her comment that she did not want to date me. Why do I care, I wondered.

"What about when you two aren't playing? When you're both just home?"

"I never see her."

"Do you think you two could be friends?"

I thought about her saying she wanted that, but also the resentment I felt at the comment. "I don't know. I don't think she has much time for that."

"That has to be lonely."

"I don't mind. It's almost like living alone, and besides, I do have people, even if John's moving."

Meghan frowned. "No, Phoenix, I meant lonely for her."

CHAPTER TEN

Over the next few days, I thought about what Meghan had said. I never saw Kris with her friends, though of course she had some. But who were they? No one came to visit, and every call she got seemed to be about work. The one exception to this was the occasional story she told about her experiences in the BDSM scene. But we hadn't gone to any play parties together. I was open to the idea of play parties, but it was so new to me that with everything else going on, we decided not to rush into it. As a consequence, I'd yet to see Kris interact with anyone except me.

I had wondered before I moved in if it would be hard for Kris to share her home, but every day she seemed grateful I was there. Of course, this gratefulness was somewhat complicated by the fact that she generally greeted me by ordering me into the lavender room, to hit me with toys or fuck me or, one night, have me stand naked in front of her while I described all the things I'd done to make the house nice for her.

A couple of days after my chat with Meghan, I got a call I'd been wanting for weeks. A touring band wanted to book aerialists for some local shows, and Sasha and I popped up in their search. For several years, I had picked up performance gigs here and there.

Some months, I'd managed as many as two with my busy schedule and scooped up some good money. Other times I'd gone four or five months with nothing but a single cabaret put together by other aerialists, which paid less than I'd doled out in rehearsal space and costumes. I'd hoped to book at least two or three performances a month as a full-time aerialist, but since my career change, I'd been fruitless in that regard. Then, finally, I had two shows lined up in one week, and they were paying more than I made in two weeks teaching. They were relatively small shows, at a beautiful old venue in Oakland, in a month. We wouldn't even need a new act. The manager had seen video of our fabrics act and wanted us to do variations of that, slowly and on repeat, while the band played.

One of the shows was a Friday night, so I texted Kris right away to reschedule our standing date. She texted back much later with just with word, *Okay.*

While I was making dinner that night and eating it alone again, I got an unexpected impulse. I wanted Kris to see my show. Other than those early YouTube videos, she'd never seen me perform. She'd said she wanted to see me perform live. When I was up in the air, I felt my most confident. It was where I was sexiest, strongest, and most powerful. I wanted her to be in the room with that side of me.

That night when she got home, she tossed me over her shoulder and carried me to our room. There, she ordered me to undress her. She yanked me by the hair and positioned my face between her legs. She doled out instructions that I happily followed, and I got wet pleasing her. I didn't get rewarded that night though. In my excitement over my gig, I'd completely forgotten to take the laundry out of the dryer. It was all wrinkled and cold. I'd need to redo it.

Afterward, as we lay there together, I invited her to my show.

"Maybe." She shrugged. "We should talk about rescheduling that Friday session. This Saturday? We could go to a play party."

"Let me think about it." I frowned. "Do you want to come to one of the shows? You'd get to see me perform in real life finally.

There's a Friday night and a Saturday night show. I'm sure I could get you tickets."

"I'll think about it."

"I'd really like it if you came to the show." I twisted the sheet in my fingers.

She sighed. "Phoenix, you wanted me to come to your friend's party, and now there's this. This is the kind of thing I meant when I said I wasn't a good girlfriend. I don't know if I can, and I don't make promises unless I'm sure I can keep them. What time is the show?"

"Doors open at eight. We go on with the band at nine."

"Either day I'm going to be working. Maybe everything will be fine and I'll be able to leave work early one of those nights and get to Oakland before you go on. Maybe I won't be dead tired and I won't mind being in a loud room with music I might not like and crowds of people I almost certainly won't like. I'm sure you'll do a great job. But if I'm busy or I'm tired, I won't be there."

I inched away from her in the bed. "You didn't come to John's going-away party, and I didn't make a big deal out of it, even though it sucked to be there by myself. I'm not asking you to be my plus-one to everything. I'm asking this once for you to come to something that's important to me, and you won't even try."

"Do you want me to lie to you and say I'll be there no matter what?" She sounded so innocent in her question, which only made me madder.

"I'd like you to show up even if you don't feel like."

"I'm not going to do that. I'm not going to be there if I'm tired or have other things to do."

"You know, this is your company. You're the boss. If you decide to take one evening off and have fun, no one is going to fire you."

"That's not the point. I don't want to take the evening off. I have people depending on me and on the success of my company, and that's more important to me."

"More important to you than what?" I said. "Than being at something that's important to me?"

"Well, yes. You may not like it, Phoenix, but I'd rather spend my Friday working than going to a show."

"So you just don't want to go, that's it? You're not interested in my livelihood and my dreams, basically?"

She sighed. "Come on, Phe. Don't make it like this."

I threw my hands up. "Like what? Like I'd really value having you in the audience and you won't show up? Or like you're not interested in my work?"

"It's not even your show. It's you as decoration for a band."

I whipped around and jumped out of bed. I flung on clothes as I stomped around ineffectively on the soft carpet.

"Is this news to you?" she asked gently. "I told you what my limitations are before we started anything. I thought you understood."

"That's such a fucking cop-out. You can't just say, 'These are my limits,' and act like that gives you a pass. Your limits are shitty, Kris. I'm not asking you for a lot here. I'm asking you to see me perform once, to be there on the first paying gig I've gotten since I quit my day job. You said we'd also be friends. Friends show up. At the very least, they try."

"Phoenix, come here," she said and opened her arms. I plopped on the bed beside her and glared. When I wouldn't give her a hug, Kris reached for my hand. "I admire what you're doing. It's part of the reason I decided to do this with you, because I want to support you. I'd like to see you perform, but I'd rather see that when it's all about you, not some band I don't listen to. I'll try to make it if it works out, but I'm not going to pretend I'm going to drop everything else to be there. I want to be clear here. I like our arrangement. I'm having a great time. But I'm not your girlfriend. I'm not going to be there every time you'd like someone there for you. If that's not okay for you, we don't have to keep doing this. Is it important for you to have the person you're sleeping with in the audience when you perform?"

I sniffled and squeezed her hand. "I don't know."

"We agreed to date other people. Are you seeing anyone else, someone who could be there?"

I flung myself back in the bed. "No, I haven't even really tried. I don't know how to do this. I've only ever had girlfriends. I've never had…this."

"Our situation is pretty unique." Kris lay down next to me. "It's okay with me if it isn't working. I like you and I like this, but I don't want you to be unhappy. If you need us to change things, we can."

"Change things how? Like end it?"

"If that's what you want. Your emotional needs don't just disappear because we're doing this, and I know it must be hard to find time for somebody else with all this," Kris said.

"I don't know if I even want to, honestly. Besides, I don't know how to date someone when I'm already sleeping with somebody else. I've always been, I don't know, thoughtlessly monogamous."

"Do you want to learn how to be less monogamous?" She ran her fingers through my hair.

I laughed. "Who's going to teach me? You don't even have time for *one* girlfriend."

She shrugged. "I'm not an expert at all, but I have had more than one play partner at the same time before, and most of my partners had other relationships when they were with me. And even in my most monogamous relationship, we had a threesome."

"You had a threesome?" I nearly shouted.

"Yes. A few. Is that so shocking?"

"No, I guess. But I don't really know a lot of people who've actually done things like that."

"I thought that you wrote down you were interested in that?"

I bit my lip. "I've thought about it as a fantasy. I've never considered it as a real possibility." That was an understatement. I fantasized about kinky group sex practically every time I masturbated. And that had been the case since I was a teenager. But I'd never told anyone.

"Do you want to tell me more about your fantasies?" She pulled me closer to her on the bed. "I'd appreciate it."

"What do I get for it?" I answered playfully.

"What would you like?"

"Come to my show."

She cocked her head. "Okay."

"Really?"

Kris nodded. "But I want the good stuff. I want to hear the fantasies you never tell anyone, the ones you're not sure if you'd ever want in real life. Tell me what you want. And come with me to the play party."

I glanced at the clock. "Yes."

"So?" She raised an eyebrow. "Get on with it."

"Tomorrow," I hopped out of bed grinning. I pointed at the clock. It was nine thirty-eight.

"You're killing me."

"You love it." I kissed her forehead. "And tomorrow, I'll tell you whatever you want."

The next night at eight twenty-nine, Kris shoved me against the door to the lavender room and reached up under my skirt. "I want to hear it all," she said.

I'd never in my life told anyone what I thought about when I was alone with my hand between my legs. Writing that list and negotiating with Kris in the beginning was the closest I'd ever gotten. "Where do I start?"

"Do you ever think about more than one woman at a time?"

I nodded.

"Tell me."

I closed my eyes. "Ever since I can remember, I've been thinking of this particular scene. It's a little different every time, but basically, there's this hot woman who has kidnapped me, and she chains me up in a big industrial room, like a warehouse, and strips me. I feel like there are other people in the room, watching, but I can't quite see them. Sometimes, she has strangers come up and touch me and fuck me, but she's always in charge of it. She tells them what they're allowed to do, and I'm completely helpless. Sometimes only she is allowed to touch me, and she teases me and won't let me come, or won't let me touch her. Sometimes she makes me touch her. She's trying to get information out of me this whole time, and after hours and hours, I finally give her what she wants. But usually, I come before I can even think about that part."

Kris yanked my panties off and told me not to move. She strung the rope through the hooks in the ceiling. "Keep talking. I bet you have more."

"That's it for that fantasy."

"There must be others."

I chewed on my lip.

She shot me a glare. "Undress. And then tell me."

Slowly, I unbuttoned my shirt and let it drop to the floor. I unhooked my bra and let it slide off my shoulders. I was barefoot already, like I always was in the house, and wearing just a flouncy little skirt. When I reached to take it off, Kris grabbed my wrists and began binding them with rope. She tied them together with the rope strung above me.

She slipped a finger between the rope and my skin to check. When she was satisfied, Kris moved a chair in front of me and sat with her hands folded behind her head. "Now, you're going to tell me what I want to know and I'm going to play with you, and if you're very good, I might even let you come. But you need to keep talking until I tell you to stop."

I gulped and closed my eyes. "I don't know what to say."

"Yes, you do." She reached up under my skirt again to run a finger against my wet lips. Then she plunged inside me, pumping briefly before pulling out and tracing my wetness over my thighs.

"There is one other," I said. Kris moved her hands up my torso to tug at my nipples. "I'm in an outfit like this one, a little skirt and a button-down shirt, and I'm walking by an alley. This hot butch starts calling out to me, sort of menacing, and I stop, and I realize that all her hot butch friends have me surrounded. They push me into the alley. The first one, the leader, slaps me in the face. She says I'm going to get what I deserve, and she rips open my shirt and throws me against a brick wall. All the buttons pop off. I don't have a bra on. There are five or six of them, and they are all staring, and then the leader tells them to help themselves, and they all start groping me at once. I can't even tell whose hands are on my breasts, or my ass, or in me, because it's everyone at once. All these mouths and hands on me, and then the leader undoes her jeans, and they force me to the ground. I give her head while I'm on my knees in this alley. The others are still touching me, hitting me. After I make her come, she lets them all fuck me, use me in every way they can think of. Sometimes I beg them to stop, but they just make me come."

"How does that fantasy end?" Kris rose and stood behind me, squeezing my ass with both hands.

"At some point, I'm getting fucked from behind and have someone's pussy or strap-on in my face at the same time, and I always come, and that's when it's over."

"You like the thought of someone having control of you and over other people too, of someone dominating all of you."

"As a fantasy," I said.

"As a fantasy." She walked to the closet and came back with a paddle. Kris hit me swiftly over my butt and the back of my thighs for a few minutes. Then she set the paddle aside and raked her short nails over my stinging flesh.

"What else?" she said.

"There's just one more, but it's silly."

"I'm not laughing," she said.

"Sometimes, I think about a room full of beautiful women, and we're all naked and oiled up and we're climbing into something like a giant inflatable pool without any water in it. There are a dozen of us. Around the edges, there are people who've paid tons of money to watch us. All of us in the pool start wrestling and laughing and playing with each other, and going down on each other, and touching each other. We're having fun and coming and everyone is lost in a sea of this, of our bodies together. All the while, we're getting rich, because these people are paying for the show, and they want to touch us so desperately, but they can't. They can only watch."

Kris eased three fingers inside me and I moaned. "I love hearing what you think about."

"It's not things I've ever done. I've never even told anyone." I rocked against her as best I could.

"Would you want it? If I could make those fantasies come true, would you want them?"

"Maybe." My breath got faster.

"What if I could give you just the part underneath it? Where other people can see you, and I'm in control of you and who gets to touch you? If it were somewhere safe, and with just one other person, and you knew I'd take care of you?"

I was coming on her hand. "Yes," I exclaimed, from the proposition or the orgasm I wasn't sure.

Afterward, when we were lying in bed, she asked me again if I might want to explore my fantasies in real life.

"Yes," I answered, surprising myself. "But slowly."

"Of course." She stroked my cheek. "We can go to a play party and see how you feel just watching, or playing in public."

I nodded. "And you're going to be at the show?"

"Yes." She kissed me slowly, then looked at the clock. "Shit, I've got to go. I lost track of time."

I looked over. It was after ten. "We're going later every night." I smiled.

"Yeah, and I'm getting behind on work." She threw her shirt back on and hopped into her pants.

"You've been working all day and it's late. How can you possibly have more work?"

Kris gave me a peck on the neck. "I promised I'd get back to someone tonight. It's just a few emails."

I wanted to tell her she was working too hard. But I wasn't her girlfriend, and I'd already put enough pressure on her to come to my show. Kris was an adult, I told myself. She could work as much as she wanted. We didn't tell each other what to do.

CHAPTER ELEVEN

We went to a play party on a Friday night the following week. It was a queer party for all types of queer women and trans and genderqueer people. I was expecting people all dressed in leather and collars, but it wasn't like that. There were a few people in leather and some were naked, but mostly the people at the party looked like, well, queer people I might see anywhere in San Francisco. Except that some of them were making out and/ or flogging each other.

Kris was dressed in dark jeans, boots, a black T-shirt, and a leather jacket. She'd picked out my clothes as part of our play the night before, the red dress I'd worn when we met, and heels. A few people eyed us as we entered the party. Heavy fabric hung on the walls, and there were couches and chairs scattered in the various rooms. Kris greeted some people and introduced me. Everyone was friendly, in the way people are when they're meeting a friend's new girlfriend, but no one seemed to be hitting on us. Still, I felt shy, almost unable to talk.

"You okay?" Kris squeezed my hand.

I murmured that I was, but I was overwhelmed. I heard low moans through a wall, and the sound of leather slapping against skin. I wasn't sure I was ready for it all.

"Let's just walk around for a while," she said. Kris led me around through a maze of softly lit rooms. I caught glimpses of strangers touching each other and talking, laughing. We stopped in a room where a large wooden cross was set up. A woman with a shaved head was draped over it, her bare chest pressed to the wood and her wrists bound to the edges of it. Someone behind her whipped her in a steady rhythm.

Kris sat in a chair facing the pair and pulled me onto her lap. She rubbed her palm over my thigh. "Do you like seeing this?"

I nodded. My throat felt dry.

She turned me around to straddle her. "I'd like to have you, right here, with all these people around. Do you want that?" She reached up and tweaked my left nipple through my dress. She'd told me not to wear a bra.

"I don't know. I feel shy."

"Shy like you don't want to, or shy like I should push you?"

My breath sped up. "Push me," I gasped.

"No one will notice us. Everyone is busy with each other. Let me have you," she said.

I took a deep breath and nodded. Kris slipped the straps off my shoulders and pulled the front of my dress down, exposing my breasts. As she played with my boobs, I ground myself on her thigh. I listened to the other couple in the room, the thuds of the whip and the whimpers and sighs and groans from the couple. Kris whispered that I had to do this, said that she was orchestrating the whole scene, that all eyes were on me, that she was going to pass me around. I closed my eyes and imagined for a second that it was true, and as I did, I came with a shout, yelling out. When I opened my eyes, I saw Kris looking up at me, smiling. I looked around and saw that for a moment, the couple was looking at me too.

I pulled my dress up. "How are you doing?" Kris asked.

"W-whoa," I stammered. My neck felt hot.

She got me some water while I watched the scenes around in us in a daze. I couldn't believe I'd done that, but I felt sort of proud too.

Kris and I left soon after. She took me to a diner and bought us French toast. "Did we go too far?" she asked.

I chewed. "No. I'm just…It surprised me how turned on I was," I said.

"Was it worth trying?"

"Oh, hell yes."

"Do you want to do something like that again?"

"Yes. Yes, please."

"Let's get on that."

My stomach fluttered. Kris and I discussed possibilities over the next few weeks, but didn't plan anything. I was focused on preparing for my performance with Sasha.

When the night came, I spotted Kris in the crowd. Her arms were folded over her chest, her mouth was just friendlier than a frown, and I'm pretty sure she had earplugs in. But she was there.

With how well everything was going, it was no surprise that Kris and I agreed to continue our arrangement. The week after my show, Kris and I went to one of the BDSM clubs in the city to play and to meet Kris's friends Eric and Derek. The couple had been together for years, had always been heavily involved in BDSM, and often had subs that they dominated together. "We're both doms at heart," Derek said. I had trouble telling them apart at first, both of them white men in their forties with similar buzz cuts, warm smiles, barrel chests, and equal dedication to the gym. Eric had kind, dark eyes and Derek had twinkling blue ones, but from a distance, I was never sure.

When we met, they were hanging out eating jelly beans. After we talked for a while, they excused themselves to cheerfully string someone up in some elaborate suspension bondage. They were easy to talk to, and I found their arrangement fascinating. They had two or three subs at any given time, but at the end of the day, they came back to their apartment to just one another, like any other happy long-term couple.

"I really like them," I said on our way home.

She grinned. "I'm glad. They're some of my best friends."

I was glad to finally see that Kris had friends of her own. Though it wasn't part of our arrangement, I did worry that she didn't seem to have a social life. Seeing her at a couple of play parties and meeting Eric and Derek, I could see that wasn't the case.

In the weeks that followed, we fell into a nice routine of Friday night play parties. We played or hung out with her friends at the party (especially Eric and Derek), or if we were invited to, we watched wildly creative exhibitionist scenes. We didn't involve anyone else when Kris and I played, though we flirted with the idea in conversation sometimes. I wasn't quite ready for it because I was afraid of upsetting our equilibrium. I'd found a balance between work, friends, and my adventures with Kris, and a dream career that was coming together before my eyes.

The only hiccup in November was Thanksgiving. John and I had been organizing anti-colonialist Thanksgrieving dinners since the first year we met, complete with elaborate vegan main dishes (John), homemade pies (John), tons of sides (John), and weird handmade paper decorations (me). This sometimes included a turkey, brought by committed carnivore guests since John was a vegetarian who kept our oven meat-free. Once Ollie came along, our celebrations started including excellent wine. Tons of people always came over. We'd even hosted John's family once, though usually he or both of us went to their much more normal celebration after our own. I'd never been able to afford to fly home for both Thanksgiving and Christmas, and being home for Christmas always won out. The only year of my adult life I hadn't shared Thanksgiving with John was my freshman year of college, when Amanda and I spent the day eating pizza and watching sci-fi movies. My own household was never the most traditional when it came to Thanksgiving (my dad was the one who taught us to call it "Thanksgrieving"), but still, the prospect of being all alone for the holiday was overwhelmingly depressing.

Meghan and Bill were off to Bill's parents' for the holiday. Sasha's parents had bought her a ticket home to the East Coast. John and Ollie were, of course, on the other side of the country. Way too late in November, I realized I had nowhere to be.

Part of the reason I'd forgotten to make plans was that Kris hadn't mentioned it. The Sunday before Thanksgiving, we'd just finished up our afternoon session when she said we'd, of course, adjust the week's schedule for the holiday.

"What are you doing for Thanksgiving?" I asked as she got dressed.

"I'm going over to Eric and Derek's place. They have it catered every year. It's great. What about you?"

"Um, nothing, actually. I sort of forgot it was happening."

"You're not going to see your family?" She sounded surprised.

"No. Thanksgiving at my house is mostly an opportunity for everyone to get drunk and talk about genocide."

"Wow, your parents must be really interesting people."

"They met as PhD students. Political, Chicano PhD students in the late seventies. Do you know what I mean?"

"Not even remotely. But you really don't miss them over the holidays?"

I shrugged. "Sure, but I'm going to see them for ten days for Christmas. My sister and brother-in-law come with their kid. We go to my abuela's with all my cousins and tios and everyone. It's a whole thing. Thanksgiving, not so much."

"Huh. So what are you going to do for Thanksgiving then? Relax around here?"

I must have looked as miserable as I felt, because after a long, awkward silence, Kris said, "I could see if there's room at Eric and Derek's, if you want."

Was spending a major family holiday with her live-in roommate submissive really what Kris wanted? Probably not, but I couldn't fake a lack of interest. "Could you?"

"I'll call them today. I bet they can squeeze in one more." She said it so kindly I almost wept.

"Thank you."

"No problem."

I was so grateful that Kris didn't bring up the possible boundary blurring in the situation I didn't even ask another question about it. Of course, that meant I was more than a little nervous when the day rolled around. What would a kinky Thanksgiving entail? I'd literally never seen this couple outside of a play party, and I had no context for them with their shirts on. Despite Kris's urging, I had never attended a munch, a non-sexual, non-kinky get-together for folks into BDSM. I wasn't interested in hanging out with people just because we had the same sexual interests if there was no possibility of sex. I'd never hung out with kinky people as a platonic group before.

Kris assured me that I should treat it as a normal Thanksgiving. She took care of bringing some wine, and I put on my favorite velvet thrift store dress and went along for the ride. Eric and Derek's condo was gorgeous. They even had a view of the Bay out one of the massive windows.

Both of them were dressed in pressed slacks and polo shirts. It was a little jarring to see them both looking like accountants. Kris had dressed up like she was going to work, complete with a tie and a V-neck sweater, and I felt like the only person who was dressed for a silly party. They were hosting two other couples, all men in their forties and fifties styled much like Eric and Derek. In addition to being the only person in a dress, I was the only one there in my twenties, the only person of color, and it seemed the poorest person in the room by far. I felt even more nervous than I had when I thought everyone would be wearing leather.

Thank goodness that just as the wine started flowing, the doorbell rang.

"That must be Ray!" Derek said and went to buzz the person up.

"Ray's our new boi. 'Boi' with an 'i' mind you. 'They' and 'them' pronouns," Eric explained.

"What on earth?" said Teddy, one of the guests. "I can't keep up with you guys."

"It's so fun!" Eric added. "I'm learning so much. Plus, they're gorgeous."

"I don't know how I'll do talking about somebody as 'they,'" said Jeremy, Teddy's partner. "The grammar is going to kill me. 'They' is plural."

"You get used to it," Eric assured him.

"Excuse me for saying this, but I thought bois with an 'i' and that sort of pronoun…situation were lesbians," Teddy said.

"Not always! Ray's flexible. Flexible about their own gender, flexible about the gender of their partners." Eric dropped his voice to a flirty whisper. "Generally flexible."

The guys laughed. I wasn't sure what to expect from Eric's description, but as soon as I saw Ray, I knew that "gorgeous" was the right word. Ray was androgynous, both handsome and beautiful, with high cheekbones, short stylish dark hair, and the sort of lean body that looked good in everything. Ray had olive skin with freckles, and Ray's gender, ethnicity, and age were ambiguous. I had no idea if they were twenty-something or Kris's age. What I did know was that they were wearing a denim button-down shirt with ripped up, paint-splattered gray jeans, and I suddenly felt a lot less alone among the impeccably ironed grown-ups.

Ray was greeted by a chorus of hellos, including my own quiet welcome, and they answered, "Thanks for having me."

"You are by far the cutest one these two have brought around," said Ron, one half of the other couple at the table.

Ray blushed a little. "Thank you," they said, and pulled up a chair between Derek's seat at the foot of the table and my own.

"I'm Phoenix," I said, sticking out my hand.

Their hands were warm and soft, and so was their smile. "Ray."

Kris slung an arm over my shoulder and extended the other in front of me toward Ray. "I'm Kris."

Their brief handshake seemed like a conversation, communicating power dynamics and relationships.

"Oh, I'm being a bad host!" Derek said. "Introductions!" He introduced the rest of the table, facilitated chitchat about Ray's occupation (salesclerk) and others at the table (tech and design people). Then we wound around to me.

"Phoenix is a trapeze artist," Kris said proudly. "Very talented."

"Aerial dancer," I said.

"How did we not know this?" Teddy asked his partner. "Circus people are here!"

"Like in the circus?" Jeremy asked in the same moment.

"Like Cirque du Soleil?" Ray asked a second later.

"More Cirque than circus," I explained. "But I'm not that good."

"She's very good," Kris said.

"You have to say that," Eric teased her.

"How long have you two been together?" Ray asked us.

Kris and I exchanged a questioning look. Nobody had asked us that. We assumed that Eric and Derek's friends had been briefed on our situation because they didn't ask questions about that, or really about us at all. Maybe it was just that they were all old friends and were eager to catch up, but the spotlight had been comfortably off of us the whole time.

"I've been her sub for about three months," I said finally. I glanced at Kris to see how she took that tidy summary, and she gave me a little nod.

"Oh, like me," Ray said and smiled. They had impossibly perfect teeth.

"But I haven't seen you at any parties," I said.

"I haven't seen you either. I usually go with them Saturdays."

"I'm sometimes performing Saturdays, for work."

"We keep missing each other," Ray said with a grin. "I hope that isn't the case for much longer."

It was my turn to blush. Other people took over the conversation, and Ray and I exchanged a little more small talk over the delicious and extravagant meal. Ray had to cut out early to go to work, and after they left, the guys complimented Eric and Derek on their new sub. As they did, Kris eyed me carefully.

After a long afternoon and evening of food and drink and conversation, Kris and I waddled into a cab, tipsy and stuffed. "How was it?" Kris asked me, a hand on my knee.

"Great. Thank you so much for letting me come."

"It was nice to have you there." After a beat she asked, "What did you think of Ray?"

I picked at my cuticle. "They were nice. Cute."

"Uh-huh." She leaned in and whispered in my ear, "Because Derek told me Ray loves girls, and those guys love to lend out their subs."

My skin felt hot. What on earth? Was Kris really suggesting that she'd make one of my secret fantasies come true with one of the most attractive people I'd ever seen?

I didn't ask for permission. I kissed her fiercely. We made out in the back of the cab all the way home.

CHAPTER TWELVE

We didn't have much time to talk about, let alone arrange, any fantasy scenarios in the weeks that followed. Sasha and I got extremely lucky booking holiday parties, and our schedule was the fullest it had ever been. Kris had even more work than usual. We managed our daily schedule, but our longer sessions and play parties started to fall by the wayside. We promised we'd find time for at least one more extended session together before I went to New Mexico for Christmas with my family.

The last Friday before I left, I expected a play party, but instead of getting home around seven thirty and rushing us off to the night's locale, Kris stomped in just after five. I'd never seen her home so early.

"Hello?" I called from the kitchen. I'd been looking at the fridge and debating cooking up the meager options or going to the store.

"Hi," Kris answered in a nasal voice. She flopped onto the couch. I looked her over. Her nose was red and she looked pale and exhausted.

"Are you sick?" We'd managed to make it through the fall with nothing worse than a brief head cold for me. Kris had bragged that she never, ever got sick.

Kris sniffled. "I'm dying."

"Want some tea before you do?" She made a noncommittal noise and I put the kettle on.

"I was fine this morning, just a little congested," she said.

"It happens."

"Not to me!"

I walked to the living room and stood in front of her, feeling her forehead. "I don't think you have a fever, but you're clammy. Why don't you get in your pajamas and some slippers, I'll make you some tea and soup, and you relax?" I ruffled her short hair.

"We're not going to play tonight." She looked miserable.

"Clearly. Go get changed."

Kris dragged herself up the stairs. I made us both mint tea with honey and pulled a batch of tortilla soup from the freezer, one I'd been particularly proud of, along with the last portion of frozen tomato soup.

"Tomato or tortilla soup?" I asked when I heard her coming down the stairs.

"Tomato, and can I have a grilled cheese sandwich? And orange soda?"

"Do you turn into a little kid when you're sick?"

"Don't laugh." She shuffled up to a chair in the dining room. I'd never seen her flannel pajamas before, even in the laundry, and I knew why. Kristen Andersen, wunderkind and dom, was wearing baby blue jammies with monkeys printed all over. Sweet cartoon monkeys with bananas.

"This is a new side of you." I turned my back and stifled a giggle.

Kris slumped in her chair. "I don't get sick," she said. "So I don't know how to act. And these are my only pajamas. My mom bought them."

"You're fine. I'm just teasing." I poked around in the fridge. "No orange soda but there's ginger ale. A grilled cheese seems possible, though. Want it with the soup or before?"

"With the soup. In triangles." I brought her a mug of tea and a can of ginger ale. She sipped the tea and complained that it was hot.

I wanted to tease her more, but she looked so pathetic I could only feel sorry for her. Sorry and unexpectedly fond of her. "Go find something for us to watch, some bad TV or a movie. Relax."

"Phoenix?" She looked at me with huge eyes, her glasses put away for the night. "Thank you for taking care of me. Nobody ever takes care of me."

"How can they, if you never get sick?" I stirred the soup.

"I mean it."

"You're welcome. Grab a blanket and get comfortable on the couch. I'll be there in a second."

We settled in to a cheesy romantic comedy, the last of the tomato soup I'd made the month before, plenty of fluids, and grilled cheese in triangles. I tucked the blanket around Kris. We ate with just the sound of the movie.

"This is delicious." She slurped her spoonful, despite her usually faultless manners.

"Thanks."

"It's the best thing you've ever made."

"You've had this before, remember? This is leftovers."

"I never remember what I eat. I just gobble it up as fast as possible and get back to work."

"In that case I'm going to start making a lot less effort." I nudged her.

"I'm sorry. I should pay more attention." She sounded genuinely sad.

"You're okay." I rubbed her back lightly.

"Maybe my priorities are all wrong. I've been so stressed out. That's probably why I got sick." She blew her nose. "You know what I have planned for Christmas? Catching up on reports I should have read last week."

I frowned. "You're not going to see your family at all?"

She shook her head. "I see my parents once a year, for their wedding anniversary at the end of July. I call them every couple of weeks and on holidays, and that's plenty. I used to go for Christmas or Thanksgiving, but I hate traveling around the holidays. My brother and his wife live in Seattle with their kids, and my sister comes in with her kid, and I feel like I'm intruding on family time. They have this completely different relationship with my parents, and then I show up and everyone tries to catch up, but half the time I'm checking my phone or trying to write an email under the table. Besides, they always want to know about my personal life, and what do I say?"

"What *do* you say?"

"When I had a girlfriend, I'd mention her, but I haven't brought anyone home in a decade. For a while it's been, 'I'm working a lot. I'm dating but no one special.'"

"Ouch, what a cold phrase."

"They want me to get married and have kids. Any hint of a serious relationship would give them the wrong idea. Besides, I am not discussing anything kinky with them, and I haven't had a girlfriend for years; I've had *subs*. What would you say in that situation?"

I shrugged.

Kris thought for a minute. "Actually, that's a good question. What are you going to say to your family?"

"It's different. They're perfectly happy to talk about my career and what everyone is reading. They don't pry about my personal life."

"Is it denial? They're uncomfortable with you being gay so they'd rather not talk about it?"

I laughed. "No. If anything, they miss Amanda. She and my mom still email, mostly about work since they're both English lit people. Every once in a while, my mom will tell me what Amanda's doing, or ask if I've talked to her lately. I mean, Amanda and I are friends on Facebook and we parted on good terms, but there's a reason we broke up, you know? We ran out of common ground, and it's hard to keep a friendship going with your long-distance ex when you want to talk about the nitty-gritty of making a living out of art, and she wants to talk about theory and academia. Except, my parents also want to talk about theory and academia. Amanda has a serious girlfriend now, but my parents used to try to get us back together, like for years. She was the great student that I never was, and my mom sort of mentored her, so they wish they could keep her in the family. Unfortunately, no one I've dated since has been anything like that."

"So it's not that you're queer, just that you're a weird artist."

"A weird artist who isn't dating anyone they can relate to. Sometimes Carolena would get nerdy about politics, and my dad liked that for a minute. But she was so militant. Everything was revolution and reclaiming Aztlan, and my dad had been so deep in that when he was young that he was like, 'Yeah, but how are you actually learning from our mistakes?' He teaches at least one student like that every semester, so he can get cynical. As for my mom, she gets bored if arguments aren't sufficiently nuanced, and Carolena's were not."

I could see Kris trying to work something out in her head and frowning with the effort.

"You don't know what Aztlan is, do you?" I asked.

"I'm making a mental note to look it up."

Kris sneezed and I handed her a box of tissues. "It's the legendary original home of the Aztecs. But it's also what some people call the part of the US that used to belong to Mexico. Well, Spain before that. So the West or the Southwest, depending on your view. Some Chicano activists are or were really into the idea that it should be its own country. Carolena was all about it, and really liked to quote all these activists. But my dad knew those activists personally, had worked with them, had even taught one or two, and he was over it. He'd been having that conversation since the seventies."

"Wow, your family is something else." She blew her nose. "My parents usually just talk about baseball and gardening."

"It's normal to me," I said. "I don't really think about it."

"Is your sister like that too?"

"Are you kidding? She works in college administration. My brother-in-law is an adjunct at like three colleges. Their kid goes to a daycare on a college campus operated by education professors and their grad students. When I go home, I'm the only person in the house without at least a master's. Well, the only person over the age of two."

"And the rest of your family's like this too?"

I chuckled. "And then some. The rest of my family are *teachers*. My abuela, my tias, most of my tios, half of my cousins and the people they married. Everybody is a goddamn teacher. When I was a kid doing cartwheels outside, they'd be like, 'Don't you want to go in and read a book?'"

"I wonder what they'd think of me," Kris said.

"Working at a tech start-up and no grad school? Please. You know the answer."

"Wow, and I thought I was impressive. I guess you won't be mentioning me."

I raised my eyebrows. "What exactly would I tell them if I did, anyway? 'I'm living with a woman, but ours isn't a typical relationship. She has certain, ahem, requirements that I meet nicely and I get a place to live out of it'? Weird artist with a puny bachelor's degree is hard enough, but what's going on here? That is way outside the understanding of my family."

"You'd think leftist academics would be more progressive," she said.

I shook my head. "My mom did *not* get a doctorate so her daughter could get consensually slapped around for housing. She's second-wave all the way. And you're a white person with money! My dad would die. No, he'd lecture me about self-worth. This would not make sense to them, believe me."

She blushed. "They don't need to know the details. I don't know, maybe I'm your roommate then. Don't they know you moved?"

"Sure, but I made it sound like I found a place with a friend of a friend and that my roommate and I are basically ships in the night."

"That's not so far from the truth, actually."

"Except here I am, taking care of you when you're sick. Plus all the fucking."

She gave me a bright, if sickly, smile. "You're really fun, Phoenix."

I did a little dance with my arms and shoulders, illustrating how fun I was. Kris laughed.

She looked at me for a minute. "It's strange how little I know you outside of, well, what it is we do."

I cleared out dishes and took them to the dishwasher. "What do you want to know? I'm an open book. Do you want more tea or anything?"

"I'm okay," she said. "Why are you named Phoenix?"

"My mom's favorite myth." I sat back down on the couch. "She said she wanted to 'impart me with the ability to always find rebirth and renewal within myself.' English professors, am I right?"

"What's your sister's name again?" she asked with a tiny smile.

"Connie. Well, Consuelo, after my grandmother. My dad picked that one. She's always been lucky." I rolled my eyes.

"I'm named after my grandma too."

"Look at us, learning all about each other. A whole new level of intimacy."

She smiled. "We should hang out more often."

"Yeah, but you're never around for that."

Her smile faded. "Do you think I'm making the wrong choices with my life?"

"I really don't feel qualified to answer that one." I pulled my feet up under me.

"I wonder sometimes. People have been telling me for years that I work too much, that there's more to life than work. I never took it seriously because I loved working so much. But lately, I'm not sure. Seeing you so excited about what you're doing, about your shows...I miss that feeling."

"You're losing your passion?"

"I guess. Maybe it was more fun when there was less riding on it. Now that I'm so close to the top, I feel like I can't slip, but not even that. Even just holding steady would be failing. I have to keep expanding, keep going up, and it's not like it used to be. In the beginning I was working with these two great people, Sam and Amy, but then he moved on to another start-up, and she quit and had a baby a couple of years ago."

"You also lost your creative partners."

"It changed things." She sighed.

"Were they like your best friends?"

She shook her head. "We weren't exactly buddies, but we were great at developing ideas together. Sometimes we got in huge arguments and couldn't stand each other, but in the end we always came up with something great. We had very different lives, and I don't think we always understood each other, but intellectually, we all clicked."

"I get that. Sasha and I would probably not have become friends if we didn't perform together, but she's my favorite person to create with and that makes me love her. We annoy each other sometimes, but we appreciate each other very deeply and it makes us good friends. We're both better at what we do because of our work together." I drained my mug. "Maybe you need another partner."

"Maybe. I feel worn out, I guess, and I don't know if I could offer the energy I had when we started. Maybe Sam and Amy had the right idea. They worked hard and made their money, and then wanted to do something else. Amy said other eager young things were ready to take it over, and we should let them."

"You could," I said. "You could sell and pretty much be set for life, right?"

Kris gave a modest shrug. "I don't know about set for life, but I'd have a lot of options about when and how much I'd need to work. But what would I do with myself if I wasn't working?"

"Um, whatever you want?"

"What's that?" She gave me a helpless look.

"Oh, Kris, that is the saddest thing you've ever said."

"Maybe I'm just sick." She blew her nose again. "Maybe when I'm better, everything will look different."

"Sure," I said, though I doubted it. Kris's life depressed me. I didn't want to spend all my time working, and I had a hard time understanding why she did.

She looked at me, concerned. "Phe? Am I the only white person you've ever dated?"

I laughed. "We're not dating, remember?"

"Right." She looked down. To my surprise, she sounded a little sad. "I guess I'm putting it delicately."

"Beth was white," I said. "What about you? Please don't tell me it's been all white girls for you."

She shook her head. "I mean, I've had lots of different play partners."

When she didn't continue, I prompted her. "But?"

"I've only actually ever had one girlfriend, Laurie. So I guess I've only had a white girlfriend, a suburban girlfriend, a blond girlfriend, a girlfriend I met when we were both twenty. I loved her. I thought we'd be together forever. I'd always worked, but after college I started working ninety hours a week, and after a while she got tired of it. She said I needed to change or she'd be gone, and I didn't really believe her. Eventually, she left. We were together for six years."

"Shit," I said before I could stop myself. "So when you said that stuff when we met, that stuff about why you don't date, is that all based on one relationship?"

Kris sighed. "Pretty much. I was a huge geek in high school, and amazingly, a geeky dyke with glasses and acne does not get much action in high school. And I knew I wanted kink, and I didn't know how to express that. I thought there was something wrong with me. When I got to college and I found out about sex clubs? Sex clubs where women wanted me to hit them? That's all I did, other than school and work, for about a year. I did not date. I didn't even want to see scene people outside of the scene. I went to school with Laurie and she insisted on studying together. Of course she was actually just trying to get me to spend time with her. When I finally realized she was interested in me, I was shocked. I thought

I'd be the sort of person that never happens for. I fell for her as soon as I realized she liked me."

"Was Laurie into kink?"

She nodded. "I was nervous about telling her that, well, I'd never had sex without flogging somebody first. But she just laughed and said, 'I've always wanted to try that! As long as it's not the only thing we do.' It was great. We went to play parties together in Seattle, and I realized that friendships that started in a sex club weren't limited to that. Once we moved here, we just played at home, in *our* home, because I was so busy."

"And after you broke up, you never had another girlfriend? It's been like ten years."

She looked sheepish. "I worked and I had play partners. I'd go on dates sometimes, but for a long time I was very hung up on Laurie, and that wasn't fair. And then I figured that I had one big love, and that was more than lots of people get."

"Jesus, you are depressing when you're sick," I said with exaggerated exhaustion. Kris laughed. "How can you stand it?"

"I guess I got used to it." She suddenly sounded completely wiped out. "I think I'm more tired than I realized. I should probably go to bed."

"Of course. Let me know if you need anything."

She nodded. As she walked past me, our eyes met, and I could swear I saw tears.

After that Friday night, I didn't see Kris much for the rest of the weekend. She stayed in her room and slept. I occasionally brought her soup or crackers or tea, but mostly she fended for herself. We missed our usual Sunday afternoon session because she was sleeping. I found myself slacking off on household chores, and also incredibly horny.

Early Monday morning, Kris knocked on my door as I was packing.

"Feeling better?" I asked after I invited her in.

"Much, though I am taking my first sick day in a long time. Thanks for taking care of me."

"I was happy to." I turned to face her. "I had a really good time with you, just hanging out."

"Like actual friends," she said.

"We should do that more often."

"If I ever have time again." She sounded like she was joking, but there was a little sadness behind it.

I swallowed my impulse to tell her that she could make time, and zipped my suitcase. "I can't believe I'm actually ready to go two hours before I have to head to the airport. I'm usually stuffing things in a bag ten minutes after I was supposed to leave my apartment, missing the BART connection I needed, and racing through the terminal. What am I going to do with my free time?"

She raised an eyebrow. "Well, you've been letting your chores slide."

"Sorry! I'll get on that right now. I don't want to leave you with a mess."

"No, that's not what I mean," she said, her voice low. Oh.

"It's not eight thirty. I'm supposed to tell you no if it's outside our time. You wanted somebody you could have, but not any time you wanted." I fiddled with the suitcase zipper as I eyed her carefully.

"This isn't about our arrangement, Phe. It's not a requirement or a trick. This is just me thinking you're hot and wanting to play. That is, if you want to." Her voice was a little huskier than usual, a lingering result of her cold probably, but very hot.

I kept my gaze trained on my luggage as I answered, "What would this entail?"

"Well, I want to order you around a lot. But only if you're interested."

Her hair was messy and she had her glasses on. She was wearing dark jeans with a plain T-shirt, her feet bare. Sexy Kris, tall and grinning in my doorway. Of course I wanted her. I wanted to do whatever she told me to do.

"Yes," I said.

She smiled. "But tell me to stop if you don't like where I go with this."

"Obviously."

She adopted a serious expression. "You've been lazy," she said. "You haven't been doing your job."

"I'm so sorry." I played along, batting my lashes. "I'll do better."

"You certainly will, and you'll do it naked."

"Excuse me?"

"Take off your clothes."

"Kris, no, I couldn't."

"You'll do what you're told."

"Please," I faux-begged.

"Strip off your clothes, or I will rip them off."

I felt my nipples harden. I loved this. Slowly, I peeled off my sweater, slipped off my shoes, and wriggled out of my tight jeans. I kept my bra and panties on, and tried to cover myself with my hands.

"All of it," she said.

I turned my back to her and unhooked my blue lace bra, then let it drop onto my bed. I stepped out of my matching panties.

"Turn around," she said.

I faced her, still clutching my breasts and shielding my pussy with my hand.

"Go downstairs. You have a lot of work to do. The house is a mess."

"You want me to clean it? While I'm naked?"

"Obviously. Don't ask stupid questions. Go on."

I headed down the stairs. The house wasn't actually a mess. There were dirty dishes in the sink that I hadn't bothered to load into the dishwasher, a hamper of laundry I'd taken downstairs but hadn't started, and a few scattered items around the downstairs that needed to be put away. The counters could have done with a wipe and the floors needed to be swept, but that was it. I started by tossing the laundry in the washer. Kris stood behind me and watched.

She followed me to the kitchen, where I rinsed dishes and put them in the dishwasher. Kris said nothing as I tidied up. It reminded me of the beginning of our time together, that first day she watched me in my domestic service.

As I sprayed the counters and wiped them, Kris settled into a chair in the dining room where she could see me. "I always imagine you like this," she said. "Whenever I come home to a clean house or a home cooked meal, I think of you doing this for me, like I told you to, submissive and naked. Sometimes when I'm working, I get a vision of you on your knees, barely dressed, scrubbing my floor, and all I want is to come home and fuck you."

"Then why don't you?" I said over my shoulder.

"That's a good question." She waited a beat. "Put those down. Come here."

I set the cleaning supplies on the counter and started to walk toward her.

"No," she said. "Crawl."

I dropped to my knees and crawled over the cold tile of the kitchen, then the smooth, cool hardwood. I stopped in front of her, my face inches from her splayed legs.

"So pretty." She caressed my cheek.

"What would you like me to do?"

Kris cocked her head and ran her fingers through my hair, considering. Then she yanked me up by the hair and maneuvered me over her lap. My face hung down so all I could see were the legs of the chair and the curtain of my own hair falling around me, brushing the floor. My bare ass stuck up in the air, and Kris stroked it with her palm.

I expected her to say something, to tease me or tell me to count, but she didn't. She spanked me, hard, merciless, each blow heavy and stinging, all over my ass and the back of my thighs. I squirmed and she pulled my hair.

"I didn't tell you to move," she said.

Kris lightly rubbed my reddening ass and legs with her palms, soothing my burning skin. I relaxed a little and kept myself still. Then she started again, slapping with more force. I let out a shriek.

She laughed. I was loud when I came, but rarely during anything else. I certainly didn't scream just from a spanking. I wanted to tell her it was the shock of it. I wanted to cover my embarrassment. But I couldn't, so I kept myself frozen and bit down on my lip to keep from yelling out again.

After she'd made me sore, delightfully humiliated, and terribly wet, she ordered me back to my knees. I knelt before her on the floor.

"What am I going to do with you?" She cupped my face in her hands.

Kris stood up and walked to the couch, motioning for me to follow. I crawled behind her, resting on my knees in the plush of the living room rug when I knelt before her. She sat in front of me on the couch, my face directly across from her crotch.

"Unbutton my pants," she said. I did and slid them down her legs, along with her boxers.

She smiled wickedly at me and grabbed me by the hair again. Awkwardly, she angled my face to her pussy. I adjusted and started lapping her up. She was as wet as I was, which made me even hotter. I loved teasing her clit with my tongue, finding a rhythm and edging her toward release, then keeping her hovering there. Kris was quiet, just a few moans escaping her lips, and whenever she let me, I made it my secret mission to get her to scream.

But I didn't get to that time, and I didn't get to toy with her as long as I wanted either. After what felt like just a few minutes, she started to stiffen. "Don't stop," she said and pulled my hands up under her shirt. I barely touched her nipples, fumbling under her clothes, before she came, shaking a little but still quiet. When she was done, I looked up at her.

Kris looked spent and exhausted. I'd thought she was completely over her cold, but she looked a little weak. "You should lie down," I said. "Take a nap."

"Maybe I will."

"And what should I do?" I was hoping she'd tell me to get the vibrator I liked, which was her go-to command when we were short on time or she got stuck at work after eight thirty.

Kris looked at the clock. "You should take a shower and get going."

I glanced at it too. "I have plenty of time. C'mon, I'm so wet. What should I do?"

Her eyes were tired, eyelids drooping. "You didn't do your chores without being told, so you should think about that while you're punished. Take a shower and get dressed."

I frowned and wanted to argue.

"You aren't allowed to touch yourself." She sat up straighter. "Not today, and not while you're away. Not without my permission. If you want to come, you have to ask me and I'll tell you if you can."

I swallowed hard. My clit ached. I struggled with my desire to object—this wasn't what we agreed to—and my equal desire to do exactly what she said. To be controlled by her, even when she wasn't there.

"Do you want to play like that while you're gone?"

"Yes," I said. "I'll do exactly what you tell me to." I was surprised by just how much I meant it.

"Good." She kissed me. "Now, go catch your flight."

CHAPTER THIRTEEN

I hadn't expected my dynamic with Kris to stay with me when I went to New Mexico, but I spent the whole visit connected to her. As soon as I got off the plane in Albuquerque, I scrolled through the messages Kris had sent me, detailing what I could do to myself, and when, and with what. I texted back a quick, *Thank you*, tried to shake off the thrill it gave me, and went to greet my mom at the gate.

My mother wrapped me in her arms as soon as I stepped out of security. "Welcome home," she said. Right away, she started catching me up on the latest developments in her department, with my extended family, and about my hometown generally. We were halfway home before she paused for breath and asked, "How are you?"

"I'm really good. I've been booking some shows, and I'm teaching a lot of classes."

This piqued her interest. "Who are you teaching?"

"Adults who want to get fit or are curious. Some kids' classes."

"Could this be a career?"

Of course. I knew as soon as I said it where my mom would go with this information, but I couldn't stop myself. "I don't know if it's sustainable long-term. I'm running around between studios all over the place. If I could teach in one place, maybe, but there isn't really a studio that wants me to teach that many classes."

"Well, you're just starting out. Are there people who teach this as a profession?"

I held back my annoyance. "Sure, but mostly people who also perform or made a name performing already. Or people who own a studio and have been teaching freelance for years."

"We all have to pay our dues," she said.

"Mom, I like performing. I want performing to be a big part of my career. The teaching is fine, but it's not why I'm doing this."

"I never said anything against your shows," she said.

I pressed my lips together tightly. I knew what she wasn't saying but was implying: that bodies gave out quicker than minds, and I should not make my livelihood dependent on things as fallible as my muscles or my hands. She'd said tiny variations of these things a hundred times over the years.

Once we were home, we were greeted by the chaos that was my two-year-old nephew, Joaquin. Joaquin was using a metal pot and wooden spoon as a drum kit, shrieking with laughter. When he saw me, he threw these to the floor and ran at me at full toddler speed, head-butting me in the stomach in an attempted hug. "Tia Phe!" he screamed with delight.

"Hi, buddy." I lifted him up and spun him around. "Want to be upside down?"

"Yes!" he screamed again.

I flipped him and hung him upside down by the feet, quieting him immediately. It was our thing, something his parents didn't do. Connie walked across the living room to greet me. "Relative silence? I'm impressed, Phoenix." She hugged me with her upside down son between us. "How are you?"

"Good. Strong, as you can see." I flexed my impressive bicep and swung my nephew around.

"Well, thank God, because I needed a break from the drumming."

Joaquin laughed.

"Is that Phoenix?" Connie's husband, Nick, called from the kitchen.

"It is!" I called back.

He walked over to us, wiping his hands on a towel on his shoulder, his apron still on.

"It's nice to see you," he said with a genuine smile and gave me a kiss on the cheek. "And it's nice to hear this one laughing instead of trying to be a one-toddler punk band."

"You're very welcome. What are you making?"

"Your dad and I are making tamales."

I rolled my eyes. "Why does he insist on doing that? Abuela's going to make enough for a small army, and hers are way better."

Nick shrugged. "It's what we do. How was your trip?"

"Probably a lot more relaxing than yours." I shook Joaquin. "Hey, where's my dad?"

"He ran to the store."

"He's never actually prepared to cook the things he wants to cook." I shook my head but smiled.

"Down!" Joaquin said.

I spun him and then put him on the couch. "Want to learn cartwheels?"

He clapped with glee. I led him to the backyard and spent the rest of the time before dinner tumbling with my nephew. It was a little colder than I was dressed for, and I borrowed a sweater from my mom and bundled Joaquin up in his many available layers. As soon as the sun started to set, it got too cold and we were forced back indoors.

Once I was there, I remembered why I preferred to goof around outside. The house smelled wonderful, looked perfect, and everyone was gathered around passionately discussing the finer points of academic politics. The words flooded the room, excited voices spilling over each other.

Even though my dad greeted me with a bear hug, a minute later, he was back to the conversation. That felt like the perfect illustration of being with my family: welcome home, now let's out-talk each other. It made me wonder if I couldn't keep up with conversations like these because I didn't care, or if I pretended not to care because

I couldn't keep up. I loved my family, but being around them made me feel dumb. Worse, it made me feel like my priorities were all out of whack. The weird thing was, I got perfectly fine grades in high school and college, I read plenty of books (though not theory books), and I could hold my own at parties with snobby would-be intellectual grad students. But my family was something else altogether. Maybe it was because I was the youngest, but by the time I was seven or eight, I started to wonder if I hadn't gotten the sort of brains my sister had inherited from our parents. By that time, I'd been to a few other houses and realized that the conversations at our dinner table were not like other families. Ours required you to reference the thinkers you used in your argument. Other people talked about weather, and sports, and television (which we did not own).

It wasn't intentional, I knew. No one in my family ever said I was less than, but I felt like I'd stumbled in on a group that wasn't really mine. That night, I sat in a corner chair with a sleepy Joaquin in my arms, waiting patiently for everyone else to finish up their conversation so we could eat dinner and maybe talk about something that made room for me.

Eventually, they did, and we ate a delicious meal. Half the time my mind wandered, and half the time my family tried to include me by trying to make sense of what I was doing with my life. This was worse than having them talk endlessly about the latest thesis they'd all read. I felt like I was a foreign subject they were studying, not a family member. They were trying to understand me but had no way to do so, and it felt lonely.

After about fifteen minutes of dissecting questions about my life and career, I said I was full and tired from my trip and all those cartwheels. Everyone understood, and I hustled to my room. I lay down on my childhood twin bed, got out my phone, and texted Kris, *What do you want me to do?*

Immediately, she told me to lock my door and offered me very specific instructions about how to touch myself. I did exactly what she ordered. It made everything feel normal again, and I was able to sleep.

That's how I ended most nights of my visit home. All day, I tried to find a place with my family, and they tried to figure out what to do with me. Sometimes it was good and sometimes it was impossible, but in the end, I closed my door and made myself feel better with Kris.

It was even what got me through Christmas, when we went to my abuela's house with all our relatives. This meant I had the same conversation approximately fifty times. It went like this:

Relative: "So, what are you up to out there in California?"

Me: "I'm an aerial dancer, with a trapeze but not in the circus."

Relative: "That's interesting! I heard you were doing something like that. But don't you have a degree from UC Berkeley?"

Me (with forced smile): "No, I went to San Francisco State."

Relative: "Oh? Why there?"

Me: "My girlfriend at the time went to Berkeley, and San Francisco State was the closest college that I got into."

Relative (trying to hide their pity): "Right, that's why I was confused. So, what are you doing as an aerial dancer?"

Me: "I perform shows, practice a lot, and teach other people who want to learn to do the same thing."

Relative: "That's nice. And you can make a living doing that?"

Me: "I'm making it work."

Awkward pause. Here, either I started asking about their life and the conversation wrapped up in five to ten minutes, or else this happened:

Relative: "So are you thinking about grad school at all?"

Me: "No, I like what I'm doing. Grad school wouldn't really help."

Relative responded with one of the following: a) "But you can't really have a *career* with this, can you?" or b) "Well, of course," then excused themself.

My abuela chose option a. We'd all had a pretty similar conversation last Christmas when I was a receptionist trying to become an aerialist, but it didn't make it sting any less. No one (well, almost no one) was trying to be mean, but they did not get it. They didn't get me.

After the conversation with my grandma, I slipped into the kitchen and snuck out my phone to wish Kris a merry Christmas.

"Who are you texting?" Connie seemed to appear from nowhere.

"No one."

Connie arched one eyebrow. "Is it serious?"

"It's nothing."

"Who is she?"

I gave up. "It's not serious. It's just fun."

"Yet here you are, texting her in the middle of Christmas with your family."

"Just to make myself feel better."

Connie looked at me. "What do you mean?"

"You see how it is," I said with a sigh. "Everybody looks at me like a disappointment, dumb Phoenix who has only a BA from a college with the word 'State' in the name. Weird Phoenix who is doing something that doesn't make sense."

"They don't have any point of reference for what you're doing, but that isn't a comment on your intelligence."

"Really? Because that's not what I'm hearing."

Connie rolled her eyes. "Do you think you're the only person getting this treatment? I have a master's, and all they want to know is why I'm in administration when I could have been a doctoral candidate. Or poor Nick! Every year they ask him if he's tenure track somewhere yet. It rubs salt in the wound. But they're not doing it to make anyone feel bad. They're trying to catch up."

I slumped into a kitchen chair. "That's not how it feels."

"I know. It doesn't feel that way for me either," she said and sat across from me. "We left. That's what it is. The reason we get this is because we don't live within a hundred-mile radius like everyone else, so our lives are unfathomable. Think about it. Dad has been in the same place for essentially his entire life, and Mom grew up less than two hours away. They went away to get PhDs, and then they came back and have been here ever since. Dad turned down a position at Columbia and spent a decade commuting to Santa Fe before he got hired at UNM. He did that so we could be here, because family's most important. Everyone in this family sees each other constantly. Except for us."

I picked at a hangnail. "Why do you think we both moved away when nobody else did?"

She frowned a little. "I wasn't planning on moving away. I did stay, but then I met Nick and he couldn't get hired here. We went where he found adjunct positions with the possibility that one of them might eventually lead to more, and where I could find a job. I'd be here in a heartbeat if we could both get the jobs we wanted."

"I wouldn't," I said.

"Yes, you would. Maybe not here, but Santa Fe. If you could do what you wanted in your career and live there, you'd come back. You only moved away for Amanda, and you stayed because you found people you cared about. You built a life there, and that makes it hard to imagine moving. But you could build a life here too. Then things would be easier with our family."

I bit my tongue to keep from saying things I knew would start a fight, starting with *you don't know me*. I tried to keep my tone even. "Amanda was not the only reason I moved. I did want to be with her, and I also wanted to see other places, experience new things, find myself. If she'd gone to UNM, I still would have moved away. And maybe I could build a life in Santa Fe if my career supported me there, but I don't think that it would be easier for anyone to understand."

"Maybe you should try it," she said. "There's nothing keeping you in San Francisco, right? John moved away. You're living with a roommate you barely see. You're single. You don't have a job."

"I have a job," I said. "And I have a performance partner. I'm starting to build a name and a base of students and fans."

Plus, there was the little matter of free rent. Another hot dom willing to provide for me was probably not going to magically appear in Santa Fe, affirmations or no affirmations.

Connie waved my concerns away. "Don't get so emotional. It's an intellectual exercise: what would it take for you to come back?"

"Well, I'm not playing." I pouted.

"This isn't about the girl, is it?" She nodded toward my phone. "No."

"So, if your career took you somewhere else, you'd go?"

"Or course."

She shrugged. "Maybe it'll take you back here at some point, and everyone will stop bothering you." Connie looked at her watch. "We should get back."

"Go ahead. I'll be there in a sec," I said and pulled out my phone.

I can't wait for you to be back here, Kris had texted me. *No more letting Fridays or Sundays slide. I have big plans. And I miss hanging out with you.*

I felt my heart do a strange little flutter. Could I really leave as easily as I said?

CHAPTER FOURTEEN

I'd been planning to take BART from the airport, but there she was, beaming and waving at me as soon as I exited security in San Francisco.

"This is a nice surprise," I said as I hugged her.

"I wanted to thank you again for taking care of me," she said and took my bag for me.

"You weren't afraid it was too, I don't know, girlfriend-y?" I shifted my weight from foot to foot.

She frowned. "I'm picking my friend up from the airport. I thought you'd be happy."

I regretted what I'd said. "Sorry! No, of course. Thank you. I really appreciate it."

She nodded, but her smile was gone. In my head, I kicked myself for ruining a kind gesture. I tried to make up for it by distracting her with stories from my visit. It worked. By the time we were home, she was laughing at my goofy Joaquin tales. Toddlers were always entertaining.

"So, how was your Christmas?" I asked as we pulled into the garage.

Kris shrugged. "What I thought it would be. I worked."

I ran my fingers through her hair. "Poor Kris. Did you stay in your room the whole time?"

"Pretty much. And my deck."

"Do you ever, I don't know, want to spread out to the living room?" I asked as we walked into the spotless main floor. It looked like she hadn't been there since I'd left.

She shook her head. "I can't work in a space we share. I get distracted too easily."

"What about fun, though? You could play video games in the living room, put some books there, watch movies downstairs." I picked up a decorative glass orb from a shelf. "Like, are you really attached to this? More than stuff you actually use?"

She took it from me. "I don't even know what this is."

"It's expensive crap people use to fill up rooms. Want to get rid of this and put your stuff out here?"

Kris scrunched up her mouth. "You don't think it'll look messy?"

I laughed. "No, I think we can figure out a way to have things you actually like here without it looking bad. Let's clear this off."

I ran down and grabbed a few collapsed cardboard boxes from the garage and taped them up. We ruthlessly rid the impeccable downstairs of tchotchkes. Before we knew it, we'd filled up two boxes.

"It looks so empty."

"Not for long," I said and handed her an empty box. "On to your overstuffed room."

"It didn't used to be so bad," she said on our way to her bedroom. "Your room used to be my office."

"But it looked so perfect when you showed it to me. It looked like it hadn't even been touched."

She blushed. "I cleaned everything out of it the night we met. I wanted you to like it."

"You thought I'd want to do this if the room looked good enough?"

"Something like that." Kris started loading the box with the Xbox and related cables. She held up a video game with guns on the case. "Will it bother you if I play this in the living room?"

I shook my head. "First of all, this is your house—"

"You live here too," she said.

"You should feel comfortable in your own home. Besides, I've lived with roommates my whole adult life. Occasional video games in the living room is not a problem. In fact, I'd like it if you hung out in the common areas more. I never want to bother you when you're in your room, but I do like to see you sometimes."

"I like seeing you too," she said. There was a sizzle in the air. I felt myself drift toward her, pulled like a magnet to her mouth. But this was outside of our rules and the lines were feeling blurry enough already. In the heated silence, I pulled away, afraid of what it would mean to kiss her the way I wanted to.

"Well," I said with false cheeriness, "we better get all this set up." I marched down the stairs with a box. While I put books and games on the empty downstairs shelves, Kris rearranged her room. I tried unsuccessfully to set up her Xbox. When she came downstairs, the moment had passed.

"Here." I handed her the cables. "This is yours to figure out. I'm going to unpack finally and then throw together some dinner."

"Don't bother. I'll order us some pizza." She gave me a squeeze and kissed the top of my head. "Thank you."

"For what?"

"It sounds cheesy, but for making this into a home."

I shook my head and called her a nerd. She laughed. I ran up the stairs with my suitcase, yelling, "Mushrooms please!"

"Gross! Just on your half."

In my room, I felt the tears forming. *Making this into a home.* I took a deep breath, said my affirmation, and then sighed. I knew the feeling creeping up from my belly, and I knew it would only lead to trouble. What I didn't know was what to do about it.

Having a crush always made me horribly nervous. The anxiety wasn't something I could hide either. It made me clumsy and distracted, made me bite my nails and chew my lip raw. While training with Sasha the following week, I fumbled so much that she insisted we take a break in the middle of our new routine.

"What is going on with you?" she asked.

"I'm preoccupied."

"Obviously, but about what?"

I avoided her eyes.

Sasha groaned. "It's about that chick you're living with! Ew. Love problems."

"Not *love*. And not problems. I just have things on my mind," I said.

"Yeah, like what?' She chugged water and then handed me her metal water bottle.

I looked at her helplessly. What was I going to say?

"You're falling in love with her," Sasha said. I shook my head, though I was definitely crushing on Kris pretty hard. "Okay, so maybe you're not in love, but you're afraid that you're going to fall in love. Or you're upset that she's not in love with you. Whatever. I told you this would happen."

I stretched my arms and ignored her. Sasha knew me too well.

"You know what you need?" Sasha vigorously screwed the cap back on her water bottle. "You need to get your priorities back on track. You're supposed to be building an aerial career, not getting so worked up about your weird sugar mama that you fall off a fucking trapeze."

"I did *not* fall, and I'm not—"

"Luckily," Sasha interrupted me, "the Universe always provides. And you have me to help you see that." She sauntered over to her bag and pulled out her phone. When she walked back to me, she shoved it in my hand. A casting call filled the screen. It was for a multimedia, aerial version of "The Little Mermaid," based on the original Hans Christian Andersen tale without any nod to the Disney version, complete with the mermaid turning into sea foam. A short preview of the show had already debuted to great success in London, and now the company was looking for supporting parts for their upcoming US tour. They needed six sister-mermaids, who'd also play roles in other scenes, including the sea witch. My jaw dropped. The tour would provide connections to full-time aerial performers and producers, pay a salary in the ballpark of my office job days, and get me exposure all over the country. Plus, "The Little Mermaid" was my favorite fairy tale.

"You're welcome," Sasha said smugly. "I signed us up for auditions two weeks from now. The auditions, training, and first stop of the tour are going to be in San Francisco, so we don't even have to travel until June. And it gives you a nice out from your freaky situation when we go on tour."

I couldn't even form words and babbled like a fish, which was sort of fitting.

"Are you trying to thank me?" Sasha took her phone back.

"Wow. All I can say is wow."

"It's an amazing opportunity. We'd be perfect for it. Look, they want people who can perform doubles acts as well as solo pieces, and if we audition together, I'm sure we'll get it. If we get on this tour, we'll have so much momentum for our careers. We can network the hell out of it and be set by the time the tour is over."

"How long is the tour?" I asked.

"Six months. Could this have worked out any better? You left your stupid job and bam, this fell into your lap. The Universe *provides* when you trust it."

"We don't have the parts yet."

"But you're interested, right? You'll audition with me?"

I thought about it. I wasn't excited about leaving my comfortable life for six months of grueling performances and constant training, networking in every city, and being on the road for half a year. I was a homebody at heart. And how would Kris react? I shook the thoughts out of my head. Sasha was right. This was exactly the sort of thing I quit my job for. If it worked out, my aerial career would be thoroughly launched. I could build enough of a reputation that I could start getting the sort of high-paying, consistent work I'd need to make my aerial dance career a sustainable one. I hadn't touched my savings thanks to Kris, and with this I might never need to. I could make it a sustainable career out of aerials, as long as I got this part.

"Of course," I said. "And thank you. I'm so glad you signed us up."

Sasha beamed. "Good. So now you'll take this seriously? We've got a lot of work to do if we're going to kill these auditions."

Instantly, my clumsiness and preoccupation were gone. I'd worry about Kris later. At the moment, I had the biggest opportunity of my life to prepare for. Not to mention that having an end date for my arrangement with Kris would help me avoid any messy emotional entanglements. She'd been pretty clear about what she wanted and didn't, and I wasn't about to try to change that. I'd spent every relationship I'd ever had trying to coax people into who they could be, and what had it gotten me? My exes launched into success while I was alone. For once, I was going to put my own dreams first and push pesky crushes to the side.

Despite Sasha's optimism, I wasn't sure I'd get the part. Probably half the aerialists on the West Coast would want to get in on a paying, well-promoted tour. I expected fierce competition, and if I made it, I'd feel great. If I didn't, I didn't need everyone knowing I'd gotten my hopes up over nothing, so I told no one, not even my parents, about the audition.

The excitement made me a little jittery. I needed something to focus on. That something came a few days later when Kris mentioned she'd been talking to Eric and Derek about Ray and our threesome fantasy. They were eager to loan Ray out, Ray was eager to guest star, and the only question was: did I want to? I did. What better way to avoid getting too deep in a crush than to sleep with someone else? We arranged a date for the following Friday night. I couldn't think of a better distraction.

CHAPTER FIFTEEN

I felt excited as soon as I agreed, but nervous too. Nervous about submitting sexually to Kris in front of someone else, about my fantasies becoming real and what it might mean, and about the practical details of threesomes. Not to mention all the thoughts I was avoiding with the three-way in the first place.

When I finished training that Friday, I ran errands, finished the chores I had to do, and then sank myself into a hot bath. I was sore from all the extra training for the audition, and my feet and ankles were bruised from my renewed dedication to mastering toe hangs and one-ankle hangs, things I'd been struggling to do for years. Carefully, I shaved and tweezed and trimmed, exfoliated and moisturized, primped and styled every inch of myself. I tried not to think about how much I wanted this and how much I feared it wouldn't live up to what happened in my head.

Thirty minutes before Ray was set to arrive, Kris knocked on my door. "Ready?" she asked.

Kris was home early and still dressed formally from work. I was wearing nothing but a towel around my body, despite my finely applied makeup and carefully coiffed hair.

"What do you wear to a threesome?" I frowned into my closet.

"How about I pick it out for you? And have you eaten?"

I shook my head. "I think I'm too nervous."

"I got some takeout. Go have some, even just a little. I'll find something for you to wear."

"What if it's weird?" I asked.

"The takeout is delicious and not weird at all. As for the clothes, well, girl clothes are not really my area of expertise, but I don't think it'll be too bad."

"You know what I mean."

She rested both her soft hands on my shoulders. "It's going to be fine. And if it isn't? We'll stop. No one will be upset. It happens. We'll process or we'll watch a movie and pretend it never happened, whatever you want. It's not a problem."

I gulped.

"Now go." She turned back to my closet. "Eat something. I'll bring you clothes in a minute."

I went downstairs and picked at pad Thai, tasting nothing. Was I making a mistake? Would it actually be okay? The distraction it was providing didn't seem to be working at the moment. But even as my stomach churned with nerves and my mind filled with worries, my body tingled. I wanted to push myself past what I'd ever tried before. I wanted to do things I didn't normally do. I let myself fantasize about the night ahead, and suddenly, I wanted something even more unexpected.

A few minutes later, Kris came down with an outfit I would have never chosen for myself: a short black skirt with polka dots, a skimpy camisole with lace edges, and no bra or panties. I dressed obediently, feeling silly and exposed.

"It's not too, uh, little?" I gestured at my exposed skin.

She answered sharply, in her dom voice. "I picked out what I want to see you in. Isn't that clear?"

"Yes." I dropped my gaze. "Sorry."

She lifted my chin with her finger. "If you're uncomfortable, go change."

I shook my head.

"If you want to call this off, just say. And if you want to stop at any time, safe word. It'll be okay," she said gently. "I want to do this because you want it, and if you don't, let's not."

"I want to. I'm just in a weird headspace. Um, Kris, one more thing?" I stared at the ground. "I think, since we're trying this, I want something I'm not usually in the mood for, maybe. I might, I think, maybe…" Damn it, I couldn't get the words out. "It's that one day a year. You know, like, um, anal sex day."

"Really? You aren't too tense? You look really tense."

"You don't have to."

"Hey, I'm happy to. Let's see how it goes."

Ray arrived at our door a few minutes later. Kris had me wait in the lavender room while she greeted them. Kris appeared at the door in front of me, Ray trailing behind.

Ray looked exceptionally attractive, wearing black jeans, a white button-down shirt mostly unbuttoned, a leather collar, boots, and dark eyeliner. Ray's black hair looked freshly barbered, the sides close cropped and the top artfully mussed.

"Hi, Phoenix," Ray said, extending an elegant hand to me.

"Hello." I shook hands weakly. My throat felt dry.

"Eric and Derek have left me in charge tonight," Kris said. "They think Ray can follow my directions. Ray, you think you can do that?"

"Yes, Sir."

Kris and I exchanged a look. "We don't usually use 'Sir,'" I said.

Ray stared at their own boots. "I was trained heavy on protocol," they said. "But I'll follow the rules of the house."

Kris looked at me then at Ray. "Is it important to you to have a Sir in a scene?" she asked Ray.

They nodded.

"Phe, would you be comfortable if Ray followed their protocol?" she asked.

"Of course. I'll even follow it."

Kris raised her eyebrows. I knew the whole "Sir" thing wasn't her favorite, but I felt weird with Ray following that rule if I wasn't. My fantasy was that I'd be the one totally controlled, submitting to everyone.

"For tonight," I said. "If you don't mind, Kris."

"I want my subs happy." She rubbed my shoulder. Both of them were still standing, while I sat alone on the bed. "All right, you both need to call me 'Sir' then. We'll use stoplight colors for safe words. Ray, you prefer 'they' and 'them' pronouns, correct?"

"I do, Sir. Thank you, Sir."

"Phoenix and I use 'she' and 'her.' Eric and Derek told me about your other preferences when we arranged this, and I will be taking them into consideration. Anything else you want me to know, boi?"

"No, Sir."

"Phoenix, is there anything you want to say or ask before we get started?"

"Um, Ray, what language are you, uh, comfortable with for your body?" I felt awkward asking, but I'd been with Amanda during her early days of coming out and transitioning. More than once, she'd shut down and pulled away when I mistakenly used the wrong words for her body, though neither of us knew why she would suddenly stop. When I finally figured out to ask her what words she used for herself, we were both relieved. There was no way I was going to mess up the night by misgendering our guest star.

Kris nodded at Ray, encouraging them to answer. "I have a clit and a cunt, but I like it when people take my cock seriously as well. Sometimes I say 'chest' for what I have and sometimes I say 'tits.' Is that okay, Sir?" Ray asked Kris.

"Absolutely."

"If you don't mind me saying so, Sir, you have a very well trained girl here. She's trained so well, to ask," Ray said, still looking at Kris.

"She is a good girl." Kris smiled at me. "Though she won't be doing much talking tonight. For the rest of the night, she's not going to speak unless I tell her to. Anything else, Phoenix?"

"No, Sir." It would require some thought to add "Sir" to everything, but it felt strangely right for the evening.

Kris told Ray, "She's being shy."

"What should we do about it, Sir?" Ray asked.

"We should show her that being shy won't make any difference. We'll do what we like with her. Tie her hands behind her back."

I gasped with excitement.

Kris pointed Ray to the restraints. Ray selected a rope and went to work tying my wrists behind me as I sat on the bed. I was silent. Their hands were warm on my skin, and the rope tight without hurting. I glanced back and saw that Ray's knots were even better than those Kris made.

Kris slipped my lacy straps off my shoulders and yanked the front of my camisole down. "Look at her," Kris told Ray. "She acts shy, but look at her now, with her tits exposed."

I blushed. My humiliation fantasies were coming true too, and at the same time, I wanted to object, to explain that I hadn't chosen the outfit, that I never did things like this. The tension of wanting to call out, and at the same time loving it, made me wet. So did the look in Ray's eyes as they finished with the knots and came around to stare at my chest. Ray eyed me with pure hunger.

"Very nice, Sir," Ray told Kris. "You have a very pretty girl here."

"That's not all. She has a gorgeous pussy. Have a look." Kris pushed me back on the bed and lifted the hem of my skirt. I squeezed my knees together, but parted them when Kris slapped the top of my thighs. "Don't act shy," she said. "I told my friends what a good girl you were. Good girls do what they're told."

Those words made me so wet I was sure it was visible to Ray as they peered between my legs. No one spoke as Kris and Ray looked me over, running hands admiringly over my flesh, pinching and poking occasionally, adjusting me as if I were a doll.

"She's so lovely, Sir," Ray said again. "Thank you for letting me look."

"I've been told you're a very well trained boi," Kris said to Ray. "They say that you suck your Sirs' cocks, shine their shoes, clean for them, wash their clothes, and take any punishment they see fit to give."

"I do my best, Sir."

Kris picked up a riding crop. "They told me to play with you however I saw fit. I'm going to report back to them if you were a good boi or not."

"I'll be very good for you, Sir, and please you and my Sirs."

I felt my clit throb. It was like watching the weirdest, hottest porn I could think of.

"Good, because I'll going to hit you. Take off your shirt."

Ray unbuttoned their shirt, revealing small breasts with large, pierced nipples. I wondered if I could fit each one in my mouth, if I'd be allowed to. Ray folded the shirt and laid it on the dresser, then knelt before Kris.

"Face Phoenix and hold on to her knees. If it hurts, squeeze her. I'm going to hit you ten times," Kris said.

Ray positioned themself and gripped one of my knees in each hand. With each whoosh of the crop through the air, Ray held my knees tighter, digging their nails into my skin as the sharp smack of the crop rang out in the room. Ray didn't make a sound though, didn't even seem to exhale. I counted the squeeze-nail dig-release cycle in my head as Kris attacked Ray's upper back. Kris had never been so rough with me, and I wondered if she didn't think I could take it. Or had Eric and Derek said Ray liked this? I watched Ray's piercings bounce with the force of the blows.

"Very good. Let go," Kris said. "Face me. Hands behind you."

Ray did and was rewarded with more quick smacks from the riding crop, another five on each hard nipple. Ray winced.

"Are you clear who's in charge?"

"Yes, Sir," Ray answered immediately.

Kris put the crop aside and ruffled Ray's hair. "Good. I bet that hurt. Put those in the girl's mouth so she can kiss them better."

Kris pulled me up to sitting. In an instant, Ray was standing in front of me, alternately shoving one nipple and then other into my mouth. I kissed gently, sucked lightly, trying to ease the sting of the crop. I flicked the silver ring in each one.

"She's helping, Sir," Ray said. I realized I was not going to be spoken to, just about, for the rest of the evening. The thought made me more aroused.

"She's very helpful. I find her most helpful when I want to come. Do you want to come, boi?"

"Yes, Sir, if I'm allowed."

"You are. The girl is good with her mouth, if you want to use it. You can fuck her cunt too, but I save her ass for myself."

"May I, Sir?" Ray held their hands above my bare breasts.

"Please, play with her all you like."

Ray massaged both my breasts, slowly twisting my nipples. They repositioned me, moving me carefully onto my back with my hands still behind me. Ray lay over me, sucking on my breasts roughly. I moaned, louder than I meant to. Nervously, I glanced up at Kris and watched her smile.

Ray undid their pants, revealing a briefs-style harness with a cock already strapped on and covered with a condom. "She's good with her mouth, Sir?" Ray asked.

"Quite. Phe, give Ray a kiss, and then get on your knees and show what you can do."

I leaned up and kissed Ray's soft lips. The kiss was very gentle, wetter than with Kris, and unexpectedly sweet. Then I awkwardly flopped myself to the ground with none of the grace of a seasoned aerialist. I arranged myself on my knees in front of Ray, who sat on the edge of the bed and, with some difficulty, took their cock in my mouth.

It wasn't the best strap-on blowjob in the world, what with my hands behind my back and my balance a little off, but it seemed to be working for Ray. Ray moaned a little and pulled on my hair, urging me to take more.

Kris knelt behind me and slid a hand under my skirt. She slipped a finger in easily because I was so slick. Then another, fucking me with a steady rhythm. She teased my swollen clit with her thumb.

"Ray, if you are going to fuck her, you ought to do it now."

Ray instantly yanked my head away. "Yes, Sir." Ray lay back on the bed.

Kris slid her fingers out of me. She stood up and pulled me with her. Looking me straight in the eyes, she said, "You're going to take our cocks now, and you're going to ask before you come. Understood?"

I nodded. Kris slapped me across the face, hard.

"Understood?"

"Yes, Sir," I said.

She smiled. "It's good having Ray around. It's teaching you some things. Let's see what their cock teaches you." She lifted me onto the bed and arranged me over Ray, straddling them. Kris didn't stop there, though. She took Ray's cock in her hand and nudged it into my dripping pussy. She even took Ray's hands and put them on my breasts. "Go on now, give the boi a ride."

Slowly, I lowered myself fully onto Ray's cock. I ground and wiggled and swayed my hips, growing more confident as I did. They looked up at me, delighted, toying with my breasts and occasionally moaning. Kris was behind me, rubbing my clit, squeezing my ass, and easing a thumb between my cheeks.

I didn't realize what else she was doing behind me, and it wasn't until she'd lubed me up and had a finger inside my ass that I thought to look back. Kris was wearing a small cock—smaller than any I'd seen before—glistening with lube. She was warming up my ass so she could fuck me there. The thought of being filled like this between the two of them gave me a jolt of pleasure.

"Are you warmed up?" Kris asked me after several minutes of slipping her gloved fingers in and out of me as I rode Ray's cock. I nodded, breathless.

She slid her small cock into my ass. Even with all the lube, the play, and how turned on I was, I felt tight at first and I cringed as just the tip enter me. "Relax," Kris told me. "Breathe."

I took a deep breath while Kris rested behind me. Ray, who had been merrily fucking away, stilled too. For a moment, we all concentrated on helping me relax. It felt calm, almost spiritual, and I felt overwhelmed with happiness. My fantasy was coming true, perfectly, even better than I could have hoped. I let go, and Kris eased in slowly. She gave Ray a tiny nod, and they went back to moving beneath me.

Once she was inside me, Kris went back to massaging my clit. Stuffed with Ray and Kris and practically high from the attention, I lost myself in the sensation. I felt like my pleasure was too big for my body, like I'd expanded. When my orgasm began to build, it took me a minute to remember to ask first.

"Please, Sir," I said. "Can I come?"

"Yes, because you asked so nicely," Kris said and stroked my clit, provoking my release. Squeezing around the both of them made me come even harder, even more than usual. Kris continued to rub my clit even as I shook and moaned and whimpered.

"She can keep going for quite a while if you don't stop," she told Ray. "She's a very fun toy."

"Thank you for sharing, Sir," Ray said. "I'm impressed."

The conversation about me kept me going, kept me coming just as much as Kris's skilled fingers. I loved it. I loved everything in the fucking world.

I don't know how long I came, but by the end, I was screaming loudly enough to surprise myself. The intensity of sensation became too much. "Please," I said, "I can't take any more."

Kris moved her hand away and Ray released my nipples, but neither of them pulled out of me.

"Should we stop, Sir?" Ray asked Kris.

"That was for her, boi. Now it's our turn," she said.

I knew Kris was going to fuck me in the ass until she came. I was relaxed and spacey, and it didn't hurt anymore. I felt full, divine. Ray moved slowly under me, but Kris sped up. She angled me forward. My hands were still tied behind me, and I couldn't balance myself. I fell forward onto Ray, who stopped moving and simply looked amazed. Ray wrapped their arms around me. Their cock was still buried in my pussy. Kris's cock, meanwhile, was slamming in and out of my ass.

I felt the shift in her movement before I heard her. I knew she was coming from fucking me like this. Her quiet gasps were confirmation, but I felt it first. It delighted me that I could know this, and everything felt magical and surreal.

She pulled out of me when she finished. Without a word, she unbound my wrists. "That was incredible, Sir," Ray said.

"What about you?" Kris asked them. "Have you come?"

Ray shook their head. "I would like to, Sir, if I'm allowed."

Kris rolled me off of Ray and onto my back. Wiped out from her orgasm, I knew she was struggling to maintain control, though she was hiding it pretty well. All she wanted right now was to lie back and rest, but she wouldn't until she had seen this thing through. Coming the way she had had taken her energy for the moment, and yet her mind was still focused on making my fantasy come true.

"See to the boi, Phoenix. Whatever way they like."

I looked at Ray, smiling in a way I hoped was an invitation.

"Um, oral pretty much always works on me," they said with unexpected shyness and took off their boots, then slipped off their harness and cock.

Kris waved me in the direction of dental dams and gloves. I rolled my wrists as I got up. Being tied up hadn't hurt, but it had left me a little stiff and unnatural with my hands. I fumbled snapping the gloves on, struggled to open the dental dam, and generally moved with less finesse than usual.

Ray spread their legs wide on the bed to reveal a bald cunt. Kris moved to a chair to watch us, her eyes half-closed. I dribbled lube onto Ray's large clit, stroked it for a second with my gloved thumb, and then added more lube. I held the dental dam over their cunt, and started to lick through the latex. I liked the noises that started pouring out of Ray almost as soon as I got to work.

"A little more pressure," they moaned. "Flick the tip of your tongue…yes, just like that. Oh, fuck, yes."

The helpful hints faded away as I got a handle on Ray's preferences. Ray got louder and louder, and more colorful in their use of pleasure-filled expletives. Ray thrashed, swore, hit the headboard with their fists, kicked the bed, and generally made me feel like I was driving them wild. I loved it and responded even more enthusiastically, which made Ray louder, which made me give more energy, which made Ray come with a full-on scream.

"Perfect," Kris said. She stroked my head as soon as Ray had collapsed and I'd gotten rid of the latex. "Good girl. You did exactly what I said. Your reward is that you get to come again."

I was shocked. I felt sure the night was over. "I couldn't possibly," I said, then I caught myself after a beat and added, "Sir."

Kris slapped me in the face, even harder than she had earlier. "You're going to follow my directions."

"Yes, Sir."

Without another word, she took off my camisole and bound my wrists again. This time she secured me to the eyehooks, with me kneeling on the ground. Ray, still a little groggy from their orgasm, watched with interest from the bed.

"I was going to make this easy for you," Kris said. "But you questioned me, so you need to be punished a bit first. Boi, get the flogger and come here."

Ray jumped up and followed the directions right away. Ray was still naked except for the collar, while Kris was almost fully dressed. She went over to the dresser and replaced the small cock with the large blue one she'd introduced me to before we even lived together.

"You're going to flog her until I tell you to stop," Kris told Ray. "Then we will make her come."

Ray obediently began flogging my back. They did not start gently, the way Kris always did, but with the kind of heavy strokes that exhaust the arm when you give them. I jumped.

"I know it hurts," Kris said sympathetically as she shoved her cock in my mouth. I gagged and she pulled out.

"Color?" she asked me.

The sting of my back didn't make me change my answer. I wanted this, wanted whatever Kris had in store for me. "Green, Sir," I said without hesitation, even as I pulled away from another blow.

She smiled and eased into my mouth more gently. "This is happening because you didn't follow directions." She pumped away at my mouth. "Do you understand?"

I nodded with her cock in my mouth.

"Will you obey now?"

I nodded again.

"Boi, stop," she commanded Ray. "Put on a glove, then get down on your knees and play with her tits. If you're a very good boi, I'll let you have her pussy too."

"Yes, Sir. Thank you, Sir," Ray said and did as they were told.

Ray knelt back on their heels in front of me and groped my breasts, pinching my nipples, and then sucking on them intensely. Ray was awkwardly squeezed below Kris, her pussy over their head. My clit was aching to be touched again. All the while, Kris continued to fuck my mouth. "Touch her pussy," she told Ray. Ray kept their mouth and one hand working my breasts, while their other hand rubbed my clit. Meanwhile, Kris was beginning to tremble, a sign she was about the come again. She moved faster, harder, while Ray worked on me. The intensity of it knocked me over the edge. Kris came with a shiver and pulled out of my mouth just in time for me to cry out.

Ray didn't milk my orgasm for more like Kris always did, but it was just as well because I was spent. Kris sank onto the bed and ordered Ray to untie me and to clean everything up. Once I was free, I stumbled over and lay beside Kris.

"Good?" she asked.

I could only nod. Once Ray had put everything away and dressed, they lay with us too. Kris had arranged for Eric and Derek to pick up Ray later that night. The three of them were going to Ray's favorite late night diner for aftercare and pancakes. Until Eric and Derek arrived, Ray, Kris, and I lay in bed silently, dazed, cuddling passively by resting our limbs on each other. I was in the middle, exactly how I wanted.

Eric and Derek gave all of us water and lots of praise when they got to our place. They offered to take us to the diner too, but Kris and I decided to stay home. We each hugged Ray, Eric, and Derek, and then we plopped onto the couch.

"Want something to eat?" Kris asked once they'd left.

I rested my head on her shoulder. "Maybe popcorn."

"Sure. We could watch a movie or something."

I managed a handful of popcorn and the opening credits before my eyelids drooped. When I woke up, it was morning, I was tucked in my bed, and Kris had already gone to work.

CHAPTER SIXTEEN

Okay, so I woke up alone after my huge, impossible fantasy became an even better reality. It was nothing to freak out about. Sure, I felt an uneasy resentment in the pit of my stomach. I was still crushing on Kris and hurt she wasn't there the morning after. But I didn't have time to think about any of that. I had an audition to prepare for.

Sasha and I fine-tuned our routine all week, even canceling a couple of classes to fit in more rehearsal time. By the time we actually tried out, my barrel rolls and heel hangs felt as automatic as tying my shoes. Our routine for the director, Damien, and his producers was, well, flawless. My only worry afterward was that because of all that rehearsing, I was actually pretty sick of the routine, a variation of a multi-apparatus number we'd performed before. I wondered if my boredom showed.

"What the fuck ever," Sasha said when we were in her car and I told her my fears. "We nailed that. Did you see Damien's face? He would have handed us contracts right then if he could have."

"Do you really think so?" I chewed my lip.

Sasha nodded. "This is happening."

"Should I tell Kris?"

Sasha groaned. "Does everything have to be about your weird fuck-buddy roommate?"

"It's just, if I might be going on tour..."

"Stop making lesbian drama for yourself. You had a great audition; you're feeling good about it, right?"

"Yeah, I guess."

"So embrace that feeling! What would telling her do right now? Best-case scenario is she'll be happy for you, maybe buy you dinner. But the chick is already letting you live rent free because of your magic coochie or whatever, so I don't think dinner is going to make that big a difference in your life. Worst-case scenario is she'll be mad you decided to try out for a tour and you get in a big fight. What if she wants you to move out?"

"It wouldn't be like that."

"At the very least, it's going to be so much fucking processing and worrying, and I'm going to have to hear about how you're not sure about it, blah blah blah. Tell her when we get the call that we're hired. There's no point in creating stress for yourself about something that hasn't even happened yet. It's not like she needs to split the rent."

"I just feel bad keeping secrets from her."

Sasha rolled her eyes and then softened a little. "Do what feels right," she said. "Don't get in your own head about it."

What felt right though? Telling her felt like what I should do. What I wanted to do was say nothing, though, and that's what I did. I didn't tell anyone else about my audition either. Maybe I didn't want to jinx it. Maybe it felt wrong to tell people when I wasn't telling Kris. But whatever it was, I didn't say a word about it, even when I was hanging out with Meghan a few days later and she asked me about work.

"You mean my thing with Kris?" I shifted uncomfortably.

"No," she answered with a laugh. "I mean your actual work, your aerials. How's that going?"

"Oh, fine. I'm teaching, doing a few shows, plugging along." I glanced at the clock in the coffee shop. "Speaking of work, I need to get dinner ready for my not-actual job."

"You're like a housewife," Meghan said with a raised eyebrow.

"That's the fantasy. So right now I'm a faux-housewife who needs to go grocery shopping so I can cook."

"I need to pick up a couple of things from the store too. Mind if I tag along?"

"I'd love it." I hopped up and offered her my elbow. She took it with exaggerated grace and we strolled to the nearest Whole Foods. As we wandered the aisles, we debated whether or not to pay eight dollars for a bag of grapes. Soon our conversation turned to more personal topics. By the time we were in the checkout line, we had wound around to my situation with Kris.

"You still enjoying it?" she asked.

"Actually, the most amazing thing happened last Friday." I looked at the checkout guy. "I'll tell you later."

"Don't say something like that and then leave me hanging!" she exclaimed.

"I could call you later."

"I don't want to wait until later. Tell me now."

"Unless you want to help me make dinner, it's going to have to wait."

"I could help," Meghan said. "If all I have to do is chop stuff."

I doubted that. Though I was no John, I managed fine with recipes, but Meghan's culinary skills were only slightly better than Kris's. Besides, I wasn't sure about having people helping me with my chores. But my desire to talk and Meghan's puppy dog eyes won out.

"Yes, please," I said finally. "I'd love some help. Do you have time?"

"Absolutely. Bill has plans tonight, and honestly, I was probably just going to order a pizza and rewatch *Angel*."

"Thanks for choosing me over vintage Joss Whedon."

"Well…" Meghan said. We'd left the store and were strolling toward my place. "So what's this amazing thing?"

I glanced around. No one was paying any attention to us, but I lowered my voice anyway. "Long story short, we had a three-way."

Meghan's eyebrows shot up and she tipped an imaginary cap my way.

"Some friends of Kris's have this really cute sub and it was this whole scene, with Kris dominating both of us. It was basically like my fantasy come to life." I blushed.

"That's awesome!" Meghan punched me in the arm playfully. "I'm so happy for you."

"Yeah, me too actually. I've always wanted to, but I'd always been worried that having a threesome would mess up my existing relationship, but everything is fine." Of course, actually things were a little awkward with Kris because I was still quietly resentful that I'd woken up alone that morning, but I didn't feel like getting into that with Meghan.

"That's really great, Phoenix. But I've got to ask, why didn't you ever try being the guest star to some other couple if you were worried about shaking up a relationship? You'd get all the fun without having to deal with the emotional fallout."

"Because my fantasy isn't about being the novelty, it's about getting security and novelty at the same time. And besides, whether or not you remember it, I was a serial monogamist who only had sex in the context of serious relationships until recently."

"Oh yeah," she said with a laugh. "I keep forgetting that because you've made such a seamless transition to this whole thing."

"I didn't really expect it to go so well myself. Maybe I'm built for this. It's better than most of my relationships in a lot of ways. I'm not getting lost in a girlfriend for a change. There's so much less drama." I said it with such conviction that I almost believed it myself.

"Is there anything you miss, though? About having a girlfriend instead of having this?" Meghan asked.

I bristled to cover up how much I actually wanted more. I wanted to kiss when we did things like organize the shelves. I wanted to not wake up alone. I wanted us to spend more time together, talking and just hanging out. I wanted to tell her to stop working so much. I wanted to eat dinner with her and talk about our days and our hopes and our fears. I wanted to be allowed to fall for her. Instead of the truth I said, "I miss the casual affection. And I miss saying that I have a girlfriend. But for the most part, I'm pretty happy with what I have right now."

She nodded. "I'm glad it's working out."

"Thank you again," I said.

"Oh, any time."

We got to my place and started cooking. Meghan washed and chopped while I threw together a stir-fry. I realized too late that it would probably be cold by the time Kris got home. I sent her a text explaining that I'd overestimated how long it takes to fry vegetables and tofu, and that Meghan was visiting and I hoped that was okay.

To my surprise, she texted back asking me to keep dinner warm for a little bit, promising to be home soon, and telling me to invite Meghan to stay for dinner. Who was this person, I wondered, and what had she done with Kris?

"Um, Meghan, you don't want to stay for dinner, do you?" I asked.

"That sounds sort of like an invitation, but also like you want to me to turn you down." Meghan feigned serious thought for a minute. "I like giving folks a hard time, so I'm going to accept this invitation and tell you I'd be delighted."

I must have looked nervous because she patted my hand. "If that's okay?"

"It is! I'm just surprised Kris is on board. I don't think she ever has anyone over, let alone one of my friends. And she says she's on her way over, but I don't think she's ever left work this early on a weeknight except when she was sick."

"It's seven o'clock," Meghan said. "I always leave by six thirty and I'm a lawyer."

"You're not a corporate lawyer. You're the kind that doesn't make money," I said.

"What I'm saying is, I'm in a profession that's all about working ridiculous hours, and even I think that working as much as she does is ridiculous."

"I'd never argue with you on that."

"Do you ever tell Kristen that?"

"Uh, do you understand the deal here? I'm her sub. She doesn't want career advice from me."

"Bill's my sub and he gives me his opinion all the time."

"That's different. You too are *married*. It's not a twenty-four seven thing. You play and then you're equal partners."

"This isn't a twenty-four seven thing. Doesn't Kristen always want somebody who's independent in addition to submitting?"

"Independent is not the same thing as telling her what to do. She wants me to have my own life, which I have, and I stay out of hers."

In the middle of this little debate, Kris opened the door. "Hi, guys!" she called. She strode into the kitchen with a big smile on her face and a bouquet of flowers in her hand. She kissed me on the cheek, handed me the flowers, and walked over to Meghan and gave her a hug. Stunned, I wandered over to the cabinet to find a vase.

"It's nice to see you, Meghan," she said.

"Thanks for having me. I always appreciate being fed without having to cook."

"Meghan's being modest. She helped with dinner." I freed the flowers from the cellophane wrapping. Kris smiled, so apparently having help wasn't against our rules.

"Thanks, Meghan. How's life?"

Meghan and Kris caught up as I quietly served up food, poured wine, and wondered what the hell was going on. The conversation stayed superficial and pleasant for most of the meal. Then when Meghan started her second glass of wine she said, "I hear you work too much."

My face felt hot and I looked away.

"I suppose I do," Kris said. "But I'm thinking of changing that."

"That sounds mysterious," Meghan said.

"I'm thinking of selling my company."

Had I been holding anything, I would have dropped it. My mouth fell open. "What?" I gasped.

"Yeah, I talked to some lawyers today about what that might look like. When I got your message, I thought, why not try out what it would be like if I didn't have so much responsibility?" She sounded proud of herself.

"What do you think?" Meghan asked.

"Completely worth it." She raised her glass. "Good food, good company. It was definitely a reason to leave work."

My face burned again, but with jealousy and anger instead of embarrassment. My company wasn't worth leaving work for, but Meghan's was? They'd met a handful of times before that night. Even catching one of my performances wasn't a priority to Kris and I'd had to bug her into going, but dinner with an acquaintance was worth leaving work for? I quietly gathered the dishes and started rinsing them to avoid facing Kris and Meghan. How could Kris tell all this to someone she barely knew when she'd never even mentioned the idea to me?

"So have you decided to sell?" Meghan continued. It felt like I wasn't even in the room.

"I'm leaning that way. It might take some time though."

"That's exciting! What a big change. What are you going to do instead?"

"I'm not sure. I've worked nonstop for my entire adult life. Maybe I'll travel, or sleep in, or whatever normal people do."

"What inspired this?"

"Phoenix, actually." Kris tried to catch my eye and then smiled when I met her gaze. "Phe, you're so good balancing your life. You make time for the things that you enjoy. It made me wonder if there are other things I might want to try."

"Actually, I worked ridiculous hours for years and made huge sacrifices to have a career I didn't hate. It must be really nice to make a ton of money doing something you love and then be able to sell your company and retire whenever you feel like," I snapped.

Meghan and Kris exchanged surprised looks. I didn't even care. "Well, I should probably get going," Meghan said cautiously. "Thank you for dinner, Phoenix. It was great."

"You're welcome." I still sounded snippy.

She gave me a hug anyway, and mouthed "Call me" as she headed out.

"Do you need help?" Kris asked me when Meghan left.

"All done."

"I know that our plans turned out a little differently than they usually do, but it's about eight thirty. Do you want to…?"

In all the months we'd been involved, I'd never turned her down when the appointed hour rolled around. I'd never even considered it. That night, I pursed my lips, over-enunciated the word, "no," and went to bed.

CHAPTER SEVENTEEN

K ris didn't press about my little outburst. She didn't even ask. But she handled me differently, like I was something fragile or explosive. The connection that had been growing between us seemed to dissolve. Once again, we only saw each other in that lavender room. We played harder in the days that followed, but with more distance between us. I did my chores and went about my life, internally kicking myself for ruining everything. At least I had an end in sight—if I got hired for the tour.

I was standing in front of the dairy case in Whole Foods the next week worrying about the tour gig when someone tapped me on the shoulder.

"Hi, Phoenix," Ray said shyly.

What was the etiquette in a situation like this? Before Kris, all the sex I'd had in my life had been with long-term sweethearts. I'd never had a one-night stand, let alone whatever this was with Ray.

"Um, hi, Ray. How are you?"

"Good! Good. How are you?"

"Good." Then Ray rambled for a while about why they were at Whole Foods. "…And I don't normally shop here because it doesn't support unions, but you know, it's more convenient since I don't have a car, and anyway, we do want organic, so my Sirs told me to just stop worrying about it and go buy some eggs already. So, you know, here I am."

"Uh-huh," I said.

"You live really close by, right?"

"Yeah, I can walk here."

"I come here all the time. Like, too much. Maybe I could hit you up next time I'm around? And we could get coffee?" Ray bounced from foot to foot.

There was something about Ray's lack of bravado, the total contrast from Kris's typical confidence, that charmed me. Also, Ray was cute and we'd had hot sex and I didn't know anyone else in a situation like mine, so I said yes. I gave Ray my number, Ray called so I had theirs, and we went our separate ways. By the time I got home, Ray and I had already arranged a coffee date for the following week.

I didn't tell Kris. Why would I? We weren't talking outside of our scenes. It was becoming a silent war in the house, each of us trying to say as little as possible to the other.

Things were weird with Meghan too. After our dinner—or rather, my post-dinner pouting—we hadn't seen each other. She had a big case, but she wanted to talk. After making coffee plans with Ray, I called her back. We finally nailed down a lunch date for that Saturday, but then I casually mentioned my lunch plans to Sasha and she mistook it as an invitation. Sasha and Meghan knew each other a little through me and were friendly, and the three of us hung out every once in a while, so Sasha's misunderstanding made sense.

What did not make sense was that I didn't correct her. She wouldn't have been offended and would barely have grumbled about it, but I said nothing. I told Meghan at the last minute via text with a weak apology, giving her no chance to change plans. Honestly, I didn't really want to be alone with Meghan. I loved her, but I felt strange about Kris's openness with her for reasons I didn't understand. To avoid dealing with these feelings, I'd brought Sasha, who always took up a room. And I'd brought a story that I knew would distract my lunch companions.

They both knew about the threesome, and I knew my plans with Ray would keep the conversation away from my unusual reaction at dinner the other night. Which it did, though not in the way I expected.

"That is a fucking terrible idea," Sasha said as she stabbed at her salad. "Cancel that shit."

"I've got to say, Sasha's right," Meghan said. Then she sighed in a way that she only did when she was exceptionally annoyed.

"What's so bad about coffee?" I asked.

"I don't know, Phoenix. What is bad about having a one-on-one coffee with your threesome friend? When, you know, the person who isn't invited is the one paying your rent?" Sasha punctuated this with an eye roll.

"Did you tell Kristen?" Meghan asked.

"No. I also didn't tell her I was having lunch with you. I am allowed to hang out with people. I don't have to report back to her on every little thing. We're not even really a couple." I sounded like a brat even to my own ears.

"It's rude, Phoenix," Meghan said. "It's a complicated situation, and you could do some real damage."

"It's coffee!"

"With someone who fucked you," Sasha said.

"We're not even monogamous," I said.

"Okay, but don't you think you should at least give Kristen a heads up when it's this particular person? Just out of courtesy?" Meghan asked.

"Kris and I barely talk, so why start with this?" They both stared at me, and I found myself rambling an explanation. "I feel deceitful in this bizarre situation. Look, it's amazing and I'm really lucky, but whenever I talk to anyone who doesn't already know, it's this uncomfortable web of lies. I ran into an old coworker a few weeks ago, and I told this whole story about how I'd saved so much and that's why I can do this. But the whole time I was thinking, 'Actually, I'm basically a sex worker, but not officially, because money isn't changing hands. Just rent, utilities, and access to a car.' It felt gross. I wanted to have coffee with Ray because I don't have to pretend my life is different than it is."

"Uh, hello? We're right here!" Sasha said. "You don't have to pretend with us."

"And you did save. You worked hard for this. The fact that it's less stressful financially because of the work you're doing with Kristen doesn't need to make you feel bad."

"It's the lying that makes me feel bad."

"So don't lie," Meghan said.

I raised my eyebrows. "Kris asked me for some discretion."

Meghan shook her head. "You don't have to say it's her if you want to talk about it to some random person. And that's not a reason to have coffee with Ray or to keep it a secret from Kristen."

"Luckily, I don't need a reason or anyone's permission to get coffee."

"You better hope we get on this tour," Sasha said with her mouth full. "Because when your lady finds out, she'll be kicking you to the curb. Nobody wants to play sugar mama to a cheater."

"I'm not cheating!"

"Tour?" Meghan asked.

"She didn't tell you? We auditioned for this incredible tour. It went really well." She turned to me. "You didn't tell Meghan?"

"Clearly, I did not," I growled.

"Why not?" Sasha asked.

I turned to Meghan. Her face was raw with hurt and anger. Why hadn't I told her? She was one of my best friends.

"I'm sorry," I said.

Meghan's face didn't change. If anything, she looked more wounded.

"I just didn't...I'm sure if I'm going to get it, and I didn't want to talk about it, and, I don't know. I should have told you."

"You say the lying bothers you, but it's not just your relationship with Kristen that you're omitting. Why are you acting like this?"

My jaw clenched and my cheeks felt hot.

"Uh, look, it's awkward o'clock, so I better be going," Sasha said uneasily. She left a twenty on the table for her unfinished meal and hustled off. For all her brash style, Sasha hated when emotionally charged conflict got real.

Meghan and I stared each other down until Sasha was out of earshot.

"I need someone to connect to," I said. "This is all so new to me, the power dynamics, the sex work, the full-time aerials, everything. I just need someone who understands."

"And I don't? You can't connect with me?"

"It's just different. You aren't a sub."

"Is that what this is about? Jesus, Phoenix, you can talk to Bill. Or I can introduce you to a sub you and Kristen haven't slept with. And that doesn't explain why you didn't tell me about the possibility of you *leaving* and going on tour for God knows how long. Or why you got so upset out of nowhere when I was at dinner at your place. Or why Sasha tagged along for the first one-on-one time we've had since then."

"Things are weird. Things are weird between you and me."

"If they're weird, it's because you aren't talking to me. What is going on?"

"I don't know. I don't know how I ended up in this situation. I don't know what to do."

She looked worried. "If you're unhappy with this, why are you doing it? What is happening in that house?"

"I'm not unhappy. I'm just...lost."

"Are you okay?"

"Yes, I'm all right."

"Then what's wrong?"

"Everything changed," I said.

"That's life! Things change. We all deal with it. It doesn't mean you get to treat people like this."

Tears stung my eyes. I knew she was right.

"What aren't you telling me?" she asked.

I didn't know what to say or how to say it. I shook my head.

"This isn't you, Phe. You wouldn't do something that could really hurt people."

"Coffee isn't hurting anyone," I said.

Meghan glared. "You are playing with power dynamics and keeping secrets, and it *can* hurt people. But I wasn't talking about that. I was talking about how you're acting with me. It's hurting me, and you don't even see it."

My cheeks burned and a tear leaked out of my left eye. I opened my mouth to speak, but couldn't find words.

Meghan threw her napkin on the table and stood up. "Call me when you go back to being someone who actually thinks about other people's feelings, Phoenix." She stomped away, leaving me with three half-finished meals and the bill.

Even as I furiously poked at my salad and waited on my change, part of me knew she was right. But I didn't call her. I didn't call Sasha and talk about what had happened. I didn't tell John when I talked to him, which was becoming a bad habit. Though as roommates I'd told him everything, since he'd moved I'd become more and more selective in what I mentioned to him. I hadn't told him about my growing feelings for Kris, my complicated feelings the morning after the threesome, or even about my audition. He was busy with his new home, his new job, and making friends in a new city. John and Ollie were talking about getting married (though based on history, they'd probably talk about it for another year before deciding anything). It was becoming easy to focus our conversations on that instead of about what was happening with me. I wondered briefly if not having a person to debrief with every day was part of the reason I was doing such a shitty job of processing my feelings.

I wondered if I should try to talk to Kris when she got home and hoped she would see how upset I was so I wouldn't have to broach the subject. Instead she pulled me into her like it was any other night. She didn't seem to notice the stiffness with which I held myself. She kissed me, pulled my hair, and smiled at me while nodding toward the downstairs bedroom.

I followed her. I let her fuck me while my mind stayed on my fight with Meghan. My body felt good, but I was checked out in a way I'd never been with Kris before.

I knew Meghan was right, even if I was too mad to admit it. I didn't even really want Ray, but I did want a distraction. So I texted them, a little bit flirty, and then turned off the light, turned off my phone, and missed my old life fiercely.

CHAPTER EIGHTEEN

Ray got called into work right before our coffee date, and we couldn't get our schedules to match up again for weeks and gave up. It seemed like the kind of almost-friendship that never got off the ground. I hoped we'd figure it out, and I didn't feel guilty at all, even though I didn't tell Kris. That is, I didn't feel guilty until the Friday night that followed, after Kris and I had played.

"Hey, are you okay?" she asked me as we lay in bed.

"Yeah. Why do you ask?" I said coolly.

"You've seemed upset lately, and preoccupied. Ever since we had Meghan over. Or kind of since the threesome, really."

I shrugged. "I guess."

"Do you, um, want to talk about it?"

"I'm okay."

"I think you need some cheering up. Let's go somewhere tomorrow."

I squirmed. "I thought we said we'd spend Saturdays apart. It's my day off."

"Not like that! I meant, we could go to the beach, just as friends. We could do something platonically." It was her turn to squirm. "But I understand if you don't want to, or you're busy."

She was so cute in her vulnerability. It was sweet. I felt bad for how passive-aggressive I'd been being. "Sounds great." I forced myself to smile.

Kris kissed me slowly. "Glad to hear it. When do you want to go?"

"Two o'clock?"

"Perfect. I'll take care of everything."

The next afternoon, she picked me up after my classes and drove us south of the city to a beach in Pacifica. We were silent on the ride over, and things still felt uneasy between us. The beach was mostly empty on the winter day. The sun shone, but it was cold and windy, and I was underdressed.

"Here." Kris tossed me a thick sweater from the bag she'd brought. I smiled.

"What else do you have that bag of yours?" I asked.

"Snacks, drinks, beach towel, and terrible magazines, just in case."

"How terrible?"

She showed me an array of glossy tabloids with contradictory celebrity gossip. "Whoa," I said. "That is a lot of trash."

"I don't usually read them, but twice a year? I read every one on sale at CVS."

"Look at you and your hidden shallowness."

She blushed. "I try to keep it under wraps."

"You succeed. I would have never guessed. But I like this." I picked up a tabloid. "Oooh, secret love babies."

Kris set up our beach towel and supplies while I flipped through the pages. She laughed at me. "Are you going to help at all?"

"No, I'm going to be a princess and have you do everything."

"Well, all right then." A moment later, she presented our wonderful spread, complete with drinks and snacks.

I settled in and we spent a long, lazy afternoon reading silly magazines, eating, building a sandcastle, splashing in the cold water, reapplying sunscreen, and playing rummy. And snuggling on the beach towel. I started by leaning my head on Kris's shoulder, and before I knew it, we were resting in easy cuddles and holding hands. It was an odd, unspoken intimacy. We didn't kiss, and that somehow made it stranger. We weren't being sexual or flirtatious; we were being close. Kris didn't try to talk about how difficult things had been between us, or what a jerk I'd been. I relaxed. I knew I needed to make things right, though I still didn't know how.

As the sun started to set, the evening air started getting too chilly. Kris stood up. "Princess Phoenix?" Kris offered me a hand getting up.

"Thank you." I let her draw me up. She packed everything and I skipped barefoot toward the car.

"That was so fun, Kris. Thanks for thinking of it."

"Thanks for being spontaneous. That was the most fun I've had in a long time."

"Really?" I couldn't contain my surprise.

"Yeah. When was the last time you had so much fun?"

I was half-tempted to reference our three-way, or even the sex we had all the time, but I knew what she meant. That was pleasure. It was hot and amazing. This thing on the beach? That was a totally different kind of fun.

"Actually, I feel that way, at least a little bit, whenever I'm in the air and upside down."

She whistled in admiration. "That's wonderful, to feel so happy with what you do."

"It's taken a long time. I've worked hard to be able to do something I have so much fun with."

She frowned a little. "I miss that feeling with work."

"Maybe you should take a trapeze class."

"Maybe," she said absentmindedly.

"Well, that's why you're thinking of selling, right? So you can have fun and balance in your life?"

"Right. Maybe." She paused. "I've been looking into it, but then I start to panic. What would I do if I didn't go to work? What would happen to my company if I left? I can't even bring myself to take a vacation, so how am I going to quit?"

"Why don't you take a vacation and see what happens? Trust your employees to do their jobs while you're gone. Then you'll get back and see everything's fine and be able to move on if you want."

She frowned harder. "Where would I even go?"

"Nowhere. Just the beach. You'd relax."

"I can't picture it," she said in a joking tone, but there was truth under what she said.

"Start with a day off. Just like this afternoon, but on a weekday. You can do that, right?"

She sat up taller. "Yeah."

"Good. Then you're settled."

She glanced over at me. "You're good for me, Phoenix."

I didn't know how to respond, so I bit my lip.

"Was that a weird thing to say?" she asked gently. "I know this isn't traditional, but it's been good for me. I hope it's as good for you."

I felt a sinking in the pit of my stomach, a ball of guilt weighing down the core of me. Guilt for auditioning for something that might take me away (but wasn't my career the whole point of this in the first place?) Guilt for making plans with Ray (but it was just coffee). Guilt for fighting with my friends. Guilt for reacting the way I did during dinner with Meghan and Kris. Guilt for not talking to Kris directly about all the things on my mind. Guilt for three weeks of sulking and coldness. And beneath it all, that tender affection for her that I'd been trying all this time to avoid.

Kris reached over and pushed a stray hair out of my face. I choked back tears.

"You're too good for me. I'm so sorry."

"Sorry for what?"

"For being so rude when Meghan came to dinner, and for being rude basically ever since."

"It wasn't fun. I was wondering what that was about."

"Why didn't you make me talk about it?"

"How was I going to do that? Spank you until you told me why you were pouting?"

"Something like that."

"That's not my style. I play within the arrangements we've agreed to. But when it comes to the emotional stuff outside of that, you're an adult. I trust you to talk to me, and if you don't want to talk about something, that's your choice. What you were doing was getting on my nerves, and I want you to handle things differently next time."

I swallowed back more tears. "Why are you being so nice to me when I'm being awful?"

"You aren't being awful. You were handling something badly. It happens. If you can keep it from happening next time, we can skip the unhappy part and go right to the beach."

"I can't believe that I was so obnoxious and you still took me to the beach and gave me a wonderful afternoon."

She grinned. "Some people break open when you hit them in the right place. I thought you might be the type who breaks open when you're taken care of."

I started crying in earnest then. "I think you're right." I laughed through the flood of tears. I thought about the way submitting made me feel taken care of, and how that cracked me open as much as anything else. I thought about how badly I'd been handling my feelings. I thought about everything and could not stop crying.

"Do you want to talk about it? Where all that anger you were feeling was coming from? And why you're crying?" she asked.

"I can't yet. I can't get the words."

"When you're ready." It was a command, one I intended to follow.

I started by making up with my friends. Sasha and I had already made a weary sort of peace while training together, but the next time I saw her, I apologized.

She put a hand on her hip. "It's about time. You were being a dick."

"You were being bossy," I said.

"That is a shitty apology. I'm *always* bossy. That's part of why we work well together. You're talented as fuck, but you do better when someone's pushing you. Like this audition. You would have talked yourself out of it, but I signed us up so you did it, and it'll probably be the best thing that ever happened to either of our careers. So, yeah, I was being myself, and you were being a dick."

Sasha had a point. "Fine, I was a dick." I pulled a crash mat under a trapeze so we could get started. "When are we finding out about the auditions anyway?"

"They're supposed to start letting people know on Friday."

"The day before Valentine's Day?"

"I don't think Damien's got that on his mind. More like, rehearsals start beginning of April and that'll give people six weeks to get here if they aren't already."

I groaned. "We're supposed to go to a party Friday night. I don't want to tell Kris about this on our way to a Valentine's party."

"You are ridiculous." She spun herself up to sitting on the trapeze. "If you don't get it, you don't have to tell her anything. Or you can tell her that you had an audition but didn't get it. It's not going to ruin your night just because you're a little sad for a few minutes. But we're going to get this, so you can just be happy and not get into why. Or you can tell her you had a good audition. You can tell her you got a part and not share the details. You have options. Don't get upset because you're getting good news."

"I guess you're right," I said. "I just feel bad lying to her."

"Really? How did that work when you had your date with your three-way friend? Kristen heard all about that?"

"Touché. Though that date has been postponed indefinitely."

"Besides, what's the big deal with Valentine's Day? It's a couple's holiday. Aren't you two supposed to be more like fuck buddy roommates? It's awfully romantic for something that you keep saying doesn't involve you falling in love."

"I'm just excited for the party." It was a play party.

"If you say so. Don't fall in love. Now are we working on our doubles act or what?"

With that, I climbed up and balanced from Sasha's legs.

❖

Meghan should have been next on my list of amends, but I couldn't do it yet. Instead, I gathered up all my willpower and wrote out some of what I needed to say to Kris. The evening after I apologized to Sasha, I greeted Kris by asking her if we could talk.

"That sounds ominous," she said.

I unfolded the letter. The thought of telling her everything— my growing feelings, the audition, my almost-date with Ray— overwhelmed me. I started with something smaller but no easier.

"I'm sorry for how I behaved," I read. "I felt sad that I woke up alone after our night with Ray, even though it was what I agreed to. I knew it wasn't fair to feel that way, but that's how I felt. I handled it really badly. I felt jealous that you came home early for dinner with Meghan when it was such a fight to get you to leave work to see me perform. I felt even more jealous when you opened up to her about work when you hadn't told me anything about your plan to leave your company. I felt hurt but also like I wasn't allowed to feel that or tell you about it. I don't know why I thought I couldn't tell you, but I did. I'm sorry."

She hugged me. "I wish I'd known. I would have told you about maybe selling my company that night anyway. I'd been thinking about it since Christmas, but I wasn't sure, and meeting with the lawyers was when I got serious. I thought you wanted Meghan to stay and I came home early because I thought it was important to you. And I'm sorry you felt bad after that night. I didn't know. I wish you'd told me."

"I'm telling you now."

"Try to tell me sooner next time please?"

I nodded, even though there was so much I was still not saying.

CHAPTER NINETEEN

Damian's assistant called me early Friday morning, before I was even fully dressed. I literally had half a face of foundation on.

"We're so happy to have you." She sounded so chipper it made my ears hurt. "Will you take the part?"

I thought for a second. I could delay and talk to Kris. But why? Wasn't this exactly what I quit my day job to do?

"Of course," I said.

"Great! We'll be emailing you information later today. Can I just confirm your email address?"

That was it. Years of training, years of saving, and finally, I had a job touring. It wouldn't make me rich by a long shot. It wouldn't make me a superstar. But it was the biggest break I'd ever had.

I debated telling Kris, but when the time came, I chickened out. She'd skipped work to spend the day reading graphic novels and she was so happy over the lasagna I made her that I couldn't bear to say I was leaving. We went to a play party, had a great time, and I forgot that I'd be leaving it all behind to go on tour in a few months. At the very end of the night, as we were climbing up the stairs to our home, Kris kissed me on the lips and wrapped her arms around me.

"This is the best Valentine's Day I've had ten years," she said.

"It's been one of my best too." I hugged her back. I wanted to tell her then, but I didn't want to ruin the moment.

The next day I resolved to tell her, but still couldn't work up the nerve. I had plenty of other things to handle in the coming weeks: giving notice at my teaching jobs, figuring out when I'd need to quit my work-exchange Kirkus Radix gig, and adjusting to the rehearsal schedule, which would have us busy for long days. Because we weren't the stars, our schedules wouldn't be as grueling as some, but it would still be a lot of work. Sasha was the mermaid's understudy on top of her regular role, which meant she had to be there for basically everything, effectively ending any possibility that we'd do any other duo performances while we were rehearsing. I was also the sea witch in addition to being a mermaid-sister, which meant I had a dozen lines to learn and an additional silks routines. I didn't know how I'd get dinner on the table and keep the house spotless when I was balancing that most days of the week, especially toward the final rehearsals when we'd be running through the whole show a couple of times a day.

I decided that before I'd be able to really talk to Kris, I needed to make things right with Meghan. I called her early Sunday evening, after inhaling a giant breath and practicing my apology about five hundred times.

"Hello?" Meghan answered, sounding skeptical.

"I'm sorry. I was being a jerk. I'm sorry."

"Well, I'm glad you figured that out finally."

"You were right. I was wrong. I should have talked to you. I was jealous that Kris talked to you about selling her company when she hadn't talked to me about it before, and I acted horribly. I was scared of how upset I was, and I told Sasha about lunch and let her misunderstand because I was avoiding my feelings in really shitty ways. I know it's hurt you. I'm so sorry. Do you forgive me?"

She exhaled loudly. "I can never stay mad at you, you goofball. Even when you are not yourself at all."

"I think that was first fight we've ever really had."

"I know. I was more worried than mad, actually. What do you think brought that out in you?"

I bit my lip. "Like you said, everything changed really fast, and I've been thrown. It's been so intense, and I used to process all my feelings with John and it's harder to do that texting and we're both busy. I feel like I get lost to myself, if that makes any sense."

"Because of your living situation?"

"Maybe, but I don't think it matters that much because I'm going on tour."

"What?!"

"Sasha and I both got parts. We start training in April. The show opens here in June, and a couple weeks later, we go to LA. Then it's all over the country for five months after that."

"Congratulations! It's what you wanted, right?"

"It is. I just don't know what I'm going to do about Kris."

"You talk to her about it, obviously."

I picked at my nail polish. "I was thinking of waiting a little bit."

"The longer you wait, the worse it's going to be. You have to be careful with each other's feelings."

"You said that about the whole Ray thing. But I'm the sub here. Shouldn't she be the one who has to worry about hurting me?"

I could hear Meghan suck in a calming breath. "Sometimes I forget how many gaps there are in your kinky education. Phoenix, honey, no. You're both playing with power here. You're choosing to be submissive, but she's vulnerable too. Everything's heightened when you're taking on these roles, including the emotions. She has to be a good partner, and so do you. Don't keep secrets here. Don't avoid your feelings."

"But that's not the kind of relationship we have. We don't have long talks. We do what we do, and then we go to our own bedrooms and close the door."

"Please trust me on this. Give her the information. It's the right thing to do."

"Okay. It's just hard."

"I know, but I think what happens when you bottle things up is a lot harder."

She definitely had a point. When we finished talking, I tried to call Kris. She didn't answer. Right after we'd finished playing for the afternoon, she'd gone to check on things at work, and then maybe see friends later. I was afraid I'd lose my nerve again before I saw her. I even thought about going over to her office, but that was crossing the line.

When Kris came home for dinner, she greeted me with, "I hear you're planning a date with Ray." Her tone was completely neutral, unreadable. Shit.

"We were going to get coffee, but it never happened. I should have told you first." I gulped.

"Yes, you should have told me," she said with an edge to her voice.

"I'm sorry," I said. "I thought, you know, it was just coffee, and we aren't exclusive..."

She sat on the couch. "I know you aren't used to this, but, Phoenix, that hurt. This isn't 'don't ask, don't tell.' If you're going out with someone we both know—which is a pretty small circle of people—you should mention it."

"It wasn't 'going out.' It was just coffee." I sounded whiny, I thought. I sat next to her.

"All the more reason to tell me. If it's not a big deal, why keep it a secret? We just talked about how I want you to tell me things. I wouldn't have been upset if you'd said you and Ray were going to get coffee. I think it's good for you to know other submissives. That's why I wanted you to go to a munch. And it's fine if the submissive you want to talk to is Ray, but I am pissed that I heard about it from Eric, who thought I knew, and I didn't hear it from you." She stared at me. I had to look away.

"I should have told you. I'm sorry. One of the reasons I thought it was okay not to is because we're sort of 'don't ask, don't tell' about everything with each other. I'm going to work on talking to you more, but you and I sometimes barely say five words to each other outside the bedroom. I've liked the time I've spent with you and I wish there was more of that. It's weird going from a roommate who was my best friend to a roommate I see naked but never have a meal with. I'm adjusting." I realized as I said it that I needed to do something else too. I needed a long chat with John about all the things I hadn't been saying. I needed to stop keeping everything to myself.

"You hurt my feelings."

"I won't do it again." I offered her my hand and she shook her head. "Ray and I never even rescheduled. I don't care about seeing them."

"That's *not* why I'm upset. It's the secret, Phe. Especially after you said you were going to talk to me when you're ready, and you still haven't."

I bit my lip. "I think I'm ready now. But I'm scared you won't like what I have to say."

"I will absolutely like it more than you keeping secrets."

I looked away and began, "I don't want us to date other people, or sleep with or play with other people unless we're together. I don't know the rules for balancing this and anyone else, and I don't feel like I have the energy to learn them right now. It's taken me this long to learn our rules. And honestly, I don't really want to be with anyone else."

Her eyes were shining with tears. "Really?"

"I don't want to hurt you, but I did, and I'm sorry. I'd rather just be with you. But maybe it's something you need." I picked off the last of my nail polish from my thumbs.

"I haven't been seeing anybody else. I actually prefer just one partner at a time. I'd thought, you know, I couldn't be there for you emotionally, and you might need someone who could."

"It's stressing me out. Let's not."

"Okay."

We sat there silently for a beat. Kris broke the silence with a laugh. "I haven't been in a monogamous relationship in so long. I did not see that coming."

"This isn't exactly your typical monogamous relationship." I smiled at her.

"Who's to say? People have all sorts of relationships."

"Because we don't spend time together outside of that," I waved toward the door to the lavender room. "Not consistently. I don't know when to tell you things." In my head, I geared up to tell her my other big news. It seemed like this might be my chance.

"You agreed to this. This was what we talked about. I always said what my limitations were."

"I'm not talking about lovey-dovey and cuddling and being my date. I'm talking about figuring out time regularly to have non-scene conversations with a person I live with. Honestly, I'm amazed it didn't come up sooner. We live in this house together, and I never know when we're going to both be here outside of playing together. I'm not going to tell you I'm getting coffee with Ray five minutes before you and I are supposed to go in the bedroom. I'm not in the right headspace to tell you immediately after. We have this, I clean and cook, and that's it. There's not time where we're just roommates catching up. We like spending time together, right? So why don't we set aside any time for our friendship?"

She slapped herself on the forehead. "You're right. I can't believe it. We didn't build in any way to take care of practical things or have straight talk. We aren't in an all day, every day total power exchange agreement, but all the time we've set aside, it's in the context of me dominating you. We should have time we can check in outside of that dynamic."

"Regular time. Every week at least," I said.

"Of course. I feel terrible for not thinking of this before."

"I guess it could have been a lot worse. We managed pretty well all this time."

Her expression softened. "I'm sorry, Phoenix. I've been playing around with this kind of dynamic for a long time. I should know it better by now."

"What we're doing is different from what you had before. It's a learning curve for both of us." I knew I needed to tell her about what else was on my mind, but I let her continue.

"Let's set aside some time just to talk. Maybe one of our nights at eight thirty, instead of playing? Wednesdays? What do you think?"

"That works for me. But won't you miss playing basically every night of the week?"

She blushed. "Honestly, I've always thought I was the type of person who wanted sex every day. Now that I'm having sex or at least playing almost every day, I think I could slow down a little. Not a lot, mind you. But four or five days a week doesn't sound like a bad idea."

I took her hand. "Look at you, learning things about yourself."

She laughed. "You know, I'd had play partners, but not someone I saw this often, at least not since my ex-girlfriend. When I think of what I want, half of it is from a relationship I had a long time ago, and half of it is a fantasy."

I thought for a moment. "Has this been the fantasy you'd wanted it to be? It's been six months and I've never put on a red coat."

She gave me that half-smile from her pictures. "It's been what I wanted. You have a whole other life outside of me, and then we have this together."

"Will spending time together outside of this ruin it for you?"

She shook her head. "I've liked hanging out with you. It's made me like you more. Besides, I don't think we can keep having this without it. What about you? Does it ruin the fantasy?"

"People always think that, that fantasies are better with some blank spot where they can imagine another person exactly as they want. But I don't think so."

"Do you worry we'll be disappointed with each other? When we get to know each other better?"

"Kris, we're going to be talking and hanging out for an hour a week, right? We're not suddenly trapped in a room together for days on end with all each other's annoying habits. I don't think a tiny glimpse into each other's thoughts will destroy the mystery."

She looked at her lap. "How is it for you? In terms of fantasies and everything?"

"I've had a great time. I'm glad I finally had a threesome and went to play parties. But I'd rather be able to have a conversation with you, honestly."

"Even if it means losing a night of play and sex every week?"

I tried not to laugh. "Look, I've been perfectly happy with our arrangement, but I can't keep up with the schedule forever. Two platonic nights a week, or even three, sounds just fine to me. I have a pretty high libido, and if I had nothing to do all day, maybe I'd just have sex. But I have other ambitions, and sometimes sex and kink slips on my priority list a little."

She leaned back. "I can't imagine having nothing to do all day. I think I'd lose my mind."

"Lucky there's a middle ground between working ninety hours a week and not ever having anything to do." I stretched out my legs and put my feet on the coffee table.

"I'm not great with middle ground," she said. "I'm not great at situations where I don't have control either."

"I think I noticed that."

"I'm worried, Phoenix. I'm worried that even an hour a week, you won't like me anymore."

"That's so sad." I reached to run my fingers to through her hair, but she jerked away.

"I've stuck with the things I'm good at and that I've loved. I'm not interesting. I don't have great funny stories. I'm not the best with feelings. I mean, I knew something was going on with you, but all I could manage was taking you to the beach. I should have been talking to you more, but I didn't know how. I have limitations."

"You know all those things? They get easier with practice. Sometimes it feels impossible, but that doesn't mean that's the whole story. You try it, and you get stronger at it, just like everything else."

"I did try though. I tried to be a balanced person, and I failed."

"Yeah, a long time ago."

"I tried with everything I have," she said, her voice breaking.

"Jesus, she really did a number on you, huh?"

"She cheated on me. The whole last year of our relationship. With my best friend, with the woman who'd been one of my roommates in college. I'm a pretty introverted person, but I'm also loyal. I thought Laurie might be cheating, so I talked to my friend, you know? And she kept reassuring me that I was overreacting, that things were tense because I was working so much but would get better when things calmed down at work. It never occurred to me that my friend was lying to me. Then one day my laptop was dead so I borrowed Laurie's, and her email was open. There it was, a love note from my best friend."

"Shit."

"Yeah. I confronted Laurie, and she told me that if I had been a better partner, she wouldn't have cheated. She said if I'd been paying attention, I would have figured it out sooner, and she would have stopped. I had figured it out though! I'd suspected something since the beginning of their affair, but I spent a year thinking I was crazy because the two people I trusted most lied to my face. I told her that, that I had suspected and talked to my best friend about it, and I'd been manipulated. She said, 'Whatever.'" Kris sounded defeated.

"And that was it?"

"Sort of. We argued some more. Laurie was angry I worked so much and said she felt neglected. She was mad because she thought our relationship was going nowhere. She'd asked me to marry her when we were twenty-three, and I'd said I needed time and we never talked about it again. The stupid thing was, I'd bought an engagement ring before she started cheating. We were young, but I loved her. I was building a professional life I was proud of. I thought my life was falling into place. I planned a special date so I could propose, but she canceled at the last minute with some really strange excuse. I didn't think too much of it, so I planned another date, but she canceled on me again. She said she was working late once and I went to surprise her—with the stupid ring in my pocket—she wasn't there. I realized something was wrong, and that's when I started talking to my friend that I thought Laurie was cheating. Of course, she just made me feel crazy. I put the ring away thinking we'd work it out and then get married. By the time I knew what was happening, we couldn't fix things between us. We didn't communicate about the problems we had, and before I knew it, I'd lost two people I loved."

"What happened after you confronted her?" I asked.

"She moved in with my friend. I didn't want anything to do with either of them, so I cut off contact. They were pretty much my only friends, so once they were gone, I was alone. I didn't know how to make new friends either, so I just worked. After the breakup, I moved into a little studio and poured myself in work even more than usual. I didn't do anything other than work for probably a year.

"Then I looked up one day and I had money but no one in my life. I decided to go to some BDSM events. I hadn't been since I'd moved to the Bay—Laurie and I had been pretty much private players after we left Seattle. It was horrible at first because I didn't know anyone, but I made friends, and I met a play partner, and eventually, I had something outside of work. I realized that even if I never had another girlfriend, I could still have a good life and most of the things I wanted. I felt really optimistic for a little while. So I bought this house, had it fixed up, but that's as far as I got."

"And then you got me, *living* in your house. Do you regret it?"

She gave me a little smile. "Not at all. You being here, it makes my life so much better. It makes me better. You remind me there's more to life than work, that I get to be happy. For the first time, I'm seeing that I could try something else. I could change direction."

I gave her arm a squeeze. "I'm glad. Being here has been wonderful for me too."

"Can I tell you something, though?" She looked shy. "I still miss them, my ex and my ex-friend. They hurt me, and I'm still sad they aren't part of my life. But they're married. So seeing either one of them would also mean seeing that they're a couple, and I don't know if I could stand that. Even if it breaks my heart that I don't know them anymore." She blinked back tears. "You're the only person I've ever told that."

"Oh, Kris," I said and entwined our fingers. "I'm so sorry."

"At least I have someone to tell now."

I cuddled up to her. I took a deep breath and let it out. "I have something to tell you. I auditioned for a part in an aerial play. And I found out that I got it."

"Phoenix, that's wonderful!" She wrapped up me in a hug. "Congratulations!"

"The thing is, it's a tour. Rehearsal is here and the show opens here, but then we'll travel all over the country."

"For how long?"

"We'll be traveling for more than five months."

The room fell silent. I felt Kris shift away from me slightly, even as I tried to inch closer.

"When do you leave?"

"Mid June."

Silence once again.

I asked her, "What do you want to do? Is it too much, that I'm leaving? Do we have to end this?" Dread made my stomach somersault. What if I had to find a place to live my final months in the Bay Area? Worse, what if Kris never wanted to see me again?

"Of course not. I want to make the most of the time we have together. If you want to."

I exhaled in relief. "Yes. I was so scared you wouldn't want to."

"I knew eventually there'd be an end. You'd get on your feet professionally, and you wouldn't need me anymore. Of course it happened quickly; you're very good at what you do." Her voice was full of false brightness.

"I'm not only here because I need to be. I'm here because I want to be. I'm excited for this opportunity, but I'm not excited to leave. There's an eventual end if you say there's going to be an end, but I wasn't thinking of it that way."

"Phe, come on. Did you really think you were going to spend the rest of your life in this arrangement? That you wouldn't eventually want an actual partner?"

She had me on that. "Okay, yes. But I'm having fun here. I want to actually talk to you more often and get to know you better. I'm not looking forward to leaving."

"But aren't you excited?"

"I can be two things at once."

She moved toward me again. "I'm two things at once, too."

We stayed cuddling for a long time, curled up together, not saying another word.

CHAPTER TWENTY

My life settled back into a routine over the next few weeks. I finished up my teaching gigs, put in notice for my work-trade position, trained, and performed a handful of smaller gigs. I saw my friends. I cleaned the house, cooked, and had my nights with Kris. We managed to start talking to each other on our no-sex night pretty easily. Soon, she was coming home earlier on Wednesdays and we had dinner together as we caught up. We followed that with a movie, some TV, a card game, or a short evening walk. It was surprising how comfortable we quickly became. Though I still felt that edge of a crush for Kris, leaving was making it easier to keep my feelings tamped down. I couldn't risk hurting her, knowing her history, and I doubted I was really in a place to be a good partner.

"You're sure your crush isn't getting out of hand?" John asked when we had our weekly FaceTime session one afternoon in mid March. The night after my talk with Kris, I'd finally spilled my guts to him about everything. He'd been worrying about it ever since.

"I'm sure," I said.

"Okay, because now is not the time to get your heart broken. You have a show to do."

"I won't. I promise."

"I cannot wait until your show comes to New York. Ollie's so excited. The horrible drive will be worth it."

"Please remember that any time I'm not performing, it's all one horrible drive."

"At least you get paid for it."

"And you get paid to teach adorable kids all day who sometimes sneeze in your mouth."

"Ugh, don't remind me. Logan peed on me yesterday. Maybe on purpose. I don't know with that kid."

I laughed. "I miss you so much."

"Me too."

"I want to pressure you to visit, but I guess I can't until I'm back."

"Are you sure you're going back to the Bay? You might get offered something great while you're meeting aerial people on tour." He waited a beat. "Boston needs trapeze artists, I'm sure."

"New York would have been more subtle."

"I'll remember that next time I try to lure you out here. Just keep an open mind. Not about Boston, just about opportunities that come up."

"That's kind of the last thing I want. I'm not freaking out about the tour because I keep telling myself it's only for six months."

"Well, sure, if you have a reason to go back to the Bay. But really, is anything keeping you there? Kristen? I get keeping a lid on your feelings if you know nothing can come of it, but heading back to be with her when you two haven't talked about what you really want…"

"I know," I said. "I'm just not ready to make that decision."

"When will you be?"

John and his excellent questions. I didn't have an answer for him.

❖

Kris's birthday fell the weekend before rehearsal started. I'd asked her months earlier if she wanted to do anything special and she'd shrugged me off, but when we sat down at the dining room table the Wednesday before her birthday, she had another idea.

"Would you go away with me for my birthday?" she asked.

"Are you joking?"

"Nope, I'm totally serious."

"When? Where? Uh, how?"

"Friday afternoon through Sunday. An inn in Santa Cruz. I called on a whim the other day and they'd just had a last-minute cancelation. I booked it. I know it's not something we discussed. Even if you don't want to go, I think I will. I keep thinking about that day we went to the beach in Pacifica and how much fun I had. When I first moved here, I went to Santa Cruz with Laurie and had the best time. But I never went back for some reason. I think I can start off thirty-seven by doing something fun. Do you want to go?"

"I want to."

"Can you go?"

"Yes. It's just, it's my last weekend before the chaos of rehearsal."

"We don't have to," she said quickly.

"No. I think I can. I might need us to rethink the chores though. I can't get everything done and have a weekend away with you."

"Of course. Don't worry about your chores. I've loved our arrangement, but obviously things are changing." She looked down at her hands. 'This isn't about our agreement. This trip isn't a requirement, I mean. It's something to do only if you want to. It's outside of anything else we do."

"So, it's a date?"

She grimaced. "It could be a date. Or it could be as friends. Whatever you like."

I twirled a strand of my hair around my finger. "I'm interested. Either way, I'll go."

She nodded but looked a little nervous. What did it mean if it was a date? Why did I even bring that up? I let it go without us ever deciding.

When the time came for the trip, though, any nervousness she had seemed to have been forgotten. She loaded up her car and whisked me off to Santa Cruz. Kris had, much to my surprise, made a playlist for the occasion.

"I've never thought of you listening to music," I said as our road trip kicked off with the Runaways.

"Who doesn't listen to music?"

"I just never pictured you, I don't know, putting on a song and dancing around your bedroom."

She laughed. "Is that the only way to listen to music?"

"Yes, obviously. But you know what I mean. I don't think of you doing normal people things, or having normal people interests. I think of you just working and being a dom and, like, privately watching nerdy television once in a while. Whenever you say you like a type of music, or magazines, or other simple thing, I'm shocked."

"It seems like you think of me as a person without a personality."

"You're a really hard person to get to know."

"Am I at least mysterious? Intriguing?"

"Sure, but you can be so focused on your job to the exclusion of everything else, it can be hard to engage with you."

She sighed. "I know. It's time for a change. I keep going back and forth about my work future. I want to leave. I just don't know what else I would do."

"Maybe you'd figure that out with some free time? It's hard to feel imaginative when you're drained and burned out."

"I thought this company would be huge, you know? Like publicly traded down the line."

"It still could be, though, right? Even if you move on."

"Which would mean I left before I made a fortune."

"It seems like you already made a fortune. Do you actually need more money? You don't take fancy trips, your car isn't brand new, and you aren't buying diamonds or anything. You bought your house in a recession and now it's worth, what? Well over a million dollars? Do you have some debt I don't realize? I get that you spend some money on clothes and stuff, but that can't possibly eat up what you make. How are you not set for life?"

She bit her lip. "I guess I am. I don't know. I grew up working class. My dad was out of work a couple of times when I was a kid, and we lost our house and had to move into an apartment. I had to share a room with my little sister and we drove each other crazy. My folks had to keep renting until my sister finished high school.

"I helped my parents pay off their condo a year after I bought my place. That's how I knew I'd made it. It's the reason my mom's retiring. She worked for forty-three years. Can you believe that? She got a job as a cashier when she was in high school and never stopped working for longer than two months, even when she had kids. I think she was going to work until the day she died. But then she realized she didn't have rent or a mortgage, she's sixty-two, and she could probably stop. We don't retire in my family. *Nobody* would retire in their thirties. Nobody would leave a good job without another one lined up."

"I had no idea."

"They don't know what to think about me. Not the gay thing, or even the butch thing exactly. But the nerd thing. Nobody in my family went to college. My sister's a waitress. My brother works in construction with my dad. And then there's me, a dyke who hired people to reno her house and who spends all day in front of a computer. If you ask my dad, I have no practical life skills, and in a lot of ways that's true. It's confusing to them that I can make stupid things for people's smartphones and make all this money when they worked their whole lives doing actual necessary things for a fraction of the pay. I feel uncomfortable about it too.

"And it's my presentation too. I wore a bow tie to Christmas once and everyone still makes fun of me for it. In my everyday life, having this gentleman-style with pocket squares and big glasses means I'm sexy. I'm not bragging, but I'm a well-dressed masculine of center lesbian geek, and, well...I do all right in San Francisco. I never really liked how I looked growing up and I thought that's just how it is. After college I was still cutting my own hair and wearing my brother's old jeans like I always had. Then Laurie convinced me to get a tailored suit for her sister's wedding right after we moved to California, and when I saw myself in it, I thought, wow, I'm not so bad. I got into men's fashion and liked how I could look. But back home? My family thought I was ridiculous, trying to look like some snotty rich guy. They thought it was about distancing myself from them. I only pack jeans when I go home now. They just don't know what to do with me."

"My family doesn't either. They cannot figure out why I would want to have a career that requires me to use my body instead of my brain."

"You use your brain."

I smiled. "Thank you."

"You do."

I squeezed her forearm. She patted my hand.

"When you were a little kid, what did you want to be when you grew up?" I asked.

"I wanted to make things. It didn't really matter what, just make things. But my aptitude for it is limited to programming. When I've tried to make physical things, they look like crap. What about you?"

"Oh, a ballerina, but I think that's just because I didn't know you could dance in any other way as a job. I danced my whole childhood. I have great turn out, but I'm not much of a ballerina." I attempted to show her how I could point my toes apart with my heels together. This was impossible to demonstrate while seated in the car. "Then I was too punk rock for dance in high school. Thank God I found aerials, I really missed moving around."

"We both got to live our dreams, huh?"

"I am, but do you get to make things?" I nudged her.

"I did a lot more in the beginning. Now I manage a company where other people make things." She scratched her head. "I think that's when things stopped being as fun, when I ended up managing a whole company by myself." Kris sighed. "But that's enough processing for my birthday. Now it's time for fun."

And fun was what we had. We checked into a cute inn, where we had a suite with a king-size bed and a couch that folded out, just in case. We wandered around downtown Santa Cruz for a bit our first night, got some pizza, and went to a bar where live music was playing. We were exhausted when we made it back to our room. We both stretched out on the bed mid debate about sleeping arrangements, and before I knew it, we'd slept through the night.

The next morning, we sampled the breakfast spread at the inn and spent most of Kris's birthday hanging out on the beach, checking out the sea lions near the boardwalk, and going on rides at the amusement park. We grabbed sandwiches, played a round of mini golf, and headed back to our room. Kris looked the most relaxed I'd ever seen her.

"Vacation looks good on you," I said as we plopped onto the bed. Her short hair was messy from the wind and her skin slightly pink from failure to reapply sunscreen, but she'd never looked better in my eyes. She'd left her phone charging in the room all day, and her face rested in an easy smile.

"It feels good too." She yanked off her loose tank top, leaving her in men's shorts and a sports bra. "But it also feels sweaty. Who knew it'd be this hot in April?"

"I like you sweaty," I said and ran a hand over her stomach.

She smiled—oh man, those crooked teeth—and put a warm, strong hand on my lower back, pulling me toward her. "I like this dress." She moved her palm up and down the curve of my hip, my cotton sundress inching upward as she did.

"You like it because it's a halter dress and I'm not wearing a bra," I said.

She slid her palm up my body to the side of my right breast, exposed ever so slightly. "It helps," she said. "Whenever the wind blew in, your nipples popped up." She circled one with her thumb. "And I could watch you bounce as you walked." Kris pinched my nipple through the fabric. "But mostly, I could watch your ass. You don't usually wear a thong."

"It's your birthday. And it looks better with this dress." I reached behind my neck and untied the knot holding up my dress, but didn't pull it down.

"You didn't have to. It wasn't going to be that kind of trip." She edged the fabric down past my collarbone, but no farther.

"Yet here you are, staring at my body, touching me, making me wet."

"I should have asked first." She moved away.

"Ask now."

"Phoenix, can I kiss you?"

"Yes."

She gave me a long, slow kiss. It started gently, grew more urgent, and ended as we nipped at each other's lower lips.

"Can I take off your dress?"

"No, but I'll take it off for you." I rolled her onto the bed and peeled off my sundress, tossing it to the floor. I straddled her and ran my hands over her body. She reached for my thighs, but I swatted her hand away playfully.

"You have to ask," I said.

"Can I touch you?"

I smiled. "Not yet." To tease her more, I touched my own breasts. A strangled sound escaped her throat. I responded by slipping my hand into my skimpy underwear and working my clit.

"What can I do?"

"You can take off your clothes, and I'll touch you."

"But it's my birthday."

"Exactly. You get to enjoy the show, and I'll make you come."

"But—"

"It's not eight thirty. We're not at home. Your requirements don't apply. I'm in charge right now. Do you want what I'm offering or not?" I asked her, doing my best to sound like a sassy top.

She sat up halfway, took off her sports bra, and flashed a hint of a smile. "I'm not great at not having control."

"I'm offering to get us both off. Do you want me to?" I asked.

"I can't boss you around at all?"

"I don't want that tonight. But you can touch me. If you ask nicely and I give you permission, you can touch me."

She looked amazed. "I don't know the last time I had sex without running everything."

"We don't have to. If you aren't comfortable, we don't need to have sex." It was a little challenging to say that with my almost-naked body positioned directly on top of her crotch.

"I want to. It's just strange for me, but I want to."

"Try to relax. Now, I want to do all sorts of things to you. Should I ask first about each?"

"You don't need to ask, just start slow. Can I touch you yet?"

"You aren't even naked. No." I cupped one of her breasts in each hand and buried my face in her cleavage. Using my mouth and my hands, I played with her chest until she began to moan.

"Now you should be naked," I said and scooted off of her.

"Why did you stop? I was enjoying that," she grumbled as she shed the rest of her clothes.

"I wanted you motivated to get undressed quickly." I climbed on one of her thighs. "It worked. Ready for your reward?"

"Do I get to touch you?"

I nodded.

She exhaled exaggerated relief and reached for my breasts. I returned my hands to hers, and we mirrored each other's touch. As we did, I rocked my pussy against her thigh, pressing one of my legs up against her cunt as I did. She ground against me in response.

Slowly, I moved a hand from her nipple to her clit, taking my time to stroke other neglected parts of her on my way. I angled my hand between my leg and her wet lips, and touched her as she moved her hips against me.

"Unfair," she said, her breathing ragged. "You're still wearing that thong."

"You come first. Then it comes off."

She groaned. I couldn't keep my balance and rearranged one arm on the bed to hold myself up as I touched her. I did my best to suck on her nipples, but it was impossible to keep her in my mouth with all the writhing. I marveled at her. Kris was so gorgeous, so sexy, and no one got to see her like this. No one got to make her come unless she was ordering them to. This sight of her, helpless and about to come and not running the scene, was one for me alone. I flicked her clit a little faster, pressed my thigh against her firmly, and watched her dissolve.

Kris wasn't especially loud, but she was much louder than she usually was. Unlike me, she didn't like touching to continue after she came, so once her cries softened, I released her. I put my head against her chest and listened to her hammering heart.

"Wow," she whispered.

"It's fun to let go sometimes, huh?"

"Maybe once in a while. Don't get any ideas, though. This is not a thing that'll happen every week."

"Are you kidding? I love getting ordered around and roughed up. It's been two days and I'm starting to miss it."

"If that's what you're hoping for tonight, you're going to need to give me some time."

"Nah. But tomorrow you better at least pull my hair."

She wrapped her fingers in my wild mane and yanked. I smiled at her.

"Well, now I'm inspired." I wiggled out of my (now soaking) thong and handed it to her.

"I can't believe you're offering me this during the few minutes in the day when I'm incapable of doing anything about it. Give me a second, Phe."

"Nope." I batted my eyelashes and straddled her thigh again and started grinding on her. "Touching you turned me on so much I think I can come in about a minute."

She pinched my nipples, hard like I liked it, and then tried to angle her hand to my pussy. Before she could, I was already tipping over the edge, rocking fiercely against her. She reached her hand back up, twisted both my nipples, and I came. I shook against her, clenching her thigh between both of my own. Then I fell beside her, panting.

Kris stroked my head and brushed stray tangles of hair from my face. "I didn't expect that. It's been a long time since I let go of control."

"It's not something we've done before. Spontaneous and outside of our dynamic."

"It's not something I've done since I had a girlfriend," she said quietly.

"Was it okay?"

"It was excellent. I'm having the best birthday I've had in years." She pulled me to her. With my face pressed against her bare sternum, she continued. "I'm having a good time with you. I know you're going on tour soon, so there's an end date, but I want to enjoy every minute I have with you. I'm a little sad I wasted time working so much when it drained me. I don't want to waste anymore moments."

"What do you mean?"

"I'm going to make a change about work. I've decided for sure. I'm going to sell. And I'm going to have more fun."

I felt simultaneously bursting with joy about this and also weighted with sadness. On the one hand, I wanted Kris to be happy. I was glad to be a part of her finding her way. On the other, I didn't want to be the cute little artist who woke her up to fun. I didn't want what was happening between us to simply teach her a lesson, and I didn't want to be gone by the time she found balance. I wanted to be the one to see her happy and be happy with her.

But it was her birthday, and that was plenty of processing for one night, so I cuddled up to her and said only, "Happy birthday."

CHAPTER TWENTY-ONE

The rest of our vacation in Santa Cruz was as great as the beginning had been. I didn't want to go home, both because I was having a wonderful time and because I was nervous about rehearsal starting the next day. On our way home, I got that horrible back-to-work feeling I'd gotten so many Sunday afternoons in my adult life. I felt irritable and tired and almost nauseous with dread.

Arriving at the studio for training the next day with Sasha was bizarre, because Sasha was completely perky. "This is most exciting moment in my life," she said.

"I think I'm going to throw up," I said.

When we walked in, the giant open room was rigged for our performance. A dozen long pieces of red fabric hung from the sixteen-foot ceilings all the way to the floor. That floor was covered in crash mats. At the far end of the room, a few other apparatuses were set up, including a trapeze, a lyra hoop, and a rope.

Most of the other cast members were already there. The star, Mirah, had been the star in an earlier version of the show that debuted in London the year before. It had been a much shorter take on the story, just a mermaid and a prince twirling around aerial silks, with lighting representing the ocean and the land. Sasha and I had watched the videos of it close to fifty times in preparation.

Mirah looked bored as she stretched. Despite the fact that the story wasn't Disney, they'd picked a lead with deep auburn hair, gigantic eyes, and a waist so small it looked like you could break her in the middle. Mirah had not been an aerial performer before being cast in the London version, and the show had initially gotten flak from British aerial dancers annoyed that casting was about looks more than skill. Mirah was an actress, though, with actual stage credits before she tried to shimmy up silks. Though the London show didn't have much by way of inventive choreography or technique, it was pretty. Mirah had been training for the past year, and now was perhaps more able to anchor a show that spent half of the time in the air.

The prince from the London show—another attractive actor without an aerial background—hadn't joined this one. His aerialist replacement was trying to talk to Mirah, making her look even more bored. Another actor, playing both the human father of the prince and the mer-father of the mermaids, was chatting with the guy playing all the other male roles. One was graying and one was balding, and both were incredibly fit. Sasha whispered that they were both well-known aerialists on the East Coast, but I wasn't paying much attention.

I was looking at our mermaid castmates and the actress playing the both the mer-grandmother and the angel, who was probably no older than Kris. The mermaids were giggling and nervous, all beautiful, young, and perfectly made up, wearing an expensive brand of workout clothes, with matching headbands over their blond or light brown hair. Sasha and I were wearing ridiculously patterned leggings and crop tops over our sports bras. Their headbands probably cost more than our whole outfits. Even the "grandmother" wore lipstick and size-two designer stretch pants.

"Were we supposed to put on makeup for this?" I asked.

Sasha rolled her eyes. "We'd just sweat it off. You know that."

"Then why are they?"

"Oh, they're all LA people. You know how it is." She waved the thought away.

I vaguely did from Connie's descriptions and my occasional visits. She found the fashion and beauty culture there absurd. Though I identified pretty strongly as femme, I was also a femme in the Bay Area with a second-wave feminist mom. I loved my waterproof mascara with a passion and enjoyed lipstick, but half the time I skipped foundation. My wardrobe was almost exclusively exercise stuff and thrift store dresses and skirts. Though I looked cute and even sexy, I only looked polished when I was performing. These women looked like they were in an ad.

Not to mention that that every single one of them was really, really white. My skin wasn't especially dark—my foundation was always in the "medium" range—but I was noticeably darker than any other woman there. And though I was pretty petite myself, my butt was probably the size of two of theirs put together.

My horror must have shown on my face. "So they got fancy," Sasha said with a shrug. "What's the big deal?"

"Am I the sea witch because my ass is bigger than everybody else's? Or because I'm the only one who's not whiter than paper?"

"The sea witch is the only one other than the lead who gets an aerial solo! They might be more dolled up for rehearsals, but you got the best female role other than her." She nodded at the ethereally pretty Mirah. "And I'm her understudy. We got cast and we know what the fuck we're doing. Act proud about it."

With that, she sauntered into the middle of the room and started stretching dramatically, showing off her unusual flexibility.

I trailed after her, stealing uncomfortable glances at everyone around me.

Damien and his team arrived shortly after we did. This included the purple-haired choreographer, Geoffrey. In addition to being a dance choreographer of many years, Geoffrey had been an aerialist, and had put on a few interesting, experimental short shows in New York. Sasha nudged me when he walked in. He was one of those "right people" Sasha and I would meet on tour.

We began with Damien breaking down the show more thoroughly for all of us. His vision was this: the show opened with a gorgeous, lengthy "underwater" aerials scene with all merfolk, followed by Mirah hearing about humans from her older sisters, who'd been allowed to visit the surface, and the sisters aerially acting out the things they saw. Then she and her grandmother discuss humans and how they got to go to heaven after death, unlike mermaids. Mirah then goes to the surface, sees a prince, rescues him from drowning via elaborate silks duo act, and watches him be comforted on "land" (a trapeze) by a human girl. Then Mirah goes to the sea witch and asks to become human, followed by a silks sequence from my sea witchy self. Next was a dramatic sequence in which our mermaid lead gets human legs and a shot at a soul if the prince marries her, but she loses her voice. Then intermission.

The second act was a series of on-land events, sans aerials, but filled with dance. The mermaid dances for the prince, and the prince enjoys this but still marries the human princess his father had selected for him—the very one who'd comforted him after his rescue by the mermaid. Our star was then met by her sisters—us in short-hair wigs/Sasha free of her long-hair wig— and offered a knife. Her sisters tell her they gave their hair to the sea witch in exchange for an end to the mermaid's spell, as she will turn to sea foam once the prince marries another. They tell her that if she kills the prince, she can be a mermaid again. She won't do it, so her body dissolves thanks to very special lighting effects. Then she ascends to heaven thanks to a harness, and is met by an angel on silks, who tells her that her pure love has won her a soul after all.

We watched the London video. Damien gave us commentary on how lighting and projections would be used to transform stages into an underwater world, a far away castle, and heaven. I could picture how beautiful the show would be.

We did a rough run-through of the show without any aerials or dance routines. We read our lines with the script in our hands (even though I'd memorized my lines already), and practiced who was on stage when and how much time we had for costume changes. Then it was lunch break.

After a lunch of catered salad and sandwiches, we did a quick "ice-breaker" team building exercise that did not break any ice, and then Geoffrey led us in a warm-up and aerial drills. Immediately after our warm-up and drills, Geoffrey began barking orders. We were introduced to too much information, way too fast. We muddled through a rough approximation of what we were supposed to be doing, prompting more barks from our brightly hued choreographer.

Any envy or competitiveness I'd felt melted away as I watched a couple of would-be mermaids struggle after too many attempts of it. Geoffrey was pushing way too hard.

"That isn't safe," I told Sasha, nodding at the skinniest one, Vivienne. Vivienne was shaking.

She shrugged. "And we probably should have done the aerials before lunch when we were all fresh. What can you do?"

I glared at Geoffrey. "I'm going to say something."

Before she could respond, I marched over to Geoffrey and said, "She's going to hurt herself. You can't train this way."

He looked at me like I was a bug.

I turned to Vivienne, who looked ready to cry. "Do you need a break?" I asked her.

She nodded, looking green under her makeup. "I suck at this kind of straddle up," she said, referencing the trick we'd all been working on. "But I can do—"

"Everyone's doing the same thing," Geoffrey cut her off. "The point is that you'll look synchronized."

"Why?" I asked. "We all have different strengths as performers. Why can't we incorporate those into the show?"

"Because, this is a professional performance. I know that's new to you, but it is how touring shows work. Besides," he added with a sniff, "you need to work on your ankle hangs." With that, he turned back to miserable Vivienne and started shouting again.

I wanted to punch him. I wanted to tell him that he was terrible and needed to be replaced. But who was I? I was the one who would be replaced if I pushed too hard against Geoffrey.

I slunk back to Sasha. She greeted me with raised eyebrows.

"It didn't do anything," I said.

"It annoyed him. Don't pull that shit again. We need his connections."

I winced and went back to work. We ran through most of our mermaid choreography pretty easily. It was a lot of graceful climbing, weaving in and out of the silks like they were seaweed—we were told green silks were on the way—swaying, some wraps, and a couple of drops. Drops were terrifying at first, and they always got an audience reaction, because you wrapped yourself in some of the fabric and then let go, falling toward the floor until the fabric caught you and held you up. It took me years to even try them, but by that point, I literally dreamed about them. Despite Geoffrey's treatment of some of the performers, the show was pretty smartly choreographed. By keeping many sequences simple and somewhat repetitive, the audience could marvel at the grace and fluidity of the movements while focusing on the story. The exceptional trick would really stand out, and keeping those limited would help performers avoid sloppy mistakes and injuries.

Still, the first day was awful. Geoffrey didn't speak another word to me, Vivienne looked miserable, and Mirah, who had a million things to learn, spent the whole afternoon grimacing. Plus I had to spend a huge chunk of time working on one-ankle hangs, which I hated.

"What did we sign up for?" I said to Sasha as we got in her car at the end of the day.

"Come on, that was awesome! We're surrounded by hot people, we're in the air, and we get paid. What more do you want?"

I wanted Geoffrey to be less abrasive and condescending. I wanted to feel more cohesive as a group. I wanted more say in the whole thing. I wanted each cast member to get to show off what they were best at, not just what Geoffrey had in mind. I wanted to fall asleep immediately. I wanted to cry.

But most of all? I wanted to wake up the next day and return to my hodgepodge schedule of teaching and training and scrubbing the floors, while still having the energy to make dinner and get whipped. I wanted my life as it had become. I didn't want to leave it, but it seemed too late now to keep it.

CHAPTER TWENTY-TWO

It didn't get better over the next few weeks. Sasha started the brutal process of learning Mirah's part. Mirah's coldness began to make sense, because the weight of the show was resting on her. She had a musical theater background, which was good because her role required to her to sing, dance, and act. It also required her to perform on silks, fly through the air on a harness, and suppress her English accent because her mer-family all sounded American. Sasha wasn't easily shaken, but despite her own theater background, her first week of serious understudy training left her demoralized.

Geoffrey continued to be a bully. He was rude and snapped at everyone but Damien. Though we more or less got a handle on the routine after the second week, he always found something lacking. I wanted my performances to be excellent too, but his perfectionism was driving me crazy. Once, he made the entire cast redo the opening nine times in a row, once because someone's hand wasn't placed exactly where he wanted it. We all had at least some background in putting together our own performances, and most of us were chafing at having no creative input in the show. Sasha pointed out that this was just a difference between the kind of performance we usually did and full productions with choreographers, but I still hated it.

It had an impact on my home life too. I no longer cooked or cleaned for Kris. She hired someone to come in and we ordered lots of delivery. I wanted to do it, but I was too tired after rehearsals, which often ran almost as long as Kris's workdays. We managed to maintain our eight thirty hour and a playful Sunday, but extended sessions on Friday were a thing of the past.

"I miss my old life," I said to John as I lay in bed Saturday after the third week of rehearsals, feeling sorry for myself.

"With me?"

"With Kris! I miss our routine. I miss teaching my classes and booking stupid parties where I did little tricks and wore silly costumes. I miss cleaning the house."

"That is a first, my friend," he said with a laugh.

"Then you see how serious this is."

"Come on, Phe. You don't like rehearsals because it's a new thing. When you moved in with Kris, you wanted your old life back for a while. It's what you do when things change."

It wasn't exactly the first time this possible character trait had been pointed out to me. "I know, but I don't think that's why I feel like this. I don't want to go on tour. I feel the way I did at my old job, where the pit of my stomach feels hollow whenever I think about it. I know I should be happy. I have a job I'd always thought I wanted. I'm lucky. I made it work until my big break, and now here it is, and I can launch this amazing career. I can maybe quit teaching aerials, or at least charge more because I've got more clout. I'll earn enough that I can come back from this tour and not need to live with Kris. I mean, I'll need roommates and a place to live, but I won't *need* to be a live-in submissive in order to get by. Everything is opening up. I should be happy. But I'm not."

Unexpectedly, I started to cry.

"Oh, Phoenix. That's a horrible feeling."

"What is wrong with me?" I cried. "Is it this show? Or is it me?"

"I don't know, honey. But I know you should trust yourself."

"I'm almost twenty-eight years old and I don't know how to trust myself!" Heavy tears poured from my eyes, and snot started dripping out of my nose. I was not a pretty crier.

"Yes, you do. You're great at following your instincts. You can do this."

"You're sure?"

"Absolutely. Call me later?"

"Of course. Love you."

"Love you too."

The minute I got off the phone, I started bawling again. Apparently, louder than I realized, because Kris knocked on my door.

"Are you okay?" she asked.

"You're home?" I asked her back, surprised, and still hiccupping with sobs.

"Can I come in?"

"Okay." I cried harder.

Kris came in and sat next to me on the bed. Gingerly, she rubbed my back. "What's going on?"

"Why are you home in the middle of the day?"

She gave me a stern look. "Phoenix, why are you crying?"

"I hate this stupid show!" I wailed. "The choreographer's a jerk. Sasha's got to learn everything because she's understudy to the lead, so I don't have my friend to hang out with. And it's boring. I mean, it's tiring to do over and over, and I'm worn out physically, but I already know how to do it. I have one scene that's actually technically difficult, but it's full of tricks I'm not that great at when there are so many tricks I'm amazing at! And I still don't know how to act. I know my lines, but I don't know how to sound right saying them. This whole show is going to be shit and I don't even care because I *hate* this show. Maybe we'll all quit."

Finally, I exhaled, and then started bawling again.

She looked sympathetic and wrapped me in a tight hug.

"You're doing great," she said into my hair.

"I hate this show." My face was wet and sticky. I hated crying. I sniffled loudly.

Kris grabbed a box of tissues from my bedside table and handed it to me, one arm still holding me close. I blew my nose and threw the tissue on the floor. It was not an attractive moment for me.

"I've hated my job more days than I can count."

"That's not reassuring. Aren't you leaving your job?" I felt sorry for Kris, who got all my brattiness.

"That's not the point. The point is, people can hate their job sometimes and still be great at it, and still get things they want from it, and still even love it some of the time. It's not the end of the world if you hate your job right now. It doesn't feel good, but it doesn't mean you need to quit. You have a few more weeks of rehearsals to get through, and maybe you won't hate it as much with an audience," she said.

"Maybe I'll hate it even more when we're embarrassing ourselves in front of an audience."

"Okay, maybe. But you don't know yet. And even if you do? It's six months. It's not the rest of your life."

I started crying again. "Six months is so long."

"Really, it's not."

"It's a long time to be away from you." I pulled away from her and covered my mouth after I said it, like I could force the words back in.

"Phoenix, really?"

I stammered, trying to explain away what I'd said, but Kris wouldn't let me.

"That's incredibly sweet," she said. "Are you saying you want to keep doing this when your tour is over?"

I nodded. "Or maybe instead of my tour."

She took my hand in hers. "This was your dream, being able to support yourself as an aerial dancer and performing like this. You've worked so hard to do this. Right now, your dream isn't turning out like you hoped. Maybe you'll try it longer and realize you need something different. Or maybe it'll get better. No one knows right now. But you need to give it a chance."

"What are you saying?"

"I'd love to have you come back here after your tour ends. You have a place with me after you finish it. But I'm not having you stay instead of going on tour."

"Excuse me? That isn't your decision."

"If you decide to quit, you can quit. But you can't stay here if you do. I'll help you get settled somewhere else if you decide to quit, but you can't live here instead of going on tour. I'm happy to support you in going after something that's important to you. I'm not willing to give you a space to be complacent. You're good at this. You can do this. It would be a waste for you to quit this show, even if you hate it."

"Why can't I just stay with you? Everything is fine!"

She stroked my cheek. "I'm here to support you, but not give you an out because you're afraid. Doing what you really want is terrifying. Sometimes if people have a way to avoid things that scare them, they hide their whole lives, and they miss out on what they want most in the world. I won't be part of you giving up your dreams because of fear."

"It's not fear. I hate it."

"Okay, then I won't be part of you giving up your dreams because you hate rehearsals." She smirked.

"What do you know about it?" I raised an eyebrow. "You want to make a change and you haven't."

"I did, actually. I think I finally found the right buyer. We're drawing up some paperwork. I'll still be an active part of the company during the sale and the transition, but then I'm done."

"Are you retiring?"

"Sort of. I'll have enough money to be flexible about work. I might take some time off and then work on projects I'm really passionate about. But I think I'm done working eighty hours a week and never taking a break."

I hugged her. "That's amazing! I'm so happy for you."

"It wasn't easy, Phe. I was incredibly afraid. There were a lot of times when it felt easier to just keep on doing what was familiar."

"I really don't want to go on this tour. I don't."

"I know."

I sighed. "Why did I even want this?"

She brushed her fingers through my hair. "You want to perform for a living, and this is the stepping stone you need. You are doing this because it gives you credibility as an aerial dancer, and it helps you get seen and meet people who might give you other opportunities or promote your work. You're doing this because every person who sees this show gets a program with your biography that directs them to your website and links to your other work. You want this because it's a challenge, because it will pay you, and because it will help you have the career you want."

"What if I don't want this career?" I asked in a small voice. "I don't love doing corporate gigs or performing at parties. I don't want to teach forever. And now that I'm in this show, I don't think I like this kind of touring theater-type show either. I like my little weird performances I put together with Sasha and other people I know. I want to do just the aerials I want to do, and nothing else. But that's not a career."

She cocked her head. "It's not a career if you only do that and refuse to do anything else from the beginning, no. But you're talking to somebody who can now basically only do the parts of her job she likes, even though I started out my career constantly panicking about how I was going to pay my student loans."

"You worked nonstop for like twenty years! And aerials are not going to make me rich enough to stop worrying about money."

"Aren't they? Do you really have to worry about money now? I mean, it seems like you've been paying all your bills just fine."

"That's different. That's because I'm your sub. You're a benefactor giving me a reprieve from my money panic."

"I'm not going to stop wanting to do that." She played with my hair.

I melted. My heart fluttered, and I got that low belly tingle I sometimes felt after very promising second dates. It wasn't a feeling of lust, but of affection. But this pull toward her only reminded me of the feelings for her that I'd been trying to ignore for months.

"Oh, Kris." I fought back tears. "You don't know that."

"I know you're important to me and I like what we have. I don't want this to end. When you're done with your tour, you can come back. Do you like how things were before you started rehearsals? Your work, us, all of it? You were happy with that?"

"Yes."

"Going on this tour is temporary. It gives you more options, but in the end, you can come back to a situation you like. You can come back to me, to doing shows you don't love along with some you do, to teaching, to training, to all of it. The way you get the career you want—the way anyone does—is plug along paying your dues, to do as much of what you love as you can manage, and be as decent a person as you can. Eventually, maybe you just get to perform exactly what you love. But right now, you're in the early stages, which can be exciting and also incredibly shitty. But it's something everybody does, and it's okay."

I flung myself at her for a hug that knocked us both back onto the bed. First, she grunted with surprise, then she laughed.

"Thank you," I said. "I needed to hear that."

"So you're not quitting?"

"No. It sucks and I hate it, but I'm pushing through."

Kris smiled. "Good. You're amazing at this. It would be a shame if other people didn't get to see that because one choreographer is a jerk."

I looked into her beautiful green eyes and I knew at that moment. I knew I shouldn't, and that the timing was wrong, and that it probably lead to nothing but heartbreak. But it was too late. I'd tried to fight the feeling creeping up on me and I couldn't any longer.

I was completely and utterly in love with Kris.

CHAPTER TWENTY-THREE

Realizing I was in love with my dom a few weeks before I went on tour was incredibly awkward and inconvenient. I felt the need to tiptoe around and hold back with Kris, because I didn't want her realizing that I'd caught full-blown feelings. It was like what had happened months earlier but a thousand times worse because I knew I should talk to her, even while I knew that doing so could be bad news for both of us.

She seemed to chalk this distance up to my nerves and exhaustion from rehearsals, and she let it go. Unfortunately, my nerves and exhaustion were also real, and I desperately wanted the encouragement and support—not to mention the release of kink and sex—that she offered, even though each second of attention she gave me made me flush with emotion.

I couldn't just enjoy her attention or kindness, because I was worrying about how she felt, and how she might feel if she knew how I felt. Two weeks before my show opened, she came home early with a present wrapped in shiny silver paper. I loved presents, but as soon as I saw it, I got flustered. What did a present mean?

"Open it." Kris beamed at me and handing me the box. I was standing in the kitchen getting out plates. I fiddled with the little white takeout box.

"I hope you like it," Kris said when I didn't take the present.

"I'm sure I will," I said. I felt beads of sweat form on my upper lip. What was wrong with me? I was in love, that was what was wrong with me.

Carefully, I unwrapped the box, setting aside the silver paper on the counter. Kris bounced from foot to foot, an uncharacteristic goofy grin on her face. The thin white box was glossy cardboard with the name of very posh store embossed on the front. I raised my eyebrows.

Inside the box, cuddled in tissue paper, was a bright red trench coat. I lifted it carefully, like I might break it. The lining was polka dot satin, and every inch was as soft as butter to the touch. The stitches were tiny and identical to each other. It had real shell buttons, tons of discreet pockets, and a reversible belt with matching red on one side and the satin polka fabric on the other. I adored it. It was the nicest coat I'd ever touched.

"Try it on," she said with a huge smile.

I shrugged off my hoodie and surrounded myself in my new coat. It fit perfectly. Even though I was short and I typically needed every sleeve and pant leg hemmed, this coat needed no alterations. It hugged my strong arms and generous butt without being too tight. When I cinched the belt, I looked down to see my body looking like an old-fashioned movie star bombshell.

"Whoa, Kris, it's amazing. Why are all the full-length mirrors upstairs?"

I rushed up the stairs with Kris trailing behind me. In my bedroom, I twirled in front of the mirror. I looked amazing. I felt amazing.

"I love it," I said. "It's perfect."

Kris smiled, her eyes full of pride. "I hoped you'd like it."

"How'd you get the perfect size?"

She looked sheepish. "I took in your green jacket from the hall closet and had the sales lady help me. I was hoping it would be okay."

"It's a lot more than okay." I hugged her. "I can't believe it. I love this!"

She held me by the hips and looked at us in the mirror. She brushed her lips to the top of my head and kissed my hair. She whispered in my ear, "You are my fantasy come to life." Then she bit my earlobe, kissed her way down my neck.

The thought that I should hold back—that I wanted something different than she did, that I was not her fantasy come to life because I was in love with her—flashed in my mind. But a second later, that thought was washed away by the feeling of Kris's mouth on my skin. She grabbed my belt and yanked me closer to kiss me full on the mouth.

She drifted away from me for a moment and looked into my eyes. "Yeah?" she asked softly.

"Green," I said and leaned in for another kiss. Kris rested a palm against my hip and tenderly caressed me through the fabric. I lost myself kissing her. Before I knew it she was nipping at my lower lip, teasing me with her tongue, and angling me toward my bed.

"Isn't part of your fantasy that I say no to you?"

"My fantasy is that you do whatever you want. And that sometimes you'll give me control for a little while, because you want to."

"I do want you to," I whispered. I wanted more than anything to lose myself in the sensations she could give me. "I want to be yours right now, however you want me."

"I want to make it hurt, and then make you come," she said. "And I want you to get me off."

"Green, green, green."

She grabbed me by the hair and kissed me hard. "Everything off but the coat. Put on some heels. Meet me downstairs in three minutes."

Kris swaggered out of the room. I pulled off my yoga pants and panties, and unbuttoned my coat to ditch my loose T-shirt and my sports bra. Then I wrapped myself in the coat again, tied the belt, and climbed into my tallest heels. I tottered down to the stairs and into the lavender room.

She was lying on the bed, looking at her watch. "You barely made it in time," she said.

"But I made it." I climbed on top of her and I slid my hand under her pants and into her boxer briefs. She was already drenched. I maneuvered her clothes down past her ass to avoid the pinch of fabric as I went to work on her clit. I stroked her there, steady and direct, for a minute before she stopped me and pulled her pants back up.

"It's not time for that yet, princess," she said.

"What's it time for then?"

"It's time for me to hit you. Stand up. Take off the coat for me."

Slowly, I dropped the perfect coat to the ground.

"On your knees. Don't move."

I held my breath while she went to the closet to find the implements she wanted. I wanted to wiggle out of my heels, but I didn't dare without permission. I heard the slap of leather against her hand. It was a heavy paddle.

"Remember in the beginning when I tried everything out on you?" she asked.

"Yes." I was dripping.

"Today, I want to break you open."

"Yes please." As answer, she slammed the paddle against my ass. I cried out. Kris hit me again with the paddle a dozen more times, with her full strength again and again.

"Color?" she asked.

"Green." I ached but wanted more.

Kris trailed the paddle up my back, swatting me with it as she went. She kept it irregular enough to prevent me from bracing myself. Then she trailed the paddle down, over my stinging ass, along the back of one thigh, then the other. Each leg got several smacks, but none as hard as the paddling she gave my ass.

I thought she was done, but then she started rubbing the paddle against my slick pussy. Kris hit me once there, making me yelp.

"Ow!" I shouted.

She laughed. "Want me to kiss it and make it better?"

"Yes."

"Take off the heels, put the coat back on, and I will." She lay back on the bed.

I kicked off my shoes, wrapped myself in my new coat, and lowered myself over her mouth. I felt her hot, gasping breath on my sensitive skin.

"This won't take long," I said. "If you want me to come."

"There's nothing I want more, except maybe to slap you."

I scooted off her, gave her a kiss on the lips, and offered her my face.

Kris slowly stroked my cheek. Then she slapped me hard, leaving my face stinging. I exhaled and climbed back on her face. The coat fell around my thighs, obscuring her almost completely. I rocked against her tongue as her hands roamed over me. I came faster than even I'd expected. It felt too soon almost, and I felt a tinge of regret that I hadn't lasted longer—hadn't had more of her like this—when I started to shake and cry out.

I collapsed next to her, both of us panting. Kris laced her fingers between mine. Before my breathing had even steadied, she was guiding my hand back into her pants.

"Give me a second," I said.

"No. Get me off."

However tired I felt in that moment, there was nothing I wanted more than to follow her orders. I slithered on top of her. She shoved her pants down and I angled my fingers inside her as my thumb pushed steady on her clit. Kris was as wet as I had been. Gracelessly, I pulled up her shirt and sports bra and took one of her nipples in my mouth as I fucked her cunt, circled her clit. Within minutes, I had her writhing and pulling at my hair.

When she finished, she kissed me on the mouth. "Good girl," she said.

"I do what I'm told." I batted my eyelashes at her. She pulled me close and I rested my head on her chest. "I know I shouldn't say this, but sometimes I wish I weren't leaving," I said.

"Sometimes I wish that too. But you'll come back, right?"

"Yeah." I wanted to tell her then that I loved her and that I didn't just want to come back to what we'd had. I wanted to come home to her as her girlfriend. But I didn't want to upset her so instead I said, "I really love my coat."

She kissed my hairline. "It suits you."

"It makes me feel powerful. Like I could do anything."

"Good, because you can."

"Even handle my choreographer problem?"

"You know what I notice? Sometimes you like teaching and sometimes you hate it, you usually love performing, but what you really seem to be happiest doing is putting together your routines with Sasha."

"I guess that's true. I love figuring out a new way of putting things together, and it's a lot easier for me to learn a trick because I want to perform it or I know it will work best than it is because somebody else says I have to. And it's most fun when I'm collaborating with somebody as equals." I lazily drew shapes on her stomach. "I like to keep my submission in the bedroom not the workplace, you know?"

"Well, the bedroom, the kitchen, the bathroom…"

I gave her a playful shove. "Okay, I like being creative in my performances. What's your point?"

"What would you do if this were your show? If you were in charge?"

I thought for a minute. "If it were my show, I would have turned over some creative control to the cast and credit their contributions. If it were my show, I would have a choreographer who'd been an aerials teacher, so they had a sense of how to instruct people and not just how to put together routines that look great, because I'd want to get the best performances out of the individuals. I'd play to people's strengths. I'd make a point to hire more diverse performers. But really, I'd want to do something smaller and more original. I love this story, but I'd want to tell something we haven't already heard tons of times before. I'd want to put on a beautiful show with a deeper message."

"Why don't you?" she asked. "You could make the show you really want."

"It would cost a ton. Rehearsal space, costumes, paying the performers, the crew, sets, lighting, advertising, plus we'd need a venue."

"What if it wasn't a lot of performers, though? Just you, maybe Sasha, maybe a few other people who are really dedicated?"

I realized that we'd have access to rehearsal space most of the time we were touring. Sasha usually made our costumes with my help anyway. And since I hadn't touched my savings living with Kris, I had money to use. Did I want to create a show? Not just some routines for gigs, but a full-length show of my own?

"You are a fucking genius," I told Kris.

She laughed. "I try."

We had that Monday off for Memorial Day and I spent the time pricing out various costs and sketching out ideas. It occurred to me that with some luck and a lot of work, we could put on a show. At lunch on Tuesday, I pulled Sasha aside.

"After this run is over, what are your plans?" I asked.

She shrugged. "Whatever the Universe has in store for me. Come back here maybe and go back to the same things with a better network, unless I find something really appealing on the road. What about you?"

I smiled. "I want to create a show. Our own show. Something we can direct and star in and make exactly what we want."

She laughed. "Are we starting an aerial theater company?"

"Why not? We have six months of good money. For the whole time we're on the road we have access to a rehearsal space that we don't have to pay for, tons of exposure, and we'll be networking with everyone in aerials all over the country. We could find producers just by going to work. What better time to start putting together a show?"

She cocked her head. "We could do this, actually. It'd be a great way to establish ourselves. Come off a big show and immediately have our own? We could get into festivals. We could probably even get funding."

"Right? So are you in?"

Sasha nodded. "Everything we need comes our way," she said.

CHAPTER TWENTY-FOUR

The last Saturday before the show opened, Kris hosted a going-away party for me. It took me completely by surprise. She didn't tell me it was happening until Friday night while we were in the kitchen eating takeout.

"I thought if you knew about it earlier, you'd feel like you needed to help with it, and you don't," she said.

"Who did you invite?" I asked nervously.

"Only people I've heard you talk about. Sasha, Meghan and Bill, and Eric and Derek. I hope that's okay, because they're my friends."

I breathed a sigh of relief. "That's perfect. I had a panic moment when I thought I'd be spending my last Saturday night off with a million people."

"Is there anyone else you want me to invite? I could call Ray…"

I shook my head. "That's a perfect group. Low-key and simple and fun. Where are we all meeting?"

"What do you mean? We're having it here." She looked concerned. "Did you want it to be somewhere else?"

"No, I just—you never have people over. I thought it was something you didn't do."

"I have people over."

I patted her hand. "Not since I've lived here."

She frowned. I could see her searching for an occasion to prove me wrong, but she came up empty. "Really? I haven't had anyone over in almost ten months?"

"I don't think so, Kris."

She looked unhappy. "It was worse before you lived here. I lived at work. Sometimes I just slept there. And when I was home, I didn't leave the upstairs. Sometimes I'd leave work on Saturday and realized that I hadn't had a single conversation about anything but work in a week. Then I went to a play party or saw a play partner, maybe talked to a friend or called my parents, and tried really hard to be social until I felt too exhausted to stay awake. I'd crash and wake up worrying about work and start it all over again. I didn't have anyone come to this house once—anyone at all—for six months."

"It's different now," I said. "You're making changes in your life. It's not going to go back to that just because I don't live here."

She squeezed my hand. "What am I going to do without you?"

I blinked back tears. What was unsaid and seemed unsayable hung in the air like a thick fog. I wanted her as my dom and my girlfriend. Plenty of people had partners in life and in BDSM. Meghan and her husband sprang to mind. But would Kris ever want something like that after what had happened with Laurie? Would she want it with me even if she did? I felt too vulnerable to ask, with a nerve-wracking final week of rehearsals and the specter of opening night ahead of me. So I hugged her and choked down the last of my tikka masala.

The party was perfect. Kris had it catered by a Burmese restaurant I loved in Oakland. She was an ideal host, chatting with everyone and getting them drinks and giving them the tour while I sat in the little backyard talking one-on-one with my friends. She'd strung up lights in the yard and packed it with colorful folding chairs. There were, technically, enough for everyone to sit in the yard, though not much room to do anything else.

For a while, we played music in the house and had a goofy dance party in the living room. We all ate tremendously and drank and laughed. I felt incredibly lucky to have these people in my life. I missed John, but Kris had even thought of that. He'd been "invited" to join us on FaceTime, and even stayed up late (with a three-hour time zone difference no less) to virtually attend and talk to me.

Sasha and I talked about the show we wanted to start working on. Bill and I told stories. I got to thank Meghan again for introducing me to Kris and making so much possible and generally being patient and amazing. Derek, who often traveled for work, gave me travel advice. The night was lovely.

Eric settled down next to me last. They'd turned the music back on in the house and we could see everyone dancing through the French doors. I laughed at Kris's uncoordinated but enthusiastic moves.

"I can't believe she did all this," I said.

"She's in love with you," he blurted. I did a double take. Eric nodded, a little drunk but completely serious.

"What makes you think that?" I thought he had to be kidding.

"She talks about you all the time. She has for months and months. When you said you were going on tour, she came over to our place crying. She said she has feelings for you, but she doesn't want to hold you back."

"That doesn't mean she's in love with me."

"I know what love looks like." He pointed to Kris, twirling Sasha. Sasha was in full-on star mode and attempting contact improv with everyone, and Kris laughed as Sasha nearly broke a vase. Kris smiled at me through the glass.

"She never says anything."

"I don't think she knows how to talk about her feelings all that well, but that doesn't mean she doesn't have them. If you talked to her, I think you two would find you feel the same way."

"What makes you think I have those feelings for her?"

He scoffed and looked me up and down. "Come on, you're saying I'm wrong here?"

I sighed. "It's not that simple."

"Why? Because you're traveling?"

"For lots of reasons. Because of that, and because she works too much, and because she has all these requirements. Emotional involvement isn't part of that."

"Doms can't fall in love?"

"What would that even look like?"

"You two get to decide that together."

"I don't know if I can."

Eric put an arm around my shoulder. "I know it's scary. I've been telling her to talk to you for weeks, but she's afraid it'll damage things or get in your way. I think you feel the same way. Somebody has to take the leap here. Honestly? I think you're the brave one."

"What if it goes badly?"

"You're leaving, Phoenix. You'll leave, and time will heal it."

"I'll try. But I still can't believe she feels the way I do."

We looked in and saw Kris waving us inside.

"Believe it," Eric said and helped me up to rejoin the party.

❖

Reassurance from Eric helped, but I still needed to sort through things. Sunday, I woke up jittery after a night of fitful dreams. I wanted to call John, but it hadn't even been twelve hours since we'd Skyped, and I figured he might need a little break.

I paced around my room until nine, deciding that was enough time between conversations. Then I opened up my computer and dialed him. When he didn't answer, I texted. I worried that wasn't urgent enough, so I texted with all caps. I was just about to call him on the phone when I saw his name flashing on my computer screen.

"Are you dying?" he greeted me. He held up his phone to the screen, displaying my desperate bid for attention.

"Sorry. It's just…love complications."

He slapped the desk his computer rested on. "Called it!" he shouted.

"I know. You were right. Except according to her friend, she feels the same way. Love all around. It's not one-sided. What should I do?" I started to pace.

"First of all, sit down. You're making me dizzy." I did. John smiled. "Second, you talk to her. 'Hey, I hear you've got a crush on me. Funny because I have a crush on you.' No big thing. Third, you go on tour and see me. Problem solved."

"What if—"

"Nope," he interrupted. "This is not a worrying situation. You don't have to plan anything out. You don't have to allow for every possible reaction she might have. You tell her you like her and you think she likes you. That's it."

"Should I think it through more?" I chewed at my cuticle.

"Absolutely not. What you say isn't going to decide her response. You aren't going to find some perfect phrase that makes her want the same thing if that's not what she actually wants. And you aren't going to make her not like you anymore if you put your foot in your mouth either. She's a grown-up and she gets to decide what she wants to do about this, just like you do."

"What do you mean?"

"I mean you don't have to act on this just because you like each other. I think you should because I think, knowing you, you'll regret it if you don't. And I think you *not* telling her about your feelings is mostly about your discomfort with change and your tendency to sacrifice what you want for the sake of what you think the women you like want. But if you decide you don't actually want to do anything about this, that it's too much right now, that's something you can choose. Your feelings aren't an obligation."

"I think I want to tell her. I've wanted to for a long time, but I thought she didn't feel the same way. But now that I think she does…"

"I get it. It's scary, huh?"

I nodded.

"When I first met Ollie, I liked him so much, but he was seeing someone. I had to wait for months for them to break up and him to get over it, and I worried for what felt like forever. First, I worried that he'd never be single, and then I worried that I was being a bad friend for having a crush on him. When he was single, I worried that he wouldn't want me or he'd find someone else before I made a move or that if I made a move too soon I'd ruin any long-term chances because he wouldn't be ready. I worried I'd ruin my friendship with him. I worried for six months."

"I remember." I smiled. "You were exhausting."

"Do you remember what you told me?"

"No. Hopefully something helpful."

"You said that if we both wanted the same thing, we'd find our way, even if it wasn't a smooth path. You told me that one way or another, I'd be okay. And you were right."

"Wow, sometimes I'm really smart."

He laughed. "Sometimes you are. Do you want to talk to her?"

I nodded.

"Just go do it then. One way or another, you'll be okay."

"Can I call you if I'm heartbroken in an hour?"

He rolled his eyes playfully. "Ollie and I have plans at two."

"Better do this quick then." I stood up.

"Good luck!"

"Thank you, John. For everything. I love you."

"I love you too. Move to Boston!"

"Ugh, snow. Besides, I have this romantic thing here to work out."

He nodded, gave me a thumbs-up, and disappeared from Skype.

Shakily, I walked to Kris's bedroom door. I took a deep breath and knocked. Nothing. I knocked again, louder. Still nothing. Had she left already? I hadn't heard her get up.

"Kris?" I called through the door, expecting silence. I decided that if she didn't answer, I'd go back to my room and take it as a sign to give up the whole thing. "Kris?"

"Out here," she called back.

I inched her door open and saw her lounging on her deck. "Hi," I said weakly.

"Come join me."

I tiptoed through her room. As I passed through, I noticed how different it looked. Kris's room was neat and tidy. The closet doors were closed. Papers were stacked up on the desk and nowhere else. A novel I'd loaned Kris sat on her bedside table. Electronics were put away. The path to the balcony door was clear.

I'd never been invited to the balcony. As far as I knew, no one had. It was Kris's private domain. Kris was stretched out with her feet up on the ledge of the balcony, a mug of coffee cooling on the side table between us. She was wearing loose shorts, a T-shirt, and sunglasses, the very picture of summer. It was one of those rare warm mornings. I carefully settled into the free chair.

"How are you?" she asked me.

"I'm all right." I fidgeted. "I wanted to talk to you about something."

"What?"

I swallowed. My mouth felt dry. "Eric mentioned that you, uh, maybe have feelings for me." She opened her mouth to interrupt, but I talked faster. "And I've been having feelings for you too. For a little while now, actually. I know I'm going to be ridiculously busy for next few weeks and then I'm leaving. I know it sounds weird, and the timing is bad, and we're living together, and we have this unusual dynamic. I know all the reasons I shouldn't be telling you this. But when I didn't talk to you about what was really going on with me before, it made things bad, and I don't want that."

"What do you want?"

"I want to know if you feel that same way I do."

"And what way is that exactly?" Her monotone was making me nervous.

"I care about you. I like you. I'm falling for you. I want more to our relationship."

She exhaled loudly. "You want me to be your girlfriend."

"I want us to see if there could be more here emotionally."

"I like things the way they are."

"I do too, and I don't want to lose this. But I think if I pretend I don't have these feelings, we're going to lose it anyway. I want to see what else we could be."

"I like you too. I really do. I just don't think this is a good idea."

I sank back in my chair, tears stinging my eyes. "Why not?"

"I'm not ready. I'd given up on the idea that I'd ever have that kind of relationships again. I'd made my peace with that. I have been thinking, with you, that maybe I could have that again. But, Phoenix, I don't know how."

"Um, we talk? We hang out? We keep having sex? We go on dates sometimes? It doesn't have to be that different, just with more outside our play. More talking, more sharing emotionally, more time."

"You're *leaving*." She turned away. "How is that going to happen when you're on tour?"

"Phones exist, Kris. Skype, FaceTime, email, texting. Distance is not a problem for getting to know each other outside of sex. I'm scared too, but that doesn't mean it's not worth trying."

"We're both in the middle of huge upheaval. I'm selling my company. In the next six months, every part of how I spend my days is going to change. I'm going to have time off for the first time in my adult life. I don't know what it's going to mean for me, or who I'm going to be. Maybe I need to be reckless for a while, travel, get a motorcycle, do all those things normal college students do that I never did. Maybe I need more friends, a hobby, therapy, something. I have no idea.

"And you're going on tour, and saying you're going to work on your own show too. What if you meet somebody you like while you're on tour?"

I scoffed.

She shook her head. "I'm serious. You'll be meeting so many people. You don't need to be tied down right now, especially not to me. I don't know what I have to offer as a girlfriend."

"I'm not asking you for anything but yourself." A tear escaped my left eye. Kris turned back to me at last.

"I don't know who that is." She wiped my tear away.

"Why can't we find out together? People change all the time. Love is getting to know somebody over and over again. I'm saying I'm on board for that. What are you afraid of?"

"When Laurie and I broke up, it gutted me. I don't think you understand how long it took me to feel okay again. I made so many mistakes. I didn't make her a priority, so I lost her. I like you so much. But I don't know if I can do things any better. I don't want to hurt you, and I'm afraid that if we try this, I will. Especially right now when everything is up in the air."

"You're not the same person you were ten years ago. You're already changing in huge ways."

Kris shook her head again. "Maybe when you're back from tour. We'll see where we both are and what we both want and then we can give it a try then. But I need to figure things out alone first. And you need to be free."

"I know what I want," I said through gritted teeth. "It's you."

"See if you still feel that way when you come back," she said. "It's not that I don't want to. But we need to be reasonable about this."

"Fuck reasonable. You say you want to be reckless? Be reckless with this! We're both so cautious all the time. For once, I want to just go for what I want."

"I'm not ready."

I wanted to yell. I wanted to beg. But you couldn't make somebody love you if they told you they weren't there. So I stood up with all the dignity I could muster. "I want big love, Kris. I want somebody who'll be all in with me."

She took my hand. "I want that too. Maybe with time."

"I'm not waiting." It was a threat to cover up my hurt.

"I'm not asking you to."

"Even if that means you might lose your shot with me?"

"I just can't right now. I'm sorry." Under her sunglasses, I thought she might be crying.

I bit my tongue, turned, and walked away.

CHAPTER TWENTY-FIVE

The next week was a blur of work. Without even trying, Kris and I barely saw each other because I was so busy. We stopped playing, because of the long hours involved in my final rehearsals and the emotional words between us. Before I knew it, it was opening night. The theater was completely sold out. This was even more impressive than a typical opening night, because ours was a specially designed and constructed portable theater just for our show. It would be going with us on tour. We had no season ticket holders, and no one who came for the first night knew for sure what they were getting into.

"Nervous?" Sasha asked me as we wiggled into our costumes.

"Hell yes. You?"

She took a deep breath and let it out with an exaggerated "ahh." "I'm releasing this experience to the Universe. Worrying about the outcome is not respectful of the Universe's power, because everything will happen the way it's supposed to."

"Okay, but are you nervous?"

"*So* fucking nervous."

We had no reason to be, though. Despite all the difficulty of rehearsals, the show went off without a hitch. No one missed a cue. Every move was executed with precision and often with grace. The audience gasped and clapped at all the right moments and sometimes when we weren't even expecting a huge response.

I realized as we performed that we had come together as a cast. We moved together perfectly. What we wore to rehearsals didn't matter. The shit Geoffrey gave us didn't matter. Once we were actually performing, we were an amazing team.

When it was time for my sea witch performance, the music began its steady beat and I slithered up the fabric. I lost myself in the movement, even those horrible one-ankle hangs I'd finally mastered. All my sadness about Kris faded away. The sounds of the audience fueled me without seeming close or pressuring. I felt completely alive in my body, no fears or concerns. All I needed to do was move, so I did, flying in the air. I wound myself up in the fabric and dropped. I made gruesome faces at Mirah and the audience. Lighting showed me pulling away her voice. I twisted and dangled by just one arm and the side of my neck. When I finished curling myself into a fabric cocoon, leaving our star thrashing on her silks, the music exploded to finish the first act, and the audience erupted with applause.

The second act involved me very little until the final moments, so I hung backstage and watched. I marveled at how well it was going. The show was gorgeous. Mirah managed a tremendous range of skills and emotions. The prince was charming and also heartbreakingly oblivious to the devotion Mirah conveyed with her eyes. We mermaid-sisters returned for the end, Sasha's long wig gone and the rest of us in short-hair wigs. I spotted several audience members crying. Mirah refused our urging, all of us in careful belly balances on low-flying trapezes at very bottom of the audience's sight line. Mirah in a harness then flew all the way to the ceiling, where an angel on silks had been waiting in the shadows. When the lights went dim, the crowd cheered. We finished to a standing ovation.

As I started to leave the stage, I spotted Meghan, Bill, and Kris waving to me, flowers in their hands. I went over to them and got big hugs from all.

"That was so cool!" Bill said.

"That was amazing," Meghan said. "You were incredible."

"Thank you so much for being here. I know how expensive these tickets were."

"Great job, Phe," Kris said, sounding sincere.

"I couldn't have done this without you," I said. "If I hadn't been living with you, I would have had to get another day job, and I don't think I could have been part of this show." I turned to Meghan. "You too. If you hadn't introduced me to Kris, I couldn't have done this. Thank you both."

They both wrapped me up in a hug and Bill joined in. "I'm glad I could help," Meghan said.

"You're awesome," Bill added.

"I'm proud of you," Kris said.

Tears threatened again, but I wouldn't give in. I was too happy with my performance. Kris and I didn't talk about anything else that night. I went to an after-party, and she was asleep by the time I got home. Something like this became our pattern for my two weeks performing in San Francisco. We often didn't see each other at home for days. We didn't play or even touch. When we were both there, we barely spoke. We'd become strangers it seemed, with insurmountable distance between us since that conversation on the deck.

But every single day I had a performance, Kris was there. I couldn't believe the amount she'd spent on tickets. Even more, I couldn't believe the time she was taking off of work. The only real moments we had were those after the show ended, before I went backstage.

"I can't believe you're here every day," I said to her one evening in the second week.

"I don't want to miss any of your performances if I can help it," she said. "They're the most beautiful thing I've ever seen."

I started to hope, despite everything I knew, that before I left she'd offer a big gesture and say she wanted to try after all. Why else would she come to all my performances? But night after night, she told me how great I was, and little else.

"You're in love with me," I told her after my second to last show in San Francisco. "That's why you're here every night."

"I'm not saying that I'm not. But it doesn't change anything."

"Why not?"

"Because everything I said still holds true." She sounded as sad as I felt.

The last night, she was there of course. But I thought about what she said, and I didn't go up to her. I just waved. Kris was generously letting me leave my things at her place while I toured with the bare essentials. I didn't even have to really move out.

Kris and I had planned a final good-bye breakfast before I left. She'd offered to drive me to Damien's place in the Sunset, where the cast was boarding a charter bus. Instead, I decided to leave in the early hours of the morning and get breakfast alone at a diner before taking a taxi to Damien's. I snuck out early with my two suitcases, thanking God that Kris was a heavy sleeper. I left her a note that read,

Dear Kris,

I couldn't face a good-bye. I'm sorry. You know how I feel, so you might understand why. I know you deserve better than a note.

Thank you for everything. I could not be doing any of this without you. I can never repay you. I am so grateful, not just for all you've done for me, but also for the time we spent together. You are an amazing person, Kris, and you deserve a full and happy life.

I know sneaking out might make you want nothing to do with me, but if you do want to talk, I'm here.

love,

Phoenix.

With that, I was off on tour.

It was strange to be both happy and heartbroken. I was thrilled with the show, with performing, with our adventures. I was also reeling from my split with Kris. Leaving a note was a coward move, and I felt embarrassed even as I felt hurt by her lack of interest. I couldn't blame her—I was traveling, the timing was bad, and only she knew if she was ready or not—but it didn't make it hurt any less.

At the same time, the tour was incredible. We went to LA first. As the crew set up our theater, we rehearsed. Other than that, we schmoozed to promote the show, and we had time to ourselves. I got to visit Connie and her family, which was a good if sometimes grating distraction from my heartbreak. The cast had access to our rehearsal space after hours, and Sasha and I used it to start playing with our own creation. We also all got temporary apartments, the fully furnished kind you rent by the week, with everyone but Mirah paired up as roommates. Sasha and I were housed together, which meant we were in nonstop creative mode. We talked about themes and blocking while I scrambled us eggs every morning. We experimented with movement after and before rehearsing. We even roped some of the other aerialists into it and got their opinions. At a party before our LA open, we started blabbering about our unnamed, totally undeveloped show to an excitable producer, who asked to see a rough version.

"Can we send you a video when we're got it a little more polished?" I asked.

"Sure. I'm always looking for new projects," she said and handed us a business card. Sasha and I managed to wait until we got home to jump up and down.

Going on tour had been the best possible move for my career. The show was already sold out most nights in LA and had strong sales in other cities just based on the buzz from our San Francisco opening. We'd visit six more cities on our tour, finishing in New York right around Christmas. Then I'd see my family before returning to San Francisco and maybe Kris. Every time I thought about that "maybe," my soaring heart sank.

Our LA opening was even better than our first night in San Francisco. We were a flawless team. The audience was responsive to everything, and jumped out of their seats to cheer the minute the lights went down. Connie and Nick yelled louder than anybody. For a second while I took my bow, I expected to see Kris in the audience, but of course I didn't.

The second night was even better. The Sunday matinee was not. In the three weeks since the show had opened, I'd learned one thing for sure: Sunday afternoons had a lot more people who hadn't read the reviews. The tickets were a little cheaper, and parents kept bringing little kids who expected Ariel. Kids who *loudly* expected Ariel and cried when the mermaid died at the end. It was not anyone's favorite, but at least it was mostly confined to one afternoon a week.

That Sunday was no different. Little kids were crying and booing us as we took our bows. We were all a little drained. I thought I was hallucinating Kris in the front for a second. Then she stood up. As we left the stage, she walked toward me.

My mouth hung open, full of questions I couldn't articulate.

"Hi," she said, handing me a bouquet of rumpled daisies. "I got these in a rush. I'm sorry."

I looked her up and down. She was dressed impeccably, with dark jeans, boots, a tucked-in dress shirt, striped blue and green tie, and a tailored blazer with a blue and green polka dot pocket square. She looked gorgeous. I, meanwhile, had a weird wig on, stage makeup, a fake-shell bra, and I was hobbling around in a mermaid tail. Not to mention that I was dripping with sweat from performing. Sure, she'd seen me like this a dozen times, but it wasn't exactly the reunion I'd been hoping for.

"What are you doing here?"

"I came to see you. Can we talk?"

I looked around at the crowd, exasperated. "You're going to get heat stroke."

"I wanted to look nice for you."

"You're missing San Francisco Pride right now. I can't believe you're missing Pride for this."

"I made a mistake," she said.

"Which was?" I arched an eyebrow at her. "Honestly, I'm not sure you did. You told me how you felt, and it hurt, but I can't fault you for that."

"The night before you left, I realized that I didn't want you to leave. I *do* want to try. I had this whole elaborate plan. I was going to make you breakfast and tell you how I felt, and I went out and got you roses. I started moving up the timeline for the sale, so I'll be done earlier and I can do some other things I want to do before you're back, and I can come see your shows whenever you want. But then I fell asleep, and when I woke up, you'd left me that note and you were gone."

"And phones don't exist?" An exiting audience member gave me a look. I glared back at him.

"I wanted to respect what you wanted. But Eric told me that it wasn't fair if I didn't tell you how I really felt. I do love you. I do want you. I'm scared. I was scared, and I freaked out." She reached for my hand.

"I think it's too late." I pulled away.

"I meant it when I said I wasn't ready. I don't know how to be a girlfriend. I'm not prepared for all these next steps in my life. But ready or not, I am in love with you, and I want to try. Could we try?" she asked softly. I could see tears in her eyes. "Please, Phoenix, can we just try?"

"That's what I wanted and you said no."

"I know. I needed time. I thought I needed a lot of time but I knew in a week that I do want to try. I wasn't kidding when I said I didn't know how to be a girlfriend. This is what I meant. Sometimes it takes me longer than it should to figure out what I want. Sometimes I don't know."

"Then say you don't know! Say you need to think about it! Don't say, 'Let's see in six months, no promises,' and show up two weeks later saying you want to try." I tried, too late, to keep my voice down. This was becoming a scene.

Kris looked away. "I'm sorry. I thought I *was* saying I didn't know."

"Yeah? Well you said it in a way that sounded like a no."

She turned back to me, her eyes brimming with tears. "I don't know how to do this, Phe."

"Nobody knows how to do this. We're all figuring it out as we go along. I know I am."

"I want to try. I'm scared."

"Scared of what though?"

"That we'll break each other's hearts."

Damn, I thought. I understood that. I'd messed up with that fear too. My hesitation melted. I offered her my hand. "I'll be careful with your heart. I'm not perfect, and I'll make mistakes, but I will be careful with your heart. And you'll be careful with mine."

She put her hand in mine. "So, we can try?"

"We can try."

"What does that look like? What do I need to do while you're on the road?"

"You don't need to do anything. But I'd like it if you asked me about my day. Tell me about your day too. And call me and text me when you miss me. Make an effort to keep in touch. Talk about your feelings. Other than that, do things you want to do and think would be good for you. I don't think you need to rush into getting another job as soon as the sale is final, but do what you want to do."

Kris's face lit up. "I always thought, you know, that it was my fault with Laurie. And maybe it was, because I stopped paying attention in some important ways. I thought it was something intrinsic about me, though, that I couldn't do enough as a partner. But I can call you. I can talk to you."

"Maybe my requirements are more reasonable?" I nudged her. Kris wrapped her arms around me. "Years and years ago, I was learning salsa, and I was learning with this guy, a friend of mine. It was so hard. We couldn't get the rhythm right, but every time the instructor would stop us and demonstrate with me, it'd be fine. Then one class my friend was sick, and I ended up dancing with a girl who'd been going to class longer and whose partner was out too. And it was the easiest thing in the world. We both had dance backgrounds so we could keep time. We were both comfortable. It was like flying. I told her I couldn't believe how easy it was. And she told me that it is with a good partner. 'You've just been dancing with the wrong person,' she said. I think, Kris, you've got an idea in your head about who you are in a relationship based on one relationship, but you were dancing with the wrong person. I don't think it has to be what it was."

She held me tighter, so our faces were inches apart. "I know that now, thanks to you. You've changed my life, you know."

"You changed mine too." I slung my arms around her. "So, I told you what I want from you. What do you want from me?"

"You to love me?"

"Already there."

"Show me some creative uses for the trapeze?" she asked. "I never told you but I've been curious about the possibilities since the first time I saw your videos."

"Why didn't you say so before? I could have shown you months ago. I'll take you to my rehearsal space right now if you like. Anything else?"

"Kiss me. We'll figure out the rest as we go along."

I did. We did.

About the Author

Elinor Zimmerman once performed trapeze and lyra hoop under the name Elinor Radical. Today she spends her time writing instead. Her work has appeared in the anthology *Unspeakably Erotic: Lesbian Kink* and *The Lesbrary*. She lives in the San Francisco Bay Area with her wife, kid, and dog.

Website: http://www.elinorzimmerman.com/

Books Available from Bold Strokes Books

Breakthrough by Kris Bryant. Falling for a sexy ranger is one thing, but is the possibility of love worth giving up the career Kennedy Wells has always dreamed of? (978-1-63555-179-2)

Certain Requirements by Elinor Zimmerman. Phoenix has always kept her love of kinky submission strictly behind the bedroom door and inside the bounds of romantic relationships, until she meets Kris Andersen. (978-1-63555-195-2)

Dark Euphoria by Ronica Black. When a high-profile case drops in Detective Maria Diaz's lap, she forges ahead only to discover this case, and her main suspect, aren't like any other. (978-1-63555-141-9)

Fore Play by Julie Cannon. Executive Leigh Marshall falls hard for Peyton Broader, her golf pro...and an ex-con. Will she risk sabotaging her career for love? (978-1-63555-102-0)

Love Came Calling by CA Popovich. Can a romantic looking for a long-term, committed relationship and a jaded cynic too busy for love conquer life's struggles and find their way to what matters most? (978-1-63555-205-8)

Outside the Law by Carsen Taite. Former sweethearts Tanner Cohen and Sydney Braswell must work together on a federal task force to see justice served, but will they choose to embrace their second chance at love? (978-1-63555-039-9)

The Princess Deception by Nell Stark. When journalist Missy Duke realizes Prince Sebastian is really his twin sister Viola in disguise, she plays along, but when sparks flare between them, will the double deception doom their fairy-tale romance? (978-1-62639-979-2)

The Smell of Rain by Cameron MacElvee. Reyha Arslan, a wise and elegant woman with a tragic past, shows Chrys that there's still beauty to embrace and reason to hope despite the world's cruelty. (978-1-63555-166-2)

The Talebearer by Sheri Lewis Wohl. Liz's visions show her the faces of the lost and the killers who took their lives. As one by one, the murdered are found, a stranger works to stop Liz before the serial killer is brought to justice. (978-1-63555-126-6)

White Wings Weeping by Lesley Davis. The world is full of discord and hatred, but how much of it is just human nature when an evil with sinister intent is invading people's hearts? (978-1-63555-191-4)

A Call Away by KC Richardson. Can a businesswoman from a big city find the answers she's looking for, and possibly love, on a small-town farm? (978-1-63555-025-2)

Berlin Hungers by Justine Saracen. Can the love between an RAF woman and the wife of a Luftwaffe pilot, former enemies, survive in besieged Berlin during the aftermath of World War II? (978-1-63555-116-7)

Blend by Georgia Beers. Lindsay and Piper are like night and day. Working together won't be easy, but not falling in love might prove the hardest job of all. (978-1-63555-189-1)

Hunger for You by Jenny Frame. Principe of an ancient vampire clan Byron Debrek must save her one true love from falling into the hands of her enemies and into the middle of a vampire war. (978-1-63555-168-6)

Mercy by Michelle Larkin. FBI Special Agent Mercy Parker and psychic ex-profiler Piper Vasey learn to love again as they race to stop a man with supernatural gifts who's bent on annihilating humankind. (978-1-63555-202-7)

Pride and Porters by Charlotte Greene. Will pride and prejudice prevent these modern-day lovers from living happily ever after? (978-1-63555-158-7)

Rocks and Stars by Sam Ledel. Kyle's struggle to own who she is and what she really wants may end up landing her on the bench and without the woman of her dreams. (978-1-63555-156-3)

The Boss of Her: Office Romance Novellas by Julie Cannon, Aurora Rey, and M. Ullrich. Going to work never felt so good. Three office romance novellas from talented writers Julie Cannon, Aurora Rey, and M. Ullrich. (978-1-63555-145-7)

The Deep End by Ellie Hart. When family ties become entangled in murder and deception, it's time to find a way out... (978-1-63555-288-1)

A Country Girl's Heart by Dena Blake. When Kat Jackson gets a second chance at love, following her heart will prove the hardest decision of all. (978-1-63555-134-1)

Dangerous Waters by Radclyffe. Life, death, and war on the home front. Two women join forces against a powerful opponent, nature itself. (978-1-63555-233-1)

Fury's Death by Brey Willows. When all we hold sacred fails, who will be there to save us? (978-1-63555-063-4)

It's Not a Date by Heather Blackmore. Kade's desire to keep things with Jen on a professional level is in Jen's best interest. Yet what's in Kade's best interest…is Jen. (978-1-63555-149-5)

Killer Winter by Kay Bigelow. Just when she thought things could get no worse, homicide Lieutenant Leah Samuels learns the woman she loves has betrayed her in devastating ways. (978-1-63555-177-8)

Score by MJ Williamz. Will an addiction to pain pills destroy Ronda's chance with the woman she loves or will she come out on top and score a happily ever after? (978-1-62639-807-8)

Spring's Wake by Aurora Rey. When wanderer Willa Lange falls for Provincetown B&B owner Nora Calhoun, will past hurts and a fifteen-year age gap keep them from finding love? (978-1-63555-035-1)

The Northwoods by Jane Hoppen. When Evelyn Bauer, disguised as her dead husband, George, travels to a Northwoods logging camp to work, she and the camp cook Sarah Bell forge a friendship fraught with both tenderness and turmoil. (978-1-63555-143-3)

Truth or Dare by C. Spencer. For a group of six lesbian friends, life changes course after one long snow-filled weekend. (978-1-63555-148-8)

A Heart to Call Home by Jeannie Levig. When Jessie Weldon returns to her hometown after thirty years, can she and her childhood crush Dakota Scott heal the tragic past that links them? (978-1-63555-059-7)

Children of the Healer by Barbara Ann Wright. Life becomes desperate for ex-soldier Cordelia Ross when the indigenous aliens of her planet are drawn into a civil war and old enemies linger in the shadows. Book Three of the Godfall Series. (978-1-63555-031-3)

Hearts Like Hers by Melissa Brayden. Coffee shop owner Autumn Primm is ready to cut loose and live a little, but is the baggage that comes with out-of-towner Kate Carpenter too heavy for anything long term? (978-1-63555-014-6)

Love at Cooper's Creek by Missouri Vaun. Shaw Daily flees corporate life to find solace in the rural Blue Ridge Mountains, but escapism eludes her when her attentions are captured by small town beauty Kate Elkins. (978-1-62639-960-0)

Somewhere Over Lorain Road by Bud Gundy. Over forty years after murder allegations shattered the Esker family, can Don Esker find the true killer and clear his dying father's name? (978-1-63555-124-2)

Twice in a Lifetime by PJ Trebelhorn. Detective Callie Burke can't deny the growing attraction to her late friend's widow, Taylor Fletcher, who also happens to own the bar where Callie's sister works. (978-1-63555-033-7)

Undiscovered Affinity by Jane Hardee. Will a no strings attached affair be enough to break Olivia's control and convince Cardic that love does exist? (978-1-63555-061-0)

Between Sand and Stardust by Tina Michele. Are the lifelong bonds of love strong enough to conquer time, distance, and heartache when Haven Thorne and Willa Bennette are given another chance at forever? (978-1-62639-940-2)

Charming the Vicar by Jenny Frame. When magician and atheist Finn Kane seeks refuge in an English village after a spiritual crisis, can local vicar Bridget Claremont restore her faith in life and love? (978-1-63555-029-0)

Data Capture by Jesse J. Thoma. Lola Walker is undercover on the hunt for cybercriminals while trying not to notice the woman who might be perfectly wrong for her for all the right reasons. (978-1-62639-985-3)

Epicurean Delights by Renee Roman. Ariana Marks had no idea a leisure swim would lead to being rescued, in more ways than one, by the charismatic Hudson Frost. (978-1-63555-100-6)

Heart of the Devil by Ali Vali. We know most of Cain and Emma Casey's story, but *Heart of the Devil* will take you back to where it began one fateful night with a tray loaded with beer. (978-1-63555-045-0)

Known Threat by Kara A. McLeod. When Special Agent Ryan O'Connor reluctantly questions who protects the Secret Service, she learns courage truly is found in unlikely places. Agent O'Connor Series #3. (978-1-63555-132-7)

Seer and the Shield by D. Jackson Leigh. Time is running out for the Dragon Horse Army while two unlikely heroines struggle to put aside their attraction and find a way to stop a deadly cult. Dragon Horse War, Book 3. (978-1-63555-170-9)

Sinister Justice by Steve Pickens. When a vigilante targets citizens of Jake Finnigan's hometown, Jake and his partner Sam fall under suspicion themselves as they investigate the murders. (978-1-63555-094-8)

The Universe Between Us by Jane C. Esther. Ana Mitchell must make the hardest choice of her life: the promise of new love Jolie Dann on Earth, or a humanity-saving mission to colonize Mars. (978-1-63555-106-8)

Touch by Kris Bryant. Can one touch heal a heart? (978-1-63555-084-9)